YOUR SONS O ZION

YOUR SONS O ZION

A NOVEL BY
THEODORAH VILLION

WinePressPublishing
Great Books, Defined.

WinePress Publishing (PO Box 428, Enumclaw, WA 98022) functions only as book publisher. As such, the ultimate design, content, editorial accuracy, and views expressed or implied in this work are those of the author.

ISBN 13: 978-1-4141-2062-1
ISBN 10: 1-4141-2062-1
Library of Congress Catalog Card Number: 2011924435

Dedicated to the Jewish Author who
first told me to write the book—
YHM
Thank You for Your inspiring words!

…and to my "children"
The Kingdom of Heaven belongs to such as you

I will rouse your sons, O Zion,
against your sons, O Greece,
and make you like a warrior's sword.

—Zechariah 9:13

The Characters

Daniel Cohen (also called Dani, Dan-dan)—Stationed at HaPalmach Air Force base near Tel Aviv

Hanan & Miriam—Daniel's parents from Jerusalem

Yonatan & Rachel—Daniel's eldest brother and his wife, living in Jerusalem with their five children (Shmu'el, Levi, David, Yardena and a baby)

Li'or & Ruth—Daniel's second brother and his wife who live in Galilee

Ido & Roi—Twins, the youngest brothers of Daniel's—final year at school in Jerusalem

Ester Davidor (also called Esti, Esush, Es)—lives in Tel Aviv, works at the army headquarters, HaQirya

Ester's father—Absent, referred to as "abba" (daddy).

Naomi—Ester's mom, also from Tel Aviv

David (also called Dudi, Davie)—at school in Tel Aviv

Debra (also called Debs, Deb, Debush)—Ester's confidante, youngest sister of Naomi. Studies at Hebrew University in Jerusalem

Ma'ayan—Ester's friend in the army

ONE

Monday, 19 March 2007

DANIEL SLIPPED INTO his olive-green flight suit and pulled the zipper from crotch to chest. He automatically checked his pockets for gloves, wallet, and cell phone. His brown eyes held a hint of a smile as he put on his sunglasses. He remembered his preflight training. Some members of this elite corps wore their shades all day long—even inside. Even though he was tall and strong, back in those days the big brass truly intimidated him. By now Daniel had learned that harassment is the method used to weed out all candidates who should not become officers. Every thought about that period of his life was unpleasant. How he finally made it through the initiation to the flight line, only God knew!

Every day he and the other trainees wrote their mistakes in a faults book. "Oof…glad that's over!" he moaned under his breath. At the end of each week, the commander checked the books and, depending on their performance, they were penalized. Duty hours might be added or subtracted at that point. Not a fond memory. Daniel had to be near perfect at all times to avoid being washed out. Slowness was sure elimination.

1

Walking from the barracks to the squadron, he felt the nip of the wind in his short brown hair. He thought back to the time when he studied the helicopter controls in his room every evening. He reviewed how to move his hands and feet until he could do it in his sleep. Faithful practice made him believe he would be able to fly at an initial try.

Now, thinking of his first session with the instructor pilot, Daniel laughed into the crisp morning air. *Nesher*, the IP's nickname, handled most of the controls. All Daniel did was work the pedals and keep the helicopter pointed in the direction of the tree—right in front of them. Helicopter parts that had been static drawings in his flight manual vibrated and spun. His senses felt overwhelmed. He shook his head remembering how he sweated.

"What's wrong with me?" he scolded himself. For the life of him, he couldn't keep that tree in front of the bouncing monster. For some amazing reason, however, Nesher thought he did all right.

The relief was premature, however, because the next thing Daniel needed to do was to steady the machine a few feet off the ground. As he took hold of the collective with his left hand, the helicopter immediately levitated. Then he pushed it down too hard and the machine dropped. As he saw the ground rushing up, he overcompensated again and *Whoa!* They shot into the air. His instructor wasn't impressed. Daniel repeated this maneuver a few times before he learned to make slight, but constant adjustments.

The illusion that he could fly a helicopter nosedived quickly. There were just too many things to control. With relentless concentration, he pushed the pedals and worked the cyclic and collective with his right and left hands.

"Whoa, now! Whoa…whoa!" he whispered, as if to a wild horse.

Coming closer to the offices, he saw the Cobras parked on the line. What a threat they used to be in those early days! Beasts to subdue. Seeing the AH-1, he breathed deeply and smiled. "My baby." Back then it was hard to imagine flying the big bird; now it was sheer joy.

Inside the operational building, Daniel walked straight to the dressing room, where their equipment hung under each pilot's name. He pulled his vest off the hook, slung it over his shoulders, and buckled it in front. Taking his pistol and the maps from the office, he greeted the other pilot, who was ready and waiting. They walked to the line together.

The captain of the attack helicopter slid into the gunner's seat, and Daniel strapped himself into the back. He put his helmet on and pulled leather gloves over his hands. Then he began checking the positions of switches on the control panel. Soon he spoke to his copilot through the onboard sound system. "Let's go!"

Thumbs up.

Daniel opened the throttle and squeezed the trigger switch on the collective. The electric motor began to whine. Focusing, he frowned. Slowly the rotors started to accelerate, blades flashed in the morning sun. Daniel watched the temperature and pressure gauges while his colleague prepared the weapons systems on his side of the instrument panel.

"Ready?" he asked.

"In order."

Daniel brought the throttle to operating position and looked once more at the spinning blades driven by the powerful engine behind his back. The technical staff outside waved, and he saluted in response. Then he pushed the cyclic around and slowly pulled up the collective. The nose of the Cobra rose. He stabilized the helicopter and pulled forward on the controls. As the tarmac rushed past them, he felt a tingle of anticipation because this was just a routine training flight.

They were on their way!

19 March 2007: 1st *Nissan*

> Oy! One day up, one day down...Abba, please don't let this old cycle become a pattern in the New Year!
>
> Hey, if the Bible says TODAY's supposed be the first day of the year, why we do Rosh Hashanah?
>
> Anyway...Wish I didn't take a bite of that stupid cake! Would have kept me from buying more chocolate! I've been eating nonstop since two o'clock! Had ENOUGH for lunch. Why am I doing this?! Feel like a worm gnawing all day long.
>
> Good picture!

Bending over the notebook, she pushed a strand of dark hair behind her ear. Her slim hands, nails bitten, sketched a caterpillar.

> Help me, Abba! It's IN me. This constant craving. Feels like I have absolutely no control—I HATE myself! I know it's crazy, but it feels good saying that. Like a lead ball on my leg, this thing's such a drag. I deserve my chains—SLAVE! That's exactly how I feel—what kind of master is ruling over me?! Sounds like Paul.

She sat up, grabbed her Bible, and sought feverishly for the book of Romans. "Ah, chapter 4." Sliding over the verses, she glimpsed some phrases previously highlighted. She paused, her finger on verse 14. *We know that the law is spiritual; but I am unspiritual, sold as a slave to sin.*

"Exactly!" she whispered. Then reading aloud at verse 18, she confessed,

I know that nothing good lives in me, that is, in my sinful nature. For I have the desire to do what is good, but I cannot carry it out.

"This guy gets it!" She sighed and took up her journal again.

That's it! My sinful nature is the slave driver. That's what I'm supposed to hate. <u>I hate you</u>!

She underlined the words with such force that the paper tore. Covering her burning eyes, she prayed. "Abba, please help me! I don't know how to get the victory over my eating." After a while she sniffed, put the book down, and started reading through chapter 8. The Word of God began to penetrate her mind, lightening her misery.

She paused to write again:

FOR IF YOU LIVE ACCORDING TO THE SINFUL NATURE, YOU WILL DIE; BUT IF BY THE SPIRIT, YOU PUT TO DEATH THE MISDEEDS OF THE BODY, YOU WILL LIVE, BECAUSE THOSE WHO ARE LED BY THE SPIRIT OF GOD ARE SONS OF GOD. (verse 13)

Wiping away tears, she whispered, "Abba, please help me put to death the misdeeds of my body. If I make rules, I just break them. This thing is too strong for me. You said I'm more than a conqueror and that nothing can separate me from Your love. Please give me faith to believe that in spite of my failures, You love me, Abba. I know this battle is not about losing weight. Pl-e-e-ease, help me."

Ester got up, went to the bathroom, and blew her nose. Returning to her room, she threw a pillow onto the floor to kneel on and said to herself, "Debra said I need to write a proclamation."

Picking up her Bible again, she searched for the story of David and Goliath. Finding the account in 1 Samuel 17, she scanned the whole chapter.

"Wow, this is cool!" Newly inspired, she picked up the journal and found a clean page. She drew a frame around the four sides of the page, making little dots in the corners, and whispered, "Needs to look like a notice." She read verses 45–48 again and, using them as a guideline, she wrote:

Decree of Destruction

> You uncircumcised Strongman!
> You come to me with temptations and accusations,
> BUT
> I come to you in the name of Adonai Tsva'ot—the
> Commander of the armies of heaven, whom you have challenged.
> He will give you into my hands and I will fight you. I'll chop off your head.
> Yeshua has ruined your power by His death.
> By the Sword of the Spirit and the Blood of the Lamb,
> YOU WILL COME DOWN!

At the bottom, she drew two upright oval circles—one inside the other—and wrote the Hebrew letter *shin* in the middle. Smiling, she began to sing with deliberation, tapping her hand on every beat.

> *My God is stronger than your god,*
> *Afraid of you, I'm NOT!*
> *It was proven,*
> *It was proven,*
> *It was proven at the Red Sea!*

She closed her journal, picked up her Bible, and kissed it. "Abba, You are much, *much* bigger than my problems."

TWO

Sunday, 25 March 2007

E STER LOOKED OVER her commander's agenda for the day. At nine o'clock all the other soldiers in the cluster office were occupied. When her mobile phone vibrated, she grabbed it like lightning.

"Hallo?" she semi-whispered.

"*Shalom, Esush!* Happy birthday to you…"

Ester smiled at Debra's joyful song. "Thanks! Where are you?"

Debra ignored the question. "So, what are you doing to celebrate? Twenty today, right?"

"Yes! Ma'ayan brought me balloons, a rose, and a card, and at lunch we'll go out for ice-aroma."

"Glad someone's making you feel special."

"After work I'm meeting Nora and Rivka at the Azrieli mall. We'll go restauranting and do a movie."

"Anything worthwhile showing?"

"Ehmm, think we'll see *Blood Diamond*. It's about diamonds mined in African war zones and child soldiers."

"My, that's quite intense for a birthday outing, but it sounds like something you'd enjoy."

"Not so sure I'll enjoy it. They say it's rough, but I can't wait to see my friends!"

"So…how you doing?"

Ester filled Debra in on everything about the past week. She spoke so loudly that an officer got up and motioned her to leave.

"It's better," she said, walking down the passageway and outside. Hardly stopping to breathe, she continued sharing the minutest details of her life—burdens and blues, friends and fun.

Since Ester had come to *Yeshua*, Debra had become her mentor. There had always been a special bond between Ester and her mother's youngest sister, but sharing the faith forged their friendship to a David-and-Jonathan pact.

"Before I forget," Debra said, "I want you to come to my place Friday night, 6 April? It's the last *Shabbat* of *Pesach* week and I'm inviting a bunch of friends. Most of us will be having *Erev Pesach* with our families, but some of them don't have relatives here. Just a nice social. You can sleep over if you want."

"Hey, thanks! If I'm not on guard duty, I'll come."

"And tell me what's happening with the eating monster?"

"Gave Goliath a death decree."

Debra laughed. "You *what*?"

Before she could answer, someone called Ester back into the office.

"Debs, got to go. There's another phone call. Chat later." Walking at a fast pace back to the desk, Ester kissed into the phone, "*Mmwha!*"

"Who was *that*?" Ma'ayan's curious face peeked around the divider when Ester put down the green receiver. Her bleached hair spiked like a fountain at the back of her head, and her dark eyes searched Ester's.

"The psychologist."

"No!" She frowned impatiently. "I mean your cell phone."

"That was Debra."

"Oh, okay!" Ma'ayan slumped back in her chair.

Ester smiled. Her army pal had been trying her utmost to match her up with a boy. Inevitably, she thought of how Debra had avoided guys for years. Even though she was sought after, she escaped men like a slippery fish. Suddenly, her thoughts went back to the hospital room where Debra lay after she tried to end her life. She had gotten hold of a revolver and pulled the trigger on her stomach, ruining her insides.

Ester covered her face as she remembered the shock of the family standing around Debra's bed. Everyone knew what she had done, but no one could figure out why. Her straight black hair spread out over the pillow. Her skin was yellow and tubes came out of her nose. A bag of blood on a pole next to her bed dripped slowly into her veins. Machines beeped and made all kinds of noises. It was all so scary! Doctors doubted Debra had any chance of recovery, but she clung to life.

The only reason twelve-year-old Ester was finally admitted to visit Debra was because she nagged everyone constantly. "What if she dies?" she whined anxiously. She wondered who would be her friend then.

That was a long time ago, and Debra pulled through. As Ester sat staring at her computer screen, her thoughts were far away. *Debush—what a friend! More like a sister than an aunt.* As a child, Debra lived with Ester's grandparents in Jerusalem. Then, when Grandfather passed away, Uncle Doron asked Granny and Debra to live with him.

During their childhood, the two girls could not visit one another on weekends because traveling on *Shabbat* was taboo. They made up for it at big, festive Jewish gatherings. Being the social creature she was, Ester relished these gatherings. The feasts were wonderful! Especially *Pesach*. When her mom's large family got together with all the siblings, in-laws, and children, the place swarmed like an ants' nest. They would sit at a long table and read the story of Israel's exodus from Egypt. Grandpa asked the questions and the kids answered. She loved the part where they put their fingers into a wine glass and dropped wine onto their plates as he mentioned each plague. It was fun and seemed to last forever.

She thought back to one specific occasion when the reason for their get-together was Debra's *bat mitzvah*. Aunts and cousins all buzzed around her, everyone commenting on her dress and what a nice young girl she had become. Ester remembered how delighted she was when

Debra put her arm around her shoulders and they walked to the house as if they were the greatest of friends. Come to think of it, that was the first time Ester noticed Debra's developing breasts. She confessed recently that it was more or less about that time their older cousin Moshe began to "fiddle" with her. At first he was just overly sweet, but then he began to touch her in places she didn't want to be touched. She was about fourteen when she told her mom, Ester's grandma, about the sexual abuse. Granny asked if Deborah was sure this was really happening.

"Duh?! She wouldn't tell her mom something so shocking for no reason! Something bad *had* happened to Debbie!"

Debra was ashamed, but she didn't know what to do about it. It was impossible to relate to her family during that period. Ester remembered how aloof and angry Debra seemed to be. By the time she was sixteen, she had lost a tremendous amount of weight. Every time she ate, she vomited. The sexual abuse caused her to feel dirty, and puking became her way to come clean. Debra told no one, not even Ester. The next time Ester saw her was in *Hadassah Ein Kerem* Hospital.

In their religious community, sexual misconduct was hushed up. One day Debra's "pain-pot" boiled over. It was then that she finally got the whole family's attention by shooting herself. Afterward, she slowly pulled out of the deep pit of near-death. Later, she told Ester something that happened one dark day in the hospital.

"When I was at my lowest, all life was, like, draining out of me. It seemed as if I rose through the roof and looked down at my body lying on the bed. I think I went to the place where God lives, because there was a very bright light and everything was beautiful. I felt healthy and peaceful and I had no pain. The whole thing probably lasted only minutes, but to me it felt like a long time. Then I heard a voice—maybe an angel's. It said, 'Debra, you have to return. It's not your time yet.'"

Ester remembered her account of a nurse coming into the room and standing at the foot of the bed with tears streaming down her face. "God is not finished with you," the nurse said. "There's a reason why you are still alive."

Debra was furious. *What chutzpah?!* She didn't want to live! She didn't want this woman telling her there was a reason to be alive. Didn't the nurse understand that her head was a bigger mess than her body? Debra grew increasingly bitter and more intent on self-destruction. Finally, she was discharged—to a mental hospital. Thoughts of suicide tormented Debra for months.

Ester shook her head and tried to focus. The screen of her computer had gone black. She moved the mouse to bring it to life.

"Debra's messianic, right?" Ma'ayan asked during their coffee break in the kitchen.

"Yep. She's strong in the faith."

"How did she start to believe in *Yeshu*?"

"Yeshu-*a*!" Ester corrected her. "Basically, it began when a nurse became her friend."

"Hmmm."

"Yes. Debra's life was a *big* mess and this woman got everyone to pray. Then one day, Debbie encountered God in a way that changed her."

"You mean like"—Ma'ayan snapped her fingers—"that?"

"Not really. The first experience made her feel God's love. Then this nurse told her about Yeshua, but Debra didn't want to hear. She said she was Jewish, and Jesus was for the Christians."

Ester took a big sip of coffee and stared out the window. She remembered how one day Debra was all by herself, and she felt really desperate. She decided to ask Yeshua to reveal Himself to her—if He was real. Suddenly, it was like waves of peace and warmth washed over her. She cried because she felt so much relief.

Ma'ayan sounded a tad triumphant when she asked, "So, she said she was Jewish and…?"

Recognizing the challenge in her voice, Ester lifted her chin and said, "A miracle happened. Debra decided to test Yeshua. She would throw away her cigarettes and see if He would help her quit. She never smoked again."

"Shucks, wish I could stop." Ma'ayan looked wistful.

Ester smiled and went on. "But one night, only months later, Debra's resistance crumbled and she began to *really* cry. Like she couldn't even breathe. She made a pile of tissues like *this* high!" Ester indicated with her hand. "She confessed all her sins to God, and He just melted away the walls she had put up against Him. I think that's when she was born again. She said the peace that filled her heart that night was different than anything she had ever felt before. Locking herself in her room, she started reading the Bible for days on end. Slowly, God's Word began to dissolve the negativity and heal her. Now she's a *totally* different person—few people know she was such a wreck."

Ester rinsed her cup and put it on the rack. Putting her arm around Ma'ayan's shoulders, she gave her a hug. "If Debra ever comes around, ask her to tell you the story. Let's get back to work."

THREE

3 April 2007

Last night was Erev Pesach. We went to Uncle Doron's house for the Seder. Mom let me drive all the way to Jerusalem. Yay!!

God, please help her not to be so nervous. It's enough that I am! Looks like she is ready to jump on me any time! And please let her give me the car to practise on my own.

David was quiet the whole evening. He's so moody lately. What's wrong with him?

Oy, I ate too much! Still feeling stuffed! Sometimes I'm like an alcoholic. When I get happy, I lose all restraint. Eeechsa!

Other times (when I'm in boys' company) I don't even touch a bite. No balance! Pleeeze help me to get balance, Abba!

Anyway. Today I'm fasting. I've eaten enough for three days!

Oof, it will be matzo for one whole week...Never mind, I'll do rice cakes.

Was nice being with the family last night. When I see all the couples and their children, I so long to get married. God, please give me a guy... but not like the boyfriends I've had. They pressed the heart out of me, squeezed me like I was an orange, and after taking what they wanted, they threw me away. I need someone who really loves me.

Pesach is great! Wish all my relatives could know Yeshua. It makes so much sense when you know He's the Lamb that was killed for God's household. Only Debra, Mom, and myself believe. Three of forty people! Abba, PLEASE save my family! Yeshua, show Yourself to Granny before she dies.

I missed abba last night! Sometimes I get so fr...upset! Abba, please help me to forgive him. Was such a crap time to walk out—it crushed David.

I read somewhere that your father is supposed to give you:

1)   identity
2)   security
3)   authority...and...

I forgot the last one.

IDENTITY for sure! David hasn't a clue who he is. It's like he craves masculine attention. ADULT, male attention is what he needs! His one friend gives me the creeps. I'm sure that guy's gay. Please let him leave my brother alone, please!

"I want Abba hold me!"

(Eema says this is what two-year-old Corin says at the nursery school all the time.)

I WANT ABBA HOLD ME!!!

FOUR

Wednesday, 4 April 2007

DEBRA AND HANNA, a Dutch girl who studied with her at Hebrew University, shared an apartment. They lived in the quaint neighborhood of *Nachla'ot* in Jerusalem, next to the *Mahane Yehudah Shuk* —the Jewish market. Being so close they could hear the vendors call, and sometimes they could even smell the spices or get a waft of the fresh fish—especially on Thursdays and Fridays, when the market thronged with Arab and Jewish merchants and customers. The girls loved to shop amid the colorful mountains of fruits and vegetables and freshly baked *challah* breads at the end of the week, when all Jerusalem stocked up for *Shabbat*.

As the two sat in the apartment working over a list of names, Debra, pen in mouth, spoke. "Think we should stick to twelve."

"Agree," Hanna said. "If you want to do a Passover dinner like Jesus and His disciples, it's a good number. Can we get them all in?"

"We'll fit. We can make a low table on the floor this way." Debra demonstrated. "Everyone coming can bring a pillow."

"Why don't we do a foot washing?" Hanna suggested.

"Ehmm...I don't know. With Israelis, if you over-organize something, it becomes an event and it doesn't sit well. They'd rather just hang out." Debra educated her new friend about the culture. "Let's pray the Holy Spirit guides the evening."

Suddenly pensive, Debra said, "You know with *Pesach* we reenact the trip from Egypt and all, but every year I come away wishing I had celebrated my *own* salvation. I mean, why recite all the plagues but not personalize my own deliverance?"

"Right on!"

"It's not that I don't like the traditional way we do it, it's just… well, I want more of Yeshua."

"Hey, this week in archeology class I learned about the remains of a crucified man whose bones were found in an ossuary. The nail that went through his ankle was seven-and-a-half-inches long!"

"Wow, that's a monster spike!"

"Yep, and they found some olive wood on the nail too. All things point to the fact that Jesus was crucified on a tree and not a cross. He carried only the crossbeam."

"Amazing you should say that. I read in Acts 10:39 that Yeshua was hanged on a tree. It's these kinds of things that make me want to get much deeper into Yeshua's death." Debra went on instructing. "By the way, did you know that once *Pesach* was actually two feasts? There was a one-night wine feast and a week-long matzo feast."

"Nope. Didn't realize that."

"Hanna, I'm so glad we don't have to fit the whole account into one evening. We actually have a whole week to cover it. This year I'm going to ask God to give me new revelation about Yeshua."

Debra got up from the couch and switched on the kettle. "Nana tea?"

"Please! You grew up orthodox, didn't you?" asked Hanna.

Debra nodded, wiping the counter where she had spilled water. "And am I ever glad I don't have to do spring cleaning anymore! Actually, I do it, but I'm not obsessed."

"Ja, my mom also does spring cleaning."

"No, no, no! It's not like you think! Every year before *Pesach,* we Jews have a *major* cleanout and we get rid of everything that contains yeast.

It has to go. We search in the fridge, the freezer, the cupboards, even in skirt and pants pockets. The shops get rid of everything 'yeasty.' I tell you, we used to go with a toothpick and a toothbrush between the tiles of the floor and dig out crumbs. Man, clean was never clean enough!"

Hanna smiled at Debra's intensity. "And then they burn all the stuff outside in the street in those containers the municipality provides, right?" Hanna asked.

"Right. How did you know?"

"I saw people burning their stuff on the sidewalk. They brought their leftover bread, and the kids came to throw their Cheerios® into the fire," Hanna said. "Actually, the yeast-bit makes me think of a funny email I got this morning." Hanna moved her hand to the mouse of her laptop. She began to read.

> Two teenagers asked their dad if they could go to the theater to watch a movie that all their friends had seen. After reading some reviews about it on the Internet, he said no.
>
> "A-a-ah, Dad, why not?" they complained. "It's rated PG-13, and we're both older than thirteen!"
>
> Blah, blah, blah, they went on. So their dad replied, "The reason I don't want you to go is that the movie contains nudity and portrays immorality. God hates both as being normal and acceptable behavior."
>
> "But, Dad, those are just very small parts of the movie!"

"I'll forward the email. Basically, the story is about the way their dad teaches them that they shouldn't tolerate sin. A movie with even a little bit of immorality is not good."

Debra thought about how her own innocence had been violated, and then she remembered her peers. "Wow, my friends were so innocent! Compared to the secular kids in Israel, we didn't even know what 'immorality' was."

•   "I believe you. Whenever I see the religious girls on the bus in their school uniforms, I just *love* them! They're so beautiful and pure, with cheeks all rosy and eyes bright. They look really innocent."

Debra smiled. "They *are* beautiful. I wish they could always remain like that."

"Why do you say that? Don't they?"

"Impurity is just one kind of sin. But if you grow up looking down on other people, thinking you are better, that's just as bad. Remember the story Yeshua told about the Pharisee? He said, "'I thank You, G-o-d…'" Debra sang in a pious voice, "'…that I am not like THIS SINNER.'"

Hanna giggled.

Debra had made her point. If there are worse sins, pride is one. God resists the proud.

"Man, religion kills you! As soon as you get trapped in the 'try harder' cycle, your conscience won't let you rest. You feel you are *never ever* good enough."

Hanna's mind returned to the dinner plans. "I like *matzo*."

"Really? You're an exception."

"No, look. In my Christian upbringing, eating unleavened bread for a whole week would be a new experience. But I enjoy when we use *matzo* for Communion in church. I always imagine that as my teeth crack the bread, so Jesus' body broke on the cross. Death chewed Him up and swallowed Him." Hanna swallowed succinctly. "But He rose again, and when I eat Him, He becomes my energy."

"Amen! John 8 says Yeshua is the 'genuine bread.' At one time in my journey, I clung to that scripture."

"That round white wafer some Christians use for Communion is definitely *not* bread."

Debra laughed. "I agree. Hanna, if you hadn't shown me those wafers, I wouldn't have known that you could even eat them. They look like play discs for a board game."

Hanna shook her head. "You have some imagination, girl. Let me look at the list, please."

FIVE

Erev Shabbat, **6 April 2007**

ARIEL AND DOV were the first to arrive. Debra introduced them to Ester. "My neighbors live downstairs." They plonked two bottles of juice on the counter.

Ester stared. *Colorful friends!* The one introduced as Ariel had a blond mop with dreadlocks and several earrings. As he talked loudly, joy bubbled like shaken champagne. Ester pointed to a lion's head in full mane on his forefinger. "Cool ring!" she said.

"Yeah, there's a story…"But before he could explain, Debra chirped, "Ariel and Dov are brothers—they hang out with the street kids at Cat Square."

"Cat Square?" Ester asked.

"Yeah, that's where the youth go at night. Know where Zion Square is?

"Ehmm…at Ben Yehuda Street?"

Dov wore a sleeveless black T-shirt. As he pointed in the direction of the square, Ester noticed the gauge in his ear, the dog collar on his arm, and an interesting tattoo on his wrist. "Cat Square's on the next block."

ı *Wow! Looks macho, but way gentle.* "Where are you guys from?" Ester didn't recognize their accent.

"South Africa."

"Cool," she said again. "Welcome to Israel!"

"Thanks!" said Ariel. "We've lived other places in the world, but we *love* Israel."

"Cool." Although it seemed rather dumb to keep saying the same word, it was the only one that came to her mind. "Nice that someone likes us."

The bell rang and the door swung open. Tikvah entered, carrying two packets of Bamba. She greeted Debra. "Hey! What smells so yum?"

"Lasagne, baked with matzo instead of pasta."

"Is it kosher?" Tikvah smiled.

"Not sure. I made the white sauce with soymilk—an experiment."

Ya'el came in and put a plastic bag with a box of matzo and a jar of chocolate spread on the cupboard. "Dessert," she announced.

"Thanks." Debra gave Ya'el a caring hug. Pointing in the direction of the lounge, she said, "Put your pillow and Bible where you'd like to sit."

"Who else is supposed to come?" Tikvah tore open the pack of Bamba and put a few of the peanut butter puffed corn snacks into her mouth.

Debra thought a moment. "Five or six more," she said.

Ariel grabbed the Bamba from Tikvah's hand. "Let me see if this is kosher *le'Pesach.*" While trying to read the back of the packet in Hebrew, he dipped in and took out a big handful.

"Where I come from we have cheese curls. These peanut butter thingies are freaky," Ariel said.

"I grew up on it," said Tikvah, stuffing another bunch in her mouth.

"Yep, the kiddos lo-o-ove it." Dov also took a handful.

Two more guys walked in and greeted the others simultaneously: *"Shabbat Shalom!"* A chorus of voices responded as they exchanged kisses on the cheeks and hugs of welcome.

Ester was making tuna salad when Debra touched her shoulder. "Hey, here's Avi, and this is Daniel. He's a pilot,"

"I finished the army," Avishai said, smiling.

Ester quickly wiped her hand and stretched it, somewhat wet, toward Daniel.

"Your name?" asked Daniel.

"Ester." She smiled briefly and looked down.

Roi, Ido, Roni, and Jake were the last to join the group. They brought more juice and two tins of sweet corn. Jake walked to the lounge. Pointing to the low table, he commented, "*Sabbaba!* Whose idea was this?"

"Think Debra's," said Roni. "I like the candles—the smell." He walked to the corner and picked up a guitar. Jake took the djembe and did a quick drum roll on the vellum top with his fingers.

The boys jammed as the guests gradually migrated into the lounge from the kitchen. The atmosphere was warm and intimate. By the time Roni started singing, everybody was sitting or lying down comfortably, and they spontaneously joined in worship. The words of a hauntingly beautiful song hung in the air like a fragrant balm:

Ma Yedidot Mishkenotecha...

How lovely are your dwelling places.
He has brought me to his wine cellar,
His banner over me is love...

The presence of God was tangible. After a few more songs, Debra started: "Abba, thank You for Your love..." Unannounced, somebody translated her prayer from Hebrew to English.

"Thank You for bringing us together at this feast. Thank You for giving Yeshua to show us Your great love. Thank You for buying the whole world with Your blood. What a salvation! You are *so* awesome, God! Thank You that the people of every language and nation are precious to You."

After the "amen," she looked at Jake. "Seeing that it's right in front of you, will you say the blessing on the bread?"

Jake lifted the matzo. "*Baruch ata Adonai Eloheinu, Melech ha-olam, ha-motzi lechem min ha-aretz*" Translating in the same breath, "Blessed are You, Lord our God, King of the universe, who brings bread from the earth," he broke the matzo and passed the pieces around.

Ya'el was still chewing on her chunk when a revelation hit her. "Wow, that's powerful! Yeshua also came out of the earth!" She was the youngest believer in the room. Many things, like the resurrection, were wondrous in her eyes.

"Yes," said Jake, "and He was born in *Beit Lechem*—Bethlehem—the House of Bread."

"Not *Beit Matzo?*" Ariel's face was serious.

A few caught his joke.

"Tikvah, would you pass the juice on," said Debra.

"Daniel, please?"

He took the plastic cup in front of him and poured half a glass of juice. "Let's do it different than the traditional blessing." Daniel paged through his Bible. "Pour some for yourselves," he said as he searched for the passage. "Okay. I'm reading 1 Corinthians 11:23–28.

"For I received from the Lord what I also passed on to you: The Lord Jesus, on the night he was betrayed, took bread, and when he had given thanks, he broke it and said, 'This is my body, which is for you; do this in remembrance of me.' In the same way, after supper he took the cup, saying, 'This cup is the new covenant in my blood; do this, whenever you drink it, in remembrance of me.' For whenever you eat this bread and drink this cup, you proclaim the Lord's death until he comes. Therefore, whoever eats the bread or drinks the cup of the Lord in an unworthy manner will be guilty of sinning against the body and blood of the Lord. A man ought to examine himself before he eats of the bread and drinks of the cup."

Daniel looked up. "So let's examine ourselves. Anything you need to repent of? Is a relationship strained between you and someone else?

Make it right. Ask Abba's forgiveness. Don't drink a judgment upon yourself." Daniel spoke with unquestioned authority.

Ariel got up, walked over, and bent down next to Dov. He put his hand on his brother's shoulder and whispered in a low tone. They hugged.

Daniel spoke again. "The Word says we must confess our sins to one another and pray for each other so that we may be healed. Let's give it more time. Go ahead if you want to pray with someone."

They didn't wait. People here and there moved toward each other. When Hanna saw how open they were, she was amazed. *This is much better than having buckets of water and towels, she thought. These guys are washing one another's hearts!*

When it became quiet, Daniel lifted his grape juice again and said, "Yeshua, thank You for the new covenant in Your blood." He drank and the others did the same.

Tikvah lifted her cup and said, *"Le'chaim!"*

Someone exclaimed, "To Yeshua!"

Ya'el rested her head on Debra's shoulder. As she took a sip of the juice, tears slid down her cheeks. She ducked her head lower so her hair, falling forward, could cover her face.

"Drink the whole cup," whispered Debra. "It's all forgiven."

"Can I share something?" Ester asked hesitatingly.

"Feel free!" Debra smiled reassuringly.

Ester seemed shy and uncomfortable, but she began. "When I was at school, we learned that whatever you consume goes into your stomach, gets digested, and tiny nutrients are carried to your cells by the blood." She put one hand on her stomach and showed with the other hand how nutrients travelled to reach her arms and legs. "So when Eve ate that fruit in the garden, every cell in her body got the message: sin…sin… sin." She paused a moment. "But I believe that tonight every cell in my body just got the message: clean…clean…clean."

"Awesome!" said Ariel.

"And in the same way," Debra said, "if I eat the bread with *faith*, by the blood and wounds of Yeshua I am healed and made whole."

"Not only your body, but also your soul," Ester said softly.

"Hallelujah!" Someone else got the truth.

Debra rose to fetch food from the kitchen. Before she left, she turned and said, "The reason I told you guys to bring your Bibles is so you can look at the *Pesach* that Yeshua had with His disciples. I think the best description of the night before He was crucified is in John 13,14,15,16, and 17." She counted on her fingers. "Five chapters."

Hanna carried the hot lasagne, and Ester brought in a steaming pot of spiced rice. They placed everything on the low table. A tray of matzo spread with eggs and sliced olives appeared. The leftover Bamba, tuna salad, and corn came out as well. As they ate together, the atmosphere remained charged with God's presence. At some point, Roni picked up the guitar and began to sing the *Daiyenu*.

After the meal, some of the young people continued to worship, some discussed the Bible, and others made coffee. They lingered until late. When the last people finally left, Hanna looked at Debra. "So, did the evening fulfill your expectations?"

"Hey, I think it was great. We should do this kind of celebration every year!" She switched on the kettle. "A cup of tea, Es?"

"Please!"

There would be no buses running until after Saturday evening, so Ester stayed overnight.

They traveled in silence. When he pulled up to Avishai's apartment, Daniel asked, "You know Ester?"

"Nope, Debra's niece." Avishai opened the door.

Daniel nodded. "Okay. *Sabbaba!* See you at *Simchat Adon* tomorrow."

"*Laila tov*, Bro!"

SIX

Shabbat, 7 April 2007

IT WAS PAST NOON when Debra emerged from her cozy nest. Hanna was in the kitchen, and Ester was on the couch with her Bible. Debra filled the kettle with water, yawned, and stretched. "You been up for a long time?" she asked them.

"No," said Ester, stretching too. "I crawled out of bed ten minutes ago."

"And you?" She turned to Hanna.

"What does my dishevelled hair say?"

Debra snickered and rubbed her stomach. "Oof! I'm hungry. How about an omelette?"

"Great, I'm hungry too!" Ester got up and put her Bible aside. "Can I help with something?"

Debra opened the fridge door. "Pull out the leftovers from last night."

"I won't have eggs, but I'll join you girls in a minute," Hanna said. "Need to wash my face."

While Ester laid the table, Debra heated the pan. "Howzit going with your eating, Esush?"

"The meal was good last night. I usually don't eat much when so many people are around, but you saw what I did to the chocolate spread and the matzo after everyone was gone."

"I did. That's why I'm asking." Debra smiled.

Ester was a bit embarrassed. "Listen, how did you get balance? I mean, you've known my ups and downs."

"It was a process. Basically, over time, I realized that I needed only two meals a day. So I usually eat at eleven in the morning and four in the afternoon."

"Last night was a bit late for you then?"

"Uh-huh. This morning is also too late, but I needed the rest, so I slept in."

"How do you cope? If anything overthrows my routine, especially when I'm under stress, I lose control."

"You know, one thing I've learned is that nobody can take your choice from you. That's a gift God gave Adam and Eve in the garden. Doesn't matter *what* happens to you, you can still make a decision."

"But if someone rapes you, you have no choice about that!" Ester was a little defiant.

"True, but you can choose your attitude afterward, right? You can say, 'This thing will not ruin me, I will overcome it!'"

Hanna came in and joined them at the table while Debra continued. "My eating was an emotional crutch."

"Are you talking about anorexia?" Hanna asked.

"That's only one of the eating disorders. Bulimia is another. Mine was emotional eating." Debra took a bite of her omelette. "As I was saying, you have a *choice*."

"Oh yes." Hanna nodded.

"I discovered that not only were my emotions a crazy mess, but my will was totally broken too. I seldom felt right, so I didn't think straight. The consequence was that I hardly ever made the right choices."

"Just a moment. Repeat that. Sounds important," Ester said with a mouthful.

Debra patiently explained. "I often felt wrong because my emotions were so broken. I often thought wrong because my mind and my memories were a mess. I made wrong decisions because my will was messed up too."

"Wow, that makes so much sense."

"So God not only had to heal my memories, I asked Him to fix my will too," added Debra.

"That's what I need to do," Ester said, contemplating.

"Like in Psalm 23, *He restores my soul...*" Hanna quoted gently.

"Le' me ask you something else, Es." Debra popped an olive into her mouth. "Have you been journaling?"

"I've tried, but I'm not very faithful. I know, you said I need to do it every day."

"It's good to journal for a number of reasons. It is like a pressure valve to release your emotions. By expressing what you feel to Abba, those emotions won't mount and mount until you explode."

"Been there!" Ester said.

"Writing in my journal brings closure to my day," said Hanna.

"Especially if you write in the evenings, right?"

"The time doesn't matter," Debra said, "as long as you keep short accounts. Every time you confess your mistakes, you can start fresh the next day."

"*His mercies are new every morning!*" Hanna was enthusiastic. "Mine is not just a 'Dear Diary' or a 'Think Book'—you know, like a psychiatrist who makes you lie down and says, 'Now...tell me...what you feel....'" Hanna droned in a hypnotic voice. Ester and Debra giggled. "No, it's more like an ongoing conversation between God and me."

"I'm sure Abba loves your letters to Him." Debra smiled at Hanna. "Besides, if King David never wrote his prayers, we wouldn't have the Psalms."

"Or if Moses didn't write the Torah," Hanna responded. "And what would we do without all the stories of the New Covenant?"

Ester got the picture.

"I heard somebody say the Bible is the Jewish family journal," said Debra.

"I love that! Genesis is my *most* fa-vo-rite book." Hanna kissed her fingers.

"The two of you inspire me," Ester said. "I want to read my Bible and write in my journal right *now!*" She banged on the table. "So, what's the plan for today?"

"It's *Shabbat*." Debra pulled up her shoulders. "You can chill. Or read or listen to music…whatever. Hanna and I don't study on *Shabbat*. We just"—Debra threw her hands in the air in abandon—"Whatever!"

"About five we'll get ready to walk to the congregation,"said Debra. "Service starts at six."

"Cool!" Ester said, looking at the clock on the wall. "Two and a half hours. Free time is the biggest luxury in the army."

They cleared the dishes, and when Ester took up her books again, Debra lingered a moment. "You asked how to get balance. There are some practical steps, but we cannot change ourselves. A new diet? Forget it! No self-improvement program will last. It's like a monkey trying to pull himself out of a swamp by his hair."

Debra grabbed her ponytail with her hand and demonstrated. "We need the strong hand of God to yank us out and put our feet on the Rock." She jerked her other arm upward. "Write this verse in your journal: *Not by might, nor by power, but by my Spirit, says the Lord.*"

When they reached the building, the music was bursting from the seams. The door opened and a friendly lady held out her hand. "*Shalom,* welcome to *Simchat Adon!*"

Debra went ahead and scanned the congregation for three seats. People were standing everywhere, so it wasn't easy to see an available space. They waited at the back for a while as a band located on a low platform started playing. When the people began to worship God, Ester felt the fountain of the Holy Spirit begin to bubble inside her. It reminded her of the summer camp she attended the year before she went to the army. She did not often get the opportunity to attend this kind of meeting. The congregation sang about their faith and about not being afraid to testify. When *Kol Israel ivasha* came on the screen, Ester sang along with conviction.

> *His name is Yeshua*
> *His name is Yeshua*
> *In Israel, in Jerusalem…*
> *All Israel will be saved.*

She waved her forefinger in the air as if to say, "His name is Yeshua, not *Yeshu!*"

As the music became slower and more intimate, Ester put her hand on her heart and gave herself to the Father's embrace. She drank deeply from His love.

When the people finally sat down, Debra quickly led the girls to one of the side flanks. It was too far forward in the room to be comfortable, but at least they had a good view of all that was going on. An older man stepped onto the platform. Debra leaned over to Ester, "That's our senior elder."

Next to him stood an intelligent-looking guy with spiky hair. He was doing a terrific job translating.

"So, let us pray for our country," said the leader.

First, someone offered a passionate prayer for Israel and the government. Afterward, two younger men came to the platform. One spoke, the other translated.

Ester leaned onto the shoulder of Debra. "Married or single?" she whispered.

Debra poked her in the ribs.

When the band started up again, the people formed two lines down the aisles that reached all the way to the front. They moved forward and placed offerings in a basket. When the music subsided, one young guy stepped up and started speaking.

"Can we see a show of hands? How many of you are worshiping with Congregation *Simchat Adon* for the first time?"

Ester looked around shyly, surprised to see many newcomers raising their hands.

"It's wonderful to have you here with us! Let's make them feel welcome!" The leader enlisted the congregation to clap, and the people looked around enthusiastically, smiling at the visitors.

The leader blessed the children and sent them to their classes. Then he asked the congregation to greet one another, while they took a short break.

People got up from their seats, and Ester smiled. "I feel at home!"

"I'm glad." Debra pointed. "The bathroom's right at the back if you need it."

"Thanks. There are so many young people here." Ester seemed surprised. Just then she noticed Daniel approaching with Avishai and someone else. They all greeted each other. "This is my younger brother, Roi," Daniel said to Ester.

"Hi, Roi," she said.

"So, you came to spy on our congregation, yes?" Daniel smiled. "You like it?"

"Mmm...it's cool," was all she could think to say.

"My parents are also here." Daniel looked over the crowd. "See the tall gentleman with the blue jacket over there? That's Dad. My mom is the lady with gray hair next to him."

Ester nodded. "I see them."

When a voice over the microphone asked people to return to their seats, Daniel winked at Debra. "See you afterwards!"

The sermon was wasted on Ester. Her thoughts kept turning to the handsome pilot who had come to greet them during the break. "Oh, forget it! He won't even look at me." She tried to shrug off her feelings. By the end of the service she was swinging between extremes. She wanted to see Daniel again, but decided to avoid him. Maybe he didn't like her. After the sermon, she hooked her arm through Debra's in a subconscious attempt to support her weak self-image. When the guys approached them, she shifted to standing halfway behind Debra. This time, she didn't say a word. Clinging to Debra's arm, she walked with them out the door and to a nearby coffee shop.

Once inside the coffee shop, the young people moved chairs and made themselves comfortable. Two guys placed their orders at the counter. Ester was as mute as a crab with only two eyes sticking out of its shell. When the others began to chitchat, she finally relaxed.

"Tomorrow is Resurrection Sunday," began Hanna. "Anyone want to go to the Garden Tomb with me?"

"What for?" Avishai asked.

"The sunrise service."

"I have to be back at the base tonight," Daniel said.

"Don't know," said Avishai. "I don't like it when those people walk down the *Via Dolorosa* dragging a cross and singing with long faces."

"The sunrise service is not like that, Avi. It is Christians coming together to celebrate Jesus' resurrection." Hanna struggled to find the right words.

"Yes, but remember when you say 'Christians' or 'church,' most Israelis think you mean Roman Catholics," said Daniel for Hanna's sake.

"And the Jews think that Roman Catholicism is a false religion. When people light candles to the saints or kiss statues, the Jews say it's idolatry," added Avishai.

"They think that about any kind of Christianity, Avi. It's because they don't believe that Yeshua is God." Debra tried to restore the balance.

"That's not what we do!" Hanna was indignant. "I don't like pictures of Jesus either. The Ten Commandments say we're not supposed to make anything that resembles God."

"*Eeechs*, those men with golden plates on their heads!"

"Icons," Debra helped.

Avi was on a roll. "That's how you know for sure Jesus isn't Jewish."

"But Jesus *is* Jewish!" Hanna was becoming bewildered.

"He's pulling your leg, Gurl." Debra's voice was motherly. "The image of Jesus portrayed by Christian pictures is strange to the Jewish mind. The Torah does say that we're not supposed to make *any* image of God. Besides, no artist can ever do justice to Him."

"Do you blame us for being confused? The exposure Jews have had to the church is so wacko! Have you ever been inside the Old City—to churches like the Holy Sepulchre?" Avishai asked. "All the incense and the crucifixes and that huge stone at the entrance the people bend down to kiss? Man, I can't believe they laid Yeshua's body on that thing!"

When Avi saw that he had an audience, he continued the tirade. "For real, I've heard that the monks of the different denominations who hold services there, fought with one another over the key of the building so much that now a Muslim guy has to keep it." He put his hands in a prayer position at his chest and made a hypocritical bow.

"Yeah, the guys with the long robes," Daniel said. "Some of them must be bound by a spirit of religion, just like our ultra-orthodox Jews."

"Did you know that a Jewish lady in our congregation actually found Yeshua in a Roman Catholic church in Italy?" Debra intrigued her listeners. "Yep, she was desperate for God, and when she saw many paintings of the cross she prayed to Yeshua."

The others were sceptical. "Really?"

"Yes! Yeshua revealed Himself to her."

"God will use anything to speak to a person who is desperate," said Daniel.

"I know I'm opinionated," said Avishai, "but I really don't like those people with the crosses around their necks."

"Hey, Yeshua said, 'Don't judge.' You don't know their hearts." Daniel spoke straight.

"And that's exactly why I want you to go to the Garden Tomb." Hanna was now adamant. "It's nothing like what you're talking about. It's quiet and peaceful, and we sing lovely hymns."

"Hymns? What's that?" said Avi, determined to pester Hanna a little more.

"Quit it, Avishai!" Debra came to her rescue. "Hanna, I'll go with you."

"Ester, you want to come?" Hanna tried to draw her in.

Ester clicked her tongue. "Got to be back at *HaQirya* at ten. Not sure I'd make it to the bus in time."

"You wouldn't," said Daniel. "Wish I knew you needed to go to Tel Aviv. You could have had a ride with me. Maybe next time." He stood up. "Friends, I've got to go."

They said goodbye and dispersed.

SEVEN

8 April 2007

> Can't get Daniel out of my mind. What did he mean, "Maybe next time..."?
> Does he like me? It's driving me crazy!!!
> Started dieting this morning. Went okay.

9th

> Ooof!! Still can't focus on anything else.
> Abba, is Daniel for me ??????
> It's April. Three more months and I'm done with the army.
> Wow!...At the beginning it was so hard, thought it would NEVER end. Now
> my term's almost over.
> Want to study afterwards. Maybe something like Debra's doing...or
> physiotherapy. Would love to help people get their lives back after trauma.
> What is Your future for me, Abba?
> Will have to save money first. God, please help me get a job when I
> finish the service. A GOOD job that pays a LOT.
> You are my Abba. You know the plans for my life and You've carried me
> till now. Underneath me are everlasting arms...
> I TRUST You. xxxxx

10 April 2007

Was very hungry today. Ate almost nothing for two days, and then tonight six rice cakes with hummus AFTER dinner. Then a banana and more. Felt so stuffed! At least I went for a jog afterwards. I'm better now. Abba, help me with balance. NOT BY MIGHT or POWER, ONLY YOUR SPIRIT.

Daniel, Daniel...what's happening to me? My thoughts are running wild! What if he DOESN'T like me?!

Gotta get control here. Read in Jeremiah that the heart is wicked and deceitful. Is my heart deceiving me? Abba, help me please!!!

ESTER LEANED OVER and picked up her Bible. Paging through it, her eyes caught the words of a verse in Song of Songs:

Kiss me with the kisses of your mouth, for your love is better than wine.

"Aaaaaahhh!" she shouted, shaking her head so hard that her hair flew straight out. Closing her journal she opened her heart.

"Oh Abba…I really, *really* like Daniel. Please let him be mine. No, I can't ask that! What am I supposed to pray? Abba…Abba…please hold my heart."

Folding her arms across her body and rocking back and forth, she closed her eyes. "I want Abba hold me."

EIGHT

16 April 2007

Bible society in Gaza was bombed by Hamas today. Abba, please help the Palestinian believers who live there. Protect them and give them courage to go on in the faith, no matter how hard it is.

I also need faith, Abba! This eating thing is a mountain. But in Matthew 14:31 You said that our faith can move the mountains!

YOU OF LITTLE FAITH, WHY DID YOU DOUBT?

Forgive my unbelief. Please wash away all disappointing memories. Forgive me for doubting You, Yeshua. "YOU ARE THE MESSIAH, THE SON OF THE LIVING GOD!"

And I say to the devil that sows seeds of doubt in my heart: "GET BEHIND ME, SATAN. YOU ARE A STUMBLING BLOCK TO ME. YOU DO NOT HAVE THE MIND OF THE THINGS OF GOD, BUT THE THINGS OF MEN."

Yeshua, thank You that when I declare Your Word, it uproots the deepest problems. Please remove doubt from my heart and wash me with Your blood. Cleanse me from the unbelief my family has lived in for years.

Yeshua, You got the victory over this world. Take my hopelessness, worry, fears, and weakness. You promised to help me overcome my struggles! Thank You that when I am tired and depressed You lift my head.

Help me to believe Your Truth and to obey Your Word.

Help me to praise You even when I'm down.

Your Word also says that You will defend us and burn our enemies into ashes. MY STRUGGLE IS NOT AGAINST FLESH AND BLOOD.

HE WHO IS IN ME IS GREATER THAN HE WHO IS IN THE WORLD.

In the name of Yeshua the Messiah from Nazareth, who came in the flesh, I shall resist the devil. He will NOT rule over me!

I choose righteousness. Give me a love for good and a hatred for bad.

Help me to change all wrong habits.

Purify me by Your Holy Spirit!!!

Abba, thank You that I have the wonderful option of eternity.

Amen.

NINE

Erev Shabbat, 21 April 2007

DANIEL WAS VERY SURPRISED to notice Ester at the messianic
soldiers' conference, talking and laughing in a circle of girls. He
could not remember seeing her at any of the other gatherings. In the
past, he and Avishai would survey the young ladies, but they would keep
a discreet distance. This time was different. They hung around where the
others played games, but Daniel was distracted. He positioned himself
where he could observe Ester.

Ester got his attention the night at Debra's not just because she was
beautiful. (Praise God she was!) Daniel smiled as he remembered her in
the kitchen with the butcher's apron over her soft pink top. She didn't
try to draw his eye. On the contrary, she seemed to shy away from him.
It was the things she said during Messiah's supper. Daniel thought back.
When she opened her mouth it was like fresh water gushing from a fountain!

"Howzit, Bro!" Someone slapped him out of his dream.

"Nadav!" Daniel hugged his friend hard and kissed him on the cheek.
They had known each other since the years when Daniel's parents first
lived in Haifa. Together they attended kindergarten, primary school,
and youth camps.

After socializing, all the soldiers gathered for worship. Daniel observed how Ester lost herself in the presence of the Lord. With eyes closed and face tilted upward, she looked radiant as she sang:

Ein kamocha Elohim

There is no one like our God,
Redeemer of Israel
Messiah of the world,
We'll give honor to Your name!

Daniel liked what he saw. This girl's heart was with the Lord. It was clear that she loved Yeshua. He restrained his thoughts to focus on God. Soon, he enjoyed the worship as well. He knew from experience how much strength and refreshment these corporate times of praise carried.

After the worship, Eitan Shishkoff, a respected congregational leader from the north, took the microphone. "Because the Day of Remembrance is celebrated this week, we have decided to honor our heroes while they are still alive. You, our soldiers, are our pride and our joy! You have made contact with the rest of society by serving as combat soldiers. Many of you have made a choice for God while still at school, and you are serious disciples of Yeshua. Some of you are men and women of immense responsibility. I know men in their thirties and forties who do not come close to your worldview. You know what is important in this life…and how to give yourself for other people. We have a tremendous respect for you! We have great anticipation for your generation. We want you to know that we are behind you with all our hearts!"

The audience clapped with loud appreciation.

"We've asked a few soldiers in leadership positions to share their experiences with you tonight." Eitan introduced Alon Stern, a twenty-two-year-old who had finished the army.

"I was in the engineering corps for four years," Alon began, "so even though my national service is done, my military career is not over…right?" Alon would continue to serve in the reserves of the Israeli military for four to six weeks per year until he reached forty years of age. The audience understood that Israel had been at war since its inception, and if there was no army there would be no safe place to live. All girls were obligated to two years of service and all guys, three. Thus the whole nation was an army.

"After my training, I became an officer, and we did our duty between the northern border and the territories, mostly in the Ramallah area. I was in Lebanon for about a month and a half last summer. I wasn't walking strongly with the Lord before that time, but in the end I was different.

"During the war, I faced very difficult situations. God put me in a corner and I could not perform certain actions, except through Him." Almost too quickly, Alon concluded his testimony. "God used those circumstances to change my life dramatically. I'm really happy for that."

Eitan mentioned that there was a newsletter with more of Alon's story, and pointed to a guy at the back holding a bunch in his hand. "Feel free to take one."

The next speaker was Daniel's friend Nadav.

"I'm twenty-one and I've just finished my service. Spent three years in *Givati*. I was in a small engineering explosives unit inside the big infantry unit. We had one and a half years of training. Most of my time was spent as a commander in Gaza and down on the Egyptian border."

Nadav motioned with his head in Alon's direction and continued. "I was also in Lebanon with the war last summer…then back to Gaza, and…now I'm home!" His smile showed relief. "And really, it's difficult *not* to see God through all the situations and all the different run-ins we've had with our cousins. You can't go through that and say God doesn't exist or God is not protecting you. Sometimes we went in and we were not prepared, and sometimes we did all the wrong things, but God was still watching over us. Every time, after a contact, we looked at each other and saw that none of us had a scratch on our bodies. We looked around and said, 'Wow! That wasn't supposed to happen—God has definitely taken care of us.'"

He handed the microphone back to Eitan. "Thank you, Nadav. We were praying for you guys, and we are very glad that you are home safely."

"Now I want Michael Rosen to come forward. Michael is a strong believer and mentor to others. At the moment, he serves as our youth pastor in the congregation."

Most of the soldiers had heard Michael before.

"I finished army about a year ago. I served in a tank division as the tank driver. Although I was on the Jordanian and Syrian borders for a while, most of my time was in the Gaza strip. I was there during the disengagement and with some of the operations of the Israeli Defense Force. God was so faithful to me in the army! Some of you have heard me say this before, but God will give you grace not only to survive in the military atmosphere as a believer, but also to grow stronger and to share the gospel with other people. I was not in Lebanon during the war, but my whole unit was there, and some of those who served with me died.

"What touched my heart was to know that I had shared the gospel with each of those who died. God opened the door for me to speak to them before...before the time..." Michael looked down. His voice was broken when he spoke again. "So, my time of service was difficult, but God was faithful, and He helped me to shine the light of Yeshua. Amen."

"Amen!" echoed Eitan. "God is faithful, but He also calls *us* to be faithful, right? I remember how Gideon told us about an encounter they had in Nablus. This is Gideon Bar-David, who was a paratrooper. God had been drawing him very close to Himself while he was in the army. One day, his unit received an order to enter the city of Shechem and to operate against a terrorist group that planned to launch an attack against Israel. Gideon and his unit entered in three armored jeeps. Most of the army jeeps have thick armor around them; however the roofs aren't bullet-proof. While they were driving, his officer spotted a terrorist trying to hide in an alley close to the area of their mission. His officer decided to drive after the guy, but it was an ambush. They started taking heavy fire from different locations on the rooftops. Gideon was in the lead vehicle. It broke down, stopping the whole unit in the heart of the ambush. They tried to shoot from their jeeps, but they were pinned down under the heavy fire. They were trapped! As far as I remember, the platoon leader decided to do a rescue mission. The vehicle behind them started pushing Gideon's jeep from the alley, trying not to flip him. Gideon and the others shot from the back doors of the jeep. By a miracle, the engine started again. They managed to get out without any injured soldiers. Gideon said that while they were under fire, he had a calm assurance that nothing would happen to him because God was with him. He could *feel* the presence of the Lord. In spite of the fear and adrenaline, he trusted God. When they finished the operation and went back to the base, they found bullets on the floor of the jeep and holes in the roof right above his head. He said a shiver went through his entire body when he saw those bullet holes. Afterward, Gideon asked himself, 'Why me? Why am I still alive?' He realized it was because Yeshua had a plan for his life. It was God's mercy and love that protected him."

Avner Ben Tzion, a mature officer in the Permanent Force came up, and Eitan gave him an opportunity to speak.

"Friends, there is a great assurance in what these brothers shared with you today. You can count on the faithfulness of Yeshua to protect you when you are in danger. If God has given you promises, you can be sure that He does not want you to die before your time. So, when your life is threatened, you can call upon the Lord and pray, 'Father, remember Your promise!' Say it aloud! You stand upon the Word of God. It can be like a mighty sword in that moment. Say, 'God, remember You showed that I would become a computer engineer, or an electrician, or study medicine, or whatever.'

"Do you remember those disciples who were in the boat when the storm came on the *Kinneret*? Yeshua said, 'We are going to the other side.' If they had believed His words, they would not have been afraid. They would have known that they would see the other side regardless of the storm. If the Lord tells you something about your future, you can be sure that when the order comes to strike a contact with terrorists, you will live through the battle."

Eitan concluded, "In Psalm 50:15, God says, *Call upon me in the day of trouble; and I will deliver you, and you shall glorify me!*"

When the worship leader started to play "The Name of the Lord Is a Strong Tower," the soldiers stood to their feet. Greatly encouraged, they sang together in a loud voice.

During the refreshment break, Ester noticed Daniel, and her heart missed a beat. She turned her back to him. Her knees felt weak. She tried her best to engage in a conversation with the girl next to her, but to no avail. Before long, she asked her friend if they could go to the bathroom. They slipped out the side entrance.

Avishai motioned his head in the direction of a group of young soldiers gathered around Michael. "Wanna hear what they're saying." He walked a few paces forward and Daniel followed.

"How do the other guys take the fact that you're a believer?" asked a new recruit.

Michael smiled. "Secular soldiers think I'm weird because I don't swear, have sex, and do the things they do. And some of the religious kids really don't like me."

"But Yeshua said that this world would hate us because we are not part of it, so you need to face it," commented another soldier.

"Right," said the rookie.

"But you can ask people who pray to make a shield around you spiritually as well as physically," someone else piped up.

The young man frowned. "What do you mean?"

"Does anybody pray for you?" asked another guy.

"Yes—my congregation."

"They will pray for physical protection from attacks like bullets and stuff, but also ask them to pray for your spiritual life."

"Right," said Alon, who had just joined the circle. "Sometimes you will find yourself in a sick environment, where guys speak about things that defile your thoughts. It can be really engulfing. Also, the spiritual atmosphere in Gaza or in the territories is very oppressive. You *feel* the

43

darkness. When you have to go into zones of Islam, you sense that there are many evil forces in the air. Ask your friends to pray for double protection."

"Yes," added Michael. "One of the hardest things before operations was the feeling that I was alone. But the most encouraging was to know that there were people praying."

The young recruit slowly nodded.

Daniel turned around and swept the room with his eyes. No Ester. "I'm going outside," he said to his friend. "You coming?"

"Wait," said Avishai. "Need something to drink."

They walked to the table at the back of the room and each helped himself to cookies and a mug of steaming coffee.

TEN

Sunday, 22 April 2007

WHEN ESTER TIPPED her shoulder bag onto her bed, the newsletter from *Ohalei Rachamim* fell out. She moved her stuff to one side and flopped down on her pillow. Pulling her legs up, she settled comfortably on her back. Unfolding the brochure, she began to read.

UNDER THE SHADOW OF THE ALMIGHTY

Alon Stern was at home enjoying some well-earned time off when he heard the news of Gilad Shalit's capture. Immediately his officer training prompted him into action. Within minutes he was packed and organizing troop detail for his unit to mobilize.... Alon serves as a First Lieutenant in the IDF. This 21-year-old is second in command of a combat company of 90 soldiers. His unit is responsible to patrol along the Lebanese border. The IDF has trained and equipped Alon well, but as the second Lebanon war raged on, Alon experienced the miraculous power of God that no high-tech weapon could match.

A week into the war, Alon and his men were in a border town loading their gear off a truck when news came that five IDF soldiers on a mission in Lebanon had been killed in an ambush. In the ensuing retrieval mission, four bodies were recovered but one remained. Alon went back over the border with two tanks to recover the last fallen comrade. Hizb'Allah was also in pursuit of the body but by God's grace Alon and his men prevailed.

This was the first of many dangerous missions Alon led during the war. Time and again Alon faced ambushes, rocket attacks, booby traps, and road mines. At the start of a new and dangerous mission, Alon would broadcast over his tank's internal radio these words of hope and faith to his men: *He who dwells in the secret place of the Most High shall abide under the shadow of the Almighty. I will say of the Lord, He is my refuge and my fortress; my God; in Him I will trust. Surely He will deliver you from the snare of the fowler and from the perilous pestilence. He shall cover you with His feathers, and under His wings you shall take refuge. His truth shall be your shield, and buckler. You shall not be afraid of the terror by night; nor the arrow that flies by day; nor of the pestilence that walks in darkness, nor of the destruction that lays waste at noonday. A thousand may fall at your side, and ten thousand at your right hand; but it shall not come near you* (Psalm 91:1–7). Tanks can be cumbersome when facing guerrilla warfare. Though powerful, they are not as mobile as infantry and their huge diesel engines and track treads can be heard a long way off. Many of the villages of south Lebanon served as cover for Hizb'Allah guerrillas seeking to set ambushes for Israeli armor. Alon was all too familiar with this risk. "I was afraid. Sometimes my heart was really pumping, but I knew that nothing would happen to me. I had a sense of assurance—deep down I knew I was protected." Faith is not the absence of fear but rather setting one's will to move forward even when fearful emotions are in play. Alon's prayer for protection was "Lord, even though we are in this big noisy tank, **make us invisible….**"

Alon saw comrades die before his eyes: "The hardest part of the war was seeing the young men killed. I would be thinking what it would be like for their mothers. How would they take the news that their son had been killed?"

For Alon's own mother, Tamar, these matters were a constant motivation for prayer: "I was in my own war. I had to quickly take hold of my thoughts and force myself to believe the Word of God. Many nights I would spend on the floor on my face, crying. So often I had no words, but the Lord knows the heart. I didn't need words, my heart cry was all God needed to know what I was saying."

Tamar is an intercessor with deep experience in coming before the Lord on behalf of others, but the war took her to new depths of prayer. There are prayers that only mothers truly know. Alon's simple prayer for protection was joined in the heavenly realms by the deep cry of a mother's love. Our soldiers faced many difficulties and fought with honor and courage. More than 100 made the ultimate sacrifice for the nation by laying down their lives for *Eretz Yisrael*. Many mothers have been bereaved of their children. We honor these young fallen heroes but we do them no disservice by marveling at the answer to Alon and Tamar's prayers. Though under heavy fire and rocket attacks, not one from Alon's company of 90 men was even injured. Alon's company is part of a battalion of 700 men; not one soldier was killed from this battalion. This is truly the secret place of the Most High. One of Alon's fellow deputy company commanders could only ponder with amazement: "I don't understand how you haven't been hit yet; It is like **you guys are invisible!**"

Alon will soon finish his four years of duty and is looking forward to civilian life. But he knows being a soldier in Israel's army is to stand against spiritual forces opposed to God who are endeavoring to thwart His sure and unshakable promises. Alon explained, "I know there is a spiritual dimension to this conflict. The war was to stop *Katyushas*, but I know I was also defending Israel in the spiritual realm. Because I know God is with me I did not let fear overtake me. He gave me the confidence to do what I needed to do." Buoyed by a mother's prayers, this young man can truly say. *The Lord, He is my refuge and my fortress; my God; in Him I will trust."*

A MOTHER'S HEART

During the Lebanon war and with our son Alon in frontline combat for the entire conflict, I found myself being thrust into a place of taking hold of Yeshua in ways I had not needed to before the war. I had no choice. Deep places in me were opened up, and out of that deep place came the deep heart cry. It is in times such as these that were so totally overwhelming, devastating, and life threatening that we call out to the God of Israel with all that is within us, deep calling unto deep. When life is relatively peaceful and comfortable, the deep cry is not there. After the war, I began to see that Israel as a nation is going to very soon enter into this place of desperation, and will have no choice but to release that heart cry unto our God, the God of Israel, who is our only hope for deliverance from the wolves that surround us. A cry that He is waiting to hear from His people, so He (not the USA or other nations, or even our IDF) can deliver them. And all the earth will know that there is a God in Israel.

Tamar Stern

Ester looked at the photo of Alon between his parents. She saw that they stood next to their son, smiling proudly. He was wearing his IDF uniform, with a gun slung over his left shoulder. In the photo on the opposite page from the article, he was camouflaged for combat. His face was serious, but in his eyes there was a hint of hope. She thought, *How cool that God can make a tank invisible!*

ELEVEN

Wednesday, 16 May 2007

THE WEATHER WAS BEAUTIFUL when Ester finished her work and walked out of the office. As she often did, she opted for a longer route home to get some exercise. She walked down King David Boulevard, through Yitzhak Rabin park, past the Tel Aviv city hall, and down Ben Gurion Avenue, avoiding cyclists on their way home. She breathed deeply.

"Hmmm…Love the shade of these big trees!" she whispered to herself as she stretched her steps to get a more thorough workout.

The daily routine of walking to and from the base brought order to her life since the transfer from the *Negev* desert. She shook her head as she thought back to her first year in the south. *Abba, thank You for moving me. If my commander hadn't arranged for me to come to HaQirya, I don't know how I would have survived the army.*

Reaching the apartment, she ran up two flights of stairs in a final effort of exertion. Unlocking the door with the key around her neck, she thought, *Funny how I've changed! Before, I loved jewelry. Since barracks, the only thing I wear is this unsightly thing.*

But she didn't resent it. There was a certain kind of honor in wearing a uniform. *It's cool being in the army.* She smiled. *Now that this filly's broken in, it's okay.*

Noticing that her mother was not back from work, Ester washed her face, dried her hands, and went to the computer. A letter from Debra waited in her mailbox, and she was glad. She loved Debra's occasional writings.

Hey Esush!

Wish you could have been here for JERUSALEM DAY celebrations!

The gang arranged a picnic in Independence Park, but it was rained out. Fourteen of us ended up grilling our meat on Avishai's balcony. Today was the latest date for rain I've ever heard of in Israel. Why, in the month of May! Can you believe that?! Not only a few drops—it poured for about two hours. You should have seen it!

We ran for cover to Avi's apartment and watched the people who had come from all over the country—busloads of youth from the settlements, etc.—just for the day. It was supposed to be sunny, and parks were crowded with people doing barbeques.☺ Trying to!

When it started raining, the military was in parade on Mount Herzl…VIPs were under shelter, but the soldiers all got wet. Thousands of people were at the Wall, and everybody out on the streets in the march got soaked. You know how teens wrap the Israeli flag around them? There were many, many blue and white flags… SO beautiful to see! People were dancing in the rain. Puddles and pools of water everywhere!

Was like a huge joy in the city. Boys jumped and sang and splashed one another, it was awesome! Later we saw the settlers coming back from the Western Wall, their kipas, jeans, and long skirts still sopping wet. Yet everybody seemed happy. I think the organizers of events were bit frustrated, and traffic was stuck. Smile…what did they expect?

WE ARE PRAYING FOR AN OUTPOURING OF GOD'S SPIRIT IN
ISRAEL! You know Zechariah, Isaiah, Jeremiah, Ezekiel, and Joel all
speak about God pouring out His Spirit like rain: I will sprinkle clean
water on my people…I will pour out my Spirit…I will cause the latter
rain…showers to come down.

Today was like I saw those prophecies before my eyes!

I know, I know. I must come to visit!

Actually I miss your mom, and I haven't seen Dudi for a lo-o-ong
time!

> Give them each a kiss,
> Love u lots! Deb xxx

"Wow!" Ester smiled as she sat back in the office chair. *Today it's forty
years since the Temple Mount was liberated. The rain was like a birthday
gift from Jerusalem in heaven to Jerusalem local!*

TWELVE

Friday, 18 May 2007

Shabbat DINNER WAS FINISHED and Miriam was cleaning up in the kitchen. The twins had left to visit with friends.

"Abba, can I ask you something?"

"Sure, Daniel. What's up?" The evening was quiet and the breeze pleasant on the balcony.

"How did you and Mom meet one another?"

"The long or the short version?"

Daniel smiled. "You can tell me the whole story."

"Abba, so how do you know...?"

Daniel looked around to make sure they were alone. Finding it hard to utter the question, he cleared his throat and leaned forward on the railing. "How do you know when you're ready for a relationship?" There had been girls he fancied, but Daniel had never pursued anyone before.

His father put his arm over Daniel's shoulder and looked at the lights of Malcha Mall down below.

"Well…" Hanan breathed deeply. "I guess the first thing you realize is that you desire it."

He brought his arm down and leaned on the railing the same way Daniel did.

"Mmm…" Daniel waited for more.

Sensing his son's anticipation, Hanan tried to tune in.

"You begin to feel the need for companionship. A friend—a committed female friend—someone you could consider becoming your wife."

"Yes, Abba. That desire's been there for a long time." Daniel was a tinge impatient. "But how do you know when you are ready?"

"Well." Hanan rubbed his chin. "I think you're ready when you know *who* you are."

"Do you think I know?" Daniel asked with the kind of vulnerability a person musters only when he knows he is totally safe.

"Yes. You know who you are. I couldn't say that three years ago, but now…" Hanan thoughtfully nodded. "You know who you are."

"Why do you say that, Abba?" Daniel looked at his father with eyes searching wisdom from the most trusted person in his life.

His father was in no hurry. "Mom and I have seen you grow a lot since you went to the air force. Your character has developed. We can see it by the choices you make. You are an upright young man." Hanan contemplated for a moment and continued. "You've overcome your fear of people and you stand up for what you believe—even in the face of rejection. We are very proud of you, my boy."

"Thanks, Abba."

"And when it comes to a girl…a young lady, when you know who you are and where you are going, she can follow. Do you understand this?"

"Yes, Abba."

"That's another thing. Mom and I often pray for you boys to know your calling."

"What is my calling, Abba?" Daniel looked at his dad.

Hanan smiled. "Well, I have *some* idea, based on the specific talents God has given you. You're a good leader, and we know that He will use you to influence people. But all of us have a calling based on the command Yeshua gave—to love God and to love one another."

Hanan turned toward Daniel and looked into the eyes of his son. "We can see that you love the Lord and that you care a great deal about other people. That's our primary responsibility—those two things."

Then he contemplated Daniel's question again. Smiling, Hanan mused, "The young lady you choose will be very blessed, my son."

Daniel quickly looked down.

Hanan knew his son well. He had told Miriam some time back that he suspected a romantic consideration to be on the boy's mind. He put his arms around Daniel, and they hugged a strong manly hug.

"Thank you, Abba." Daniel's voice was strained from the squeeze.

"You're welcome, Daniel."

THIRTEEN

Sunday, 20 May 2007

TEST - ESTER, THIS YR CELL? DANIEL

ESTER LET OUT A SHRIEK that pierced the office. Several soldiers jumped up from their seats. Holding her hand over her mouth and blushing, she declared. "Sorry! It's nothing. It's okay. I'm okay!"

Clenching her cell phone tightly, she spun around and ran out the door. Outside, the breeze brought welcome relief to her flushed body. She trembled as she confirmed his question. She could almost hear her heart beating as she fixated on the screen.

Expecting another text message, she was startled when the phone rang. Shaking, she put it to her ear.

"*Shalom*, Ester?"

"Yes?"

"This is Daniel. Daniel Cohen."

"Ehmm…yes?

"Are you okay?"

"Yes…yes, why?"

"You sound out of breath."

"No, I'm okay. Really." She licked her lips and swallowed hard to relieve the dryness in her mouth.

"I was wondering…I need to come to HaQirya tomorrow. Would you like to meet me for coffee somewhere?"

"Ehmm…yes." She was baffled and did not know how to sound calm. "Would be nice."

"Do you want me to pick you up or meet you somewhere? I'll be done by four o'clock."

"Don't pick me up. I'll meet you…meet you somewhere."

"Where?"

"Ehmm…" Her mind raced through the Azrieli mall, thinking of *Café Hillel, Cafe Joe…No, all too public!*

"There's an Aroma Cafe on Yigal Alon Street, about two blocks away."

"I know—other side of the station."

"With the umbrellas."

"Right. How about 4:15?"

"Good." She sounded a bit more composed.

"Great," said Daniel. "I'm looking forward to it."

She could hear the smile in his voice.

FOURTEEN

Monday, 21 May 2007

HAVING GONE to the mirror in the bathroom for the umpteenth time, Ester walked out of the office at quarter to four. She asked permission to leave a little early rather than run the risk of Daniel driving past her while she was walking.

"Oh, this silly uniform! It fit me once, but now it's so baggy it looks like a sack." She spoke to herself as she ran across the street at the traffic light on Menachem Begin Street and onto the bridge over the railway. The adrenaline pumping through her had made it hard to sleep since yesterday. Hard to eat, hard to concentrate, hard to anything! She heard herself between panting breaths praying, "Abba, please don't let me be silly while I'm with Daniel. Please let him like me. Please help me talk sense."

Once inside, she sat at three different tables before settling for one in a far corner against the wall. She dug in her pockets for something to hold the table while she went to the bathroom. Once there, she drank water and splashed her face. No need for cheek pinching today! She dried her hands on a paper towel. Trying to regulate her breathing, she looked at herself in the mirror. "Don't look too long. Don't think too much," she told herself. She took the rubber band out of her long brown hair and first shook it forward and then threw it back. She drank some water and dried her mouth and hands—again. Ester blotted the basin area with a paper towel before walking back to the table.

Sitting down, she stared in the opposite direction away from the door. *He mustn't think I've been waiting for him.* Her heart was beating out of its box.

Peace walked in with Daniel as he rounded the corner and entered the Aroma Café. She didn't know how much he had prayed for this moment—she only felt its effect.

"Hi, Ester." He greeted her with a warm smile.

"Oh, hi," she said, feeling the color rise in her face.

They ordered from the counter—he an ice-aroma, she an orange juice.

The next two hours flew past. He learned that she worked in the sociology department of the army headquarters and that she did sociometric testing of army recruits. These assessments measure interactions between members of a group. Questions might be something like, "Who in this group do you want to be your buddy in combat? Who will you ask for advice? Who in the group do you think will be the right leader in such-and-such an assignment?" The point of the testing is to create trust and cooperation and to enhance the cohesiveness in a unit.

"So I sit in front of a computer most of the day, processing data. Sometimes I have to stand in front of group of soldiers and explain the testing procedure to them. I *hate* doing it. I feel so self-conscious!"

As they talked, Ester learned that Daniel was stationed at Palmachim, the air force base south of Tel Aviv. He flew an attack helicopter and his squadron was 160—First Cobra. Daniel told Ester that he grew up in a messianic home, but he never had the courage to tell his friends at school that he was a believer. "Actually, I resented the fact that I was living two lives. At home I was a believer, but at school I was just like everybody else. Did my level best not to appear different from the others.

Only at the end of my school career did I gather courage to let my best friend in on the secret."

She listened with understanding. Here in Israel, to believe in Yeshua was a big turn-off, and Ester had tasted the rejection of making her faith known.

"Basically, from that time, I had a chance to start a new life. I decided that when I went to the army, I'd tell the guys about Yeshua from the first moment. You know how it is," Daniel continued. "Everywhere you go, you have an interview with the commander. So that was the best opportunity to share about my faith in Yeshua. I would speak about my family, and then I would say, '...and another important thing you should know about me is that I am a messianic Jew.' Then I told them what that means."

"Wow, what courage!" Ester looked at him with admiration.

"No." Daniel brushed aside the compliment. "School was over, and these were totally different people. I was not prepared to go through the terrible struggle of having a double identity again." He thought a bit. "Actually, as soon as all my commanders knew, the information got to the rest of the soldiers, and in no time everybody knew I'm a believer. Of course, they also saw me reading my Bible."

"How did the other soldiers take it?"

"Some didn't understand it and some hated me, but there were others who had respect for my belief."

Ester was honestly amazed. "I have shared my faith with some of my friends, but my commanders don't know."

"It's better that everybody knows rather than trying to hide it and feeling horrible. For me, to come out of that hypocrisy was the best thing in the world."

Ester changed the topic. "How did you make it through the selection process? I know thousands of guys do the tests for pilots' course—medical, intelligence, and psychological tests—but only a few hundred make it to the pilots' *gibush*."

"*Gibush* was the hardest thing! Those six days were so tough. I would not have made it without the Lord."

"Why do so few recruits succeed? I mean, what do you guys physically have to do on the *gibush*?"

"This is not to boast, but I'm sure you've heard it said that becoming an Israeli pilot is the world's most demanding selection course. Basically, they want only the very best. They put you under massive pressure. During that week, they do not give you enough food and they watch how you cope. They never give you time to finish things, and they create situations of stress, trying to make you crack. You walk for hours and hours with heavy equipment, and they try to make you *kaput!* And then, when you have nothing left, they test you for problem resolution, crisis management, and so on." Daniel sighed.

"The testing part I know. That's what we have to process. Other guys fill in forms about you and grade your performance for leadership capabilities and people skills, yes? And they look for exceptional loyalty. I know. I key that data into the computer afterward."

Daniel nodded, almost relieved that he did not have to say more about it. "It was only God that got me through."

"Wow!" Ester's adoring eyes soothed his memory.

"Of the guys who started the pilots' course, most dropped out over three years. We also had to do a first degree through Ben Gurion University."

"What did you take?"

"My majors were economics and business management. They believe educated pilots are a better breed because they have a wider spectrum of thinking."

Ester slowly nodded. "Wide spectrum...I always thought I had an open mind, but in the army I realized much of my 'free thinking' was just because I was rebellious. It was so hard for me to cope with authority. In our home I made the rules. Before I came to Yeshua, I sometimes stayed out all night. My mom? Now I feel terrible, but I never listened to her."

Ester sipped the last juice from her glass with a slurp. "Submitting to a commander was very hard for me. Every time I had to salute him, something in me became stiff."

Daniel smiled at her honesty.

"Last week was my spiritual birthday—three years with Yeshua!" she exclaimed with excitement. "Felt like I was in a tomb for most of the time. But now I feel like a butterfly crawling out of a cocoon."

Daniel stretched, rubbed his stomach, and looked at his watch. "Wow! No wonder I'm hungry. You want to eat something?"

"No, thanks. I'm not hungry." She thought, *This conversation was food—I was like starved!*

Before they walked out, he bought a chicken schnitzel sandwich at the counter. "Sure you don't want anything?"

"No, really. My mom made dinner."

When they went outside, it was already dark. Daniel persuaded Ester to let him take her home. They walked to his blue Mazda 3, and he opened the door on the passenger's side. Once underway, she navigated home. When they were about three streets parallel from the sea front, they turned right on Ben Yehuda Street and stopped in front of number 182. She hopped out and was surprised when he got out of the car as well and walked around.

Daniel touched her near her elbow. "Thank you. It was great getting to know you a little better."

"Also for me." She smiled shyly.

Squeezing her arm he said, "We'll do it again."

"With pleasure." The warmth crept up to her cheeks.

Back in the car, he said through the open window, "I'll call you."

Smiling, Ester spun around and ran inside.

Earlier, Ester had told her mom she would be home late. Now she walked straight to her room to avoid conversation. Parking in front of the mirror, she put both hands to her face. "Wow! A pilot!" She shook her head in disbelief.

Ester took a quick shower and slipped into her pajamas. She tiptoed to the kitchen, heated her food in the microwave, and returned to the bedroom with her plate. Before closing the door, she stuck her head out and shouted down the passage, "G'night, Eema!"

FIFTEEN

22 May 2007

Thank You, Yeshua, for a new season in my life. You restored joy to my heart. Thank You that I can hope again. Thank You for pouring Your amazing grace on me.

You said, "IT IS NOT THE HEALTHY WHO NEED A DOCTOR, BUT THE SICK" (Matt. 9:12).

Thank You for being my Doctor! Thank You that after everything I went through, You're making me the person I was meant to be. COME, LET US RETURN TO THE LORD, FOR HE HAS TORN, AND HE WILL HEAL US; HE HAS STRUCK US, AND HE WILL BIND OUR WOUNDS (Hosea 6:1). Loving Father in heaven, I know that I am NOT the way I used to be.

Hallelujah!! Thank You for Your patience!!! Philippians 3:13–14

I LEAVE MY FAILURES NOT TO RETURN TO THE FEAR, BUT I RUN FORWARD.

Thank You that Daniel took me for coffee. It was SO nice. I will not make myself crazy about the future. One day at a time with You, Yeshua!

Help me not to return to fear again. Even if the worst happens. Even if Daniel should reject me, You are with me.

Abba, help me to share my faith, like D. does. I'm sorry that I've been afraid to say I'm a believer. Please forgive me. I do not want to be ashamed of Your Name. You're the best part of my life.

SIXTEEN

23 May 2007

It's Shavu'ot, the day when the Holy Spirit was poured out on the disciples. You are an all-powerful God! You could easily fill my heart too. Fill me with faith that will burst out of me. Faith that can move mountains. I need You with my eating, Lord! Today I feel that craving again. Is it because I feel scared? Am I eating for comfort? Fill me with hope and courage. You promised that You would pour out your Spirit on Your sons and daughters. Do it again, Abba, until we are a generation filled with holiness and power. Yeshua, fill us with Your passion. Pour Your love into our hearts until we are totally in love with You. Burning...

Bring Your fire on us, Yeshua! Melt the believers together.

I read something in Ephesians 2:11–21 about unity in the Messiah. Jews and Gentiles are ONE NEW MAN. Yeshua destroyed the hostility between us by His death. He made peace. Real peace. Now He builds us into a holy temple of God.

All of a sudden I realize the Jews cannot build a tabernacle for God alone. We need the Arab believers. Cool!!! Shavu'ot—the time when we read the story of Ruth. Wasn't she an Arab? (She was from Moab, that's in Jordan today???) This lady humbled herself and became one with the Jewish nation. She married Boaz and they were like ONE NEW MAN. Awesome!!

"YOUR GOD, MY GOD. YOUR PEOPLE, MY PEOPLE..."

Abba, I feel like I discovered a treasure. I'm sure this was always Your dream. Wow, imagine believers from all races loving one another like one big family....THAT will change the world!

SEVENTEEN

Monday, 28 May 2007

A WEEK LATER. Same place. Almost exactly the same time. Ester sat down at the table in the corner, waiting...

She inspected her hands, took a toothpick, and began to clean her nails. At least she was not as nervous as the previous week. After about ten minutes, she looked at her watch and checked the time at the counter. It was 17h12. Suddenly, her phone beeped a text message.

LATE – TRAFFIC, D

She slid down, put her feet on the opposite chair, and tried to relax. *It's going to be a while.* She felt fidgety. After five more minutes she got up and went outside.

"Guess I'm a bit tense," she said, talking to herself. "Not that I'm looking for him...just need fresh air." She scrolled down the mailbox of her cell phone for messages. Yep, there's one from Nora and one from Gad. She began a text conversation with Nora, but said nothing about the new interest in her life. *She'll make me crazy with questions. And if she hears who I'm seeing...oh my, she'll be envious! No, first see what happens.*

"Hi, Ester!" She jerked her head at Daniel's greeting. "Sorry, I didn't mean to scare you!" He laughed.

"No, it was so nice outside, I just came…" She tried her best to appear relaxed.

"Would you like to sit here?" Daniel pointed to the section under the umbrellas. Although it was not dark yet, the small lamps on the tables had been lit.

"Why not? It's a pleasant evening."

After submitting her bag to the security guard, she walked ahead. "This okay?" she asked over her shoulder, touching an empty table.

"Perfect," said Daniel. "I'm hungry. Shall I get us something to munch?"

Ester panicked for a moment. *Eat in front of Daniel?*

"What's on the menu?" She stalled for time.

"Don't know. You want me to get one?"

"Ehmm…no. Maybe just a salad—tuna. Tuna salad."

"Good. I'm getting a sandwich and an ice-aroma." He began to walk away, then turned around again. "Sorry, something to drink?"

"Nothing." She winked.

He's a bit stressed…probably the traffic. Maybe he doesn't like to be late. She picked up his car keys from the table and folded her hands over them. "Abba, please bless our time together," she prayed as she had done many times in the days preceding.

A few minutes later, Daniel was back. He sat down and began by asking about her day. It wasn't long before the intercom called his name for their order. He returned, carrying a tray with their meals. He placed a huge salad in front of Ester. "The orange juice is for you. Thought you're just too shy to ask."

"Thanks. And if it's too much?" She looked up.

"I'll finish it." He took a sip from his coffee-flavored drink, so thick he could hardly pull it up through the straw. He smiled. "You know us men! Hey…been meaning to ask—you have any siblings?"

"One brother—David."

"I have four. And two sisters-in-law." He took another sip of his ice-aroma.

"Didn't I introduce you to Roi that night at Simchat Adon?"

"Yes."

"Well, he's a twin. The other twin is Ido. They are my youngest brothers. And then there's Yonatan, the oldest. He is married and has five kids. His wife is Rachel. Li'or is second, and he's married to Ruth. They have a baby and live in the Galilee."

Daniel took a bite of his sandwich, chewed a bit, and then said, "So we're five brothers. Now tell me about your family."

Ester looked at her salad and began to pick at the lettuce leaves. "Well, it's only David and me. He's three years younger, but we're very close. My dad..." She shook her head. "He divorced my mom about four years ago, and it hit us hard. She's a believer and that's the reason he gave for leaving us. They were married for eighteen years. He chose to tell us at the time of David's *bar mitzva*. I'm...I'm really worried about my brother. He seems very dark lately. I wonder if he has thoughts of suicide."

She sipped slowly at her orange juice. "My mom was like a bird with both wings broken. Very shocked. We were all in shock. Almost like paralyzed for two or three years. It's only since she's found a job that she's becoming a person again. Works at a nursery school. It's a very hard season behind us." She stirred the juice with her straw. "Do you remember I said last week that I was in the tomb? My parents' divorce was part of it."

Daniel nodded. He had stopped eating and was looking at her with deep compassion. "Ester, I cannot even imagine what happens when a person's dad leaves the house."

Feeling his tenderness, Ester's eyes teared up. She took another sip to shift the lump in her throat. "I'm okay. I'm just worried about David."

Daniel put his hand on her arm for a moment. "We can pray for him tonight before I take you home."

"God helped me...us." Ester tried to compose herself. "In the worst times I felt so broken, but Yeshua carried me."

69

Suddenly her phone rang. "Hi, Gad. Ehmm…no, can't talk right now. I'll phone you back." She ended the call.

"Who's Gad?" asked Daniel in a typical Israeli way—no niceties.

"Oh, just a friend. Went to school with me, and he's doing army patrols in Hebron at the moment."

"Do you have many friends?" asked Daniel.

Sensing the gist of his question, she put him at ease. "I've kept contact with a few of my girl friends, but during the past three years I have been kind of…cut off." She thought for a moment. "Actually, I think it was God who cut me away from my worldly friends. The circle is definitely not as large as it used to be." Trying to lighten up, she added with a smile, "I was quite a party girl."

"That reminds me—how did you come to know Yeshua?" Daniel took another big bite and said with a full mouth, "Wanted to ask you since the first time."

"Wait," she said. "I need to eat a bit first. Please tell me about your parents."

He swallowed and smiled as if he had been asked to speak on a favorite subject. Daniel related how they made *aliyah* from America when Yonatan was four and Li'or was in diapers. He told how his dad served in the army when they first immigrated to Israel; how hard it was to learn Hebrew; and the contrast in development, quality, and service between the two countries in those early days. Daniel told how he and the twins were born in Israel.

"Last week you said you were a believer at school already. Was your family always part of a believing community?" Ester asked.

"Yes. Because my parents came to the faith when they were newlyweds, they've been part of a congregation from the beginning. Since moving to Jerusalem their congregation is Simchat Adon."

"Which was…?"

"Ten years ago."

"You and I are very different," said Ester. "My dad never allowed us to go to church or to sing about Yeshua. My mom tried to teach us

when we were little. That's before we—David and I—became wild."
Ester took a last bite, leaving about half of the salad.

"So," she said, smiling, "you want to know how I came to Yeshua."
Pushing the plate forward, she proceeded to tell him how angry she was
with God for all the suicide bombings during the *intifada*. One day a
guy named Bar, who was heavily into black magic, started arguing with
her about the power of Satan versus the power of God. Even though
she had never really known God in a personal way, she knew enough
to be indignant at Bar's claims. She attacked him with strong examples
in defense of God and tried to prove him wrong.

"I was quite shocked at what came out of my mouth," said Ester.
"Here I was, listening to myself preaching the truth. All the things my
mom told me for years just came out like a river!

"I told him about Yeshua, and he even became hopeful." Ester was
still amazed at the fact that Bar initially believed. "However, Satan put
fear in his heart for all the curses and spells he was involved with. He
was afraid of the bigger guys and the other covens. You know the story
about the seeds that Yeshua told? Some were choked by the weeds. I
think fear choked his faith."

"Wow! That was quite a powerful gate to enter the world of the
supernatural, hey?" Daniel commented.

"Actually, I was so poop-scared of manifestations or demons, I
quickly made up my mind to be on God's side," Ester said bluntly.

"Did anybody help you confess your sins at that time?" asked Daniel.

"No." She looked at him with a puzzled expression.

"Your mom?"

"I wasn't speaking to her at the time. I did phone Debra after a few
days. Told her what I had decided about God, and she sounded very
happy." Ester put her hand on her heart in a gesture of gratitude. "We
are family, but Debbie's my best friend!"

"No, the reason I'm asking," said Daniel, "is because when my
parents came to faith, they had a supernatural encounter with God,

but the pastor of their first church doubted their salvation because they didn't walk down the aisle and respond to an altar call."

"They didn't *what*?" She stared at him with a blank expression.

"Sorry, you said you aren't really used to church and such things. Sometimes at the end of a service, the pastor invites people to come forward so they can be prayed for. They call that an 'altar call.'"

The terminology didn't make sense to her, but not wanting to appear dumb, Ester simply said, "Oh." She looked at Daniel as he started eating her salad and thought, *You're like the most relaxed guy I've ever met!* As if reading her thoughts, Daniel leaned back and rode his chair. *This guy's not just trying to play cool. Somehow he is really at peace, and that makes me feel safe.*

After talking for another hour, they each drank a cappuccino and called it a day.

On the way home, Ester suddenly remembered. "Could we pray for David?"

"Of course! Go ahead."

"Right now?"

"Why not?" He smiled in her direction, "I won't close my eyes."

Daniel listened as Ester expressed her heart to God with unfeigned sincerity. Her voice was thin, and she prayed like a child. Her vulnerability flipped a switch of male instinct. His heart surged with desire to envelop her in his arms.

When he stopped in front of the apartment, he leaned his head on the steering wheel. "Abba, David needs a father's love. Will You please bring him to meet You personally?" Suddenly his prayers felt weak and as if they were going nowhere. He suppressed the emotion that rose in his throat.

After a few moments of silence, Ester whispered a soft "thank you" and wiped her nose on the back of her hand.

Then they said goodbye and he started the car.

"I'm on standby this weekend, but I might exchange my duty with someone so I can be free on *Shabbat*. I'll give you a call."

Daniel drove around the corner, pulled over, and looked at himself in the mirror. He straightened one leg, pulled a packet of tissue out of his pocket, unfolded one, and blew his nose hard. *What's happening to me, Abba? I feel so protective!*

EIGHTEEN

Shabbat, 2 June 2007

BY THE TIME Daniel was supposed to arrive, there was a big pile of clothes on her bed. Ester had tried on about everything in her closet. She finally settled for knee-length jeans shorts and a green baby-doll top. *Actually, I'm glad I'm not doing the open-stomach shirts anymore. Was always self-conscious about my belly,* she thought. *Some of the things I used to wear were so uncomfortable.* She looked in the mirror once more. *Hope I'm okay!* She turned around and viewed herself over her shoulder. Just then Daniel honked outside. She had asked him to do that so she would know when to come down. Running out on the balcony, she shouted, "Three minutes!" He was just getting out of the car. Quickly applying her lip gloss, she grabbed her cell phone and pushed the two items into her back pocket. She took a line of toilet paper, folded it in half and half again, and stuck them in her other pocket.

"Bye, Eema!" She whirled past her mother, gave her a peck on the cheek, slammed the front door, and ran downstairs.

"Bye-bye!" Naomi shouted after her.

When Ester came to the street, Daniel, who was wearing beige Bermuda shorts and a turquoise T-shirt, was leaning against the car.

"Hey, you look cool!" She greeted him and lifted her hand to slap him a high five.

"And you. Lovely in green."

The expression in her face said, "*Really?*"

"For sure!" He smiled reassuringly. "Matches your eyes." He enjoyed seeing her blush.

"Ready to go?" He pressed the central-lock on his keys.

Imitating the sound of the car's alarm, she answered on a high note, "Yep-yep!"

"Which way to the promenade?" He pointed with his left and right thumbs.

"I want to show you some of my 'places,' so let's go-o-o…right!"

They walked down Ben Yehuda Street for a little way. Ester pointed out Shuki Zikri. "This is the salon where we had our hair done as models."

"You were a model?" Daniel was surprised.

"When I was fifteen and weighed forty-eight kilograms."

"Oh my! You were skin and bones," he said, laughing. "Who did you work for?"

"Izabelle. Our agency was in the Dizengoff building." She talked energetically as they walked along. "Being a model is a bit of glamour and lots of work. For one thing, you have to exercise really hard. And before a shoot, you don't eat anything, 'cause you want a flat tummy. You're never quite sure they'll be happy with how you look. You go to, like, a hundred auditions and you may succeed in getting one job." Ester shook her head. "Made me feel quite hopeless."

They turned left on Gordon Street.

"Wow, I'm glad you're not doing that anymore," Daniel said, thinking aloud.

"Why not?" This time Ester was surprised. She always thought a man wanted a girl to look like she was walking out of a magazine—*picture perfect.*

Daniel immediately realized he was on sensitive terrain. "Look, the values of the world and the values of God's kingdom are totally opposite. In the world, when you have money or good looks, you're something. But to Yeshua, everybody is valuable. Rich. Poor. Beautiful. Ugly. Everyone has the stamp of God's image on them."

"Wow! Didn't think I'd hear that from a guy's mouth." Ester was pensive.

"Even when I see a beggar on the street," Daniel continued, "I remind myself that the image of God in him is just broken."

"Right." Now Ester's compassion was aroused. "The poor prostitutes! Do you know they sometimes have to see two to four clients an hour?"

"And the pimps take all the money, right?"

"It's horrible!" Ester was silent for a while. "We models were also like slaves to the agency bosses. We hardly ever got paid."

Walking through a narrow alley, they came out at a road where the sea was directly ahead of them. He grabbed her hand as they ran to cross the busy main street.

Relaxing on the beach was a favorite pastime in Tel Aviv—especially on *Shabbat,* when families usually hung out together. The waterfront was already crowded when Daniel and Ester arrived. They began walking south, talking as if they had known each other all their lives. They passed the landmark Opera Tower. Kakao, Mike's Place, and Yotvata were all open in spite of *Shabbat.*

"Want ice cream?" Daniel asked out of the blue.

Panicking, she said, "Le' me think." Her mind flashed back to the conversation about modeling. She quickly reprimanded herself. *No! I'm no longer part of that weight control regime!*

"Maybe frozen yogurt?" she said when she realized she hadn't eaten breakfast.

After they got his on-a-stick and hers in-a-cup, they walked to the water's edge, took off their shoes, and enjoyed the damp sand. Daniel finished his ice cream quickly, and, pretending to press his stick into the wet sand, he scooped up a handful of water and sprinkled Ester. She looked at his naughty face and laughed. "Just let me finish this!"

A few minutes later, she bent down to wash her hands. At first Daniel thought it was a trick and leaped away. Then, deciding it was safe, he approached. Ester stomped her foot and splashed him. The front of his pants was completely wet. She turned and ran away. This resulted in wild chasing and water throwing until both were thoroughly soaked and out of breath.

"Let's walk...to the Dolphinarium," Daniel said, panting, as he pointed to a building about three hundred meters away.

"That place gives me creeps." Ester shook her head and shuddered. She was referring to the night of June 1, 2001, when twenty-one youth were killed in a suicide bombing. "I was fourteen at the time. We used to hang out in this club, but that night God spared my life."

"Oh, no!" Daniel was shocked. "Were you here when it happened?"

"No. That evening I was partying in the harbor, but we heard the explosion. Even now there's such an eerie feeling around the nightclub. They painted and fixed the entrance very quickly, but I never wanted to come back."

"I'm sure most kids never wanted to come back."

"You're right."

"I know. People don't want to travel the same bus lines and don't want to eat at places with the same names when they've gone through a bombing."

"Yes, they're afraid it'll happen again. Do you blame them?"

"Not at all. The psychological damage is huge. I have a friend in Jerusalem whose father was in the Moment Café when it blew up. He was afraid to go back to his work for months. His nerves were so frazzled he couldn't even go out the front door of their apartment."

"Not to mention those who lost their sight or hearing or even limbs. They're messed up for life."

"Okay, this is becoming too morbid. Change course. Instead of the Dolphinarium, let's walk to the Honey Beach Lounge." Daniel playfully grabbed Ester's wavy ponytail and swung her hair from the back of her head to the front, covering her eyes.

"Oh, yes!" She smiled. "The white chairs and couches at the cocktail bar are cool!"

Daniel asked me to be his girlfriend!!!

Wow! It's amazing. Exactly two months ago I prayed for someone.

It's huge fun to be with him. Daniel's really good for my self-image! He is so, like, "calm"!

Tonight he met Eema. She likes him too. Said his eyes are clean. What did she mean by that?

He wanted to see my room, but I said NO! It's a balagan.

David is not home. Why's he never at home?!

Wonder what he'll think of my boyfriend...Ha-ha.

THANKYOU, ABBA!! I am so-o-o excited. I'm going out with a pilot!!! Yay!

Thank You, Yeshua ! Can't get the smile off my face.

Daniel kissed me. Not on my mouth. Told him I wasn't ready. Just my forehead. Thank You that he understood...

I LOVE You, Abba. xxxxxxxx

Laila tov, Yeshua!

Oh, of course...You don't sleep.

I'm sure You enjoy watching over us. ☺

NINETEEN

Thursday, 21 June 2007

WHEN THE DOORBELL RANG, Ester hurried to the door. Daniel stood with his keys in one hand and his bag in another. She lifted her face to kiss him on the cheek. He closed his eyes for a moment and let out a tired sigh. "Hi, sweetheart."

"Did you go to the gym first?"

"Yes, after work. Mind if I take a quick shower?"

"Of course not." Her mother's voice was behind them as she wiped her hands on a cloth.

"*Shalom,* Naomi."

"You can kiss me." She offered her cheek. "Ester, please give Daniel a towel."

"No need, I have one."

Naomi shrugged her shoulders and lifted her chin slightly. "Use mine. It's clean and dry."

"Thanks." He took the fresh maroon towel from Ester.

She led him down the passage. "Put your bag and stuff in there." She pointed to her room—this time immaculately tidy.

After the shower, Daniel appeared in the same T-shirt he had worn when he asked her to go steady.

"I have good memories here." Ester smiled as she pinched the turquoise shirt between her fingers.

He put his arms around her and hugged her tight. "I'm feeling better now. How are *you* doing?"

She kicked the bedroom door closed with her foot. "Glad you came."

"Food is ready!" Naomi shouted from the dining area. Immediately Daniel released Ester and opened the door. She giggled.

Naomi walked down the passage and banged on another door. "David!" Quicker than usual, the door unlocked and Ester's brother appeared. His shoulders were drooped and his long hair hung over his face. He stretched out his hand to greet Daniel without making eye contact. They'd met before, but today David was in an unsociable mood.

They sat down to a steaming meal of spaghetti, mince, and salad, while Ester chattered nonstop. Naomi was happy to see her so chirpy. Daniel took a second helping and tried to make conversation with David.

"Howzit at school?"

David lifted his shoulders as if to say, "I don't know." Besides grabbing the ketchup every now and then and squirting out a whole lot, he was super quiet.

"The meal is really good, Naomi. I was starved," said Daniel.

"I'm glad you like it," she answered. His compliment was a blessing.

David got up and took his plate to the kitchen.

"Take Daniel's plate also, please." Ester rolled her fork around another bite. She knew her brother. He wouldn't throw a tantrum now.

When he walked past Naomi, she gave him her plate as well, but David snorted. It was only Daniel's presence that prevented an explosion.

When all were done eating, they cleared the table and packed the dishwasher. David disappeared into his cave and Naomi went to the computer. Ester washed some fruit and took it on a side plate to the lounge.

When they sat down to talk, Daniel looked around the room. "I left my wristwatch in the bathroom. Do you know what time it is? We need to see the news," he said. "I've got to know what's happening with the Hamas takeover in Gaza."

Ester pointed to a small clock on the TV cabinet. "'Nother nine minutes." She peeled a clementine, leaned forward, and spoke in a whisper. "I think David's doing drugs."

"What? Are you sure?" Daniel frowned.

"I smelled *hashish* in his room." She handed half the fruit to Daniel. "I'm going to ask him. I know he'll tell me the truth."

"Mmm..." Daniel nodded, chewing. "See why you're worried about him. His self-image is low, right?"

"He has none. He's wasted, man!" She sighed and put a wedge into her mouth. Lifting herself from the couch, she grabbed the remote and switched on the TV.

Daniel held Ester's hand while he concentrated on the presenter. When the news ended, he leaned his head back.

"Man, when Hamas is in power it is not only bad news for Israel, it's bad news for the locals in Gaza. May God have mercy on the believers there!"

Sensing that he needed quiet, she snuggled under his arm, and together they watched the next program. At one point she took the remote and said, "Just want to check something" as she flipped through the channels. A scene with a boat and a rescue mission flashed momentarily on the screen.

"Hey, go back." Daniel leaned forward.

When the action was over, one of the guys ended up with a girl in the cabin. He undressed her and things got steamy. Suddenly Daniel said, "Switch it off!" He jumped up and walked around the couch. Hands in his pockets, he said, "That was *not* good!"

Ester tried to play innocent, but she could see by the look on his face he was not okay.

"I'm sorry," she said.

"Not your fault." He shook his head.

"Please, come sit down," she begged.

He slowly walked back around the couch, took his hands out of his pockets, grabbed a pillow, and sat down hard.

"It upset me too," she said, looking down.

It was quiet between them—awkward.

"Maybe I should tell you…" she said very softly. She lifted both her hands to cover her face.

Suddenly Daniel snapped out of his own discomfort and looked at her. He gently touched her arm. "What?" he whispered.

When she removed her hands, tears were streaming down her cheeks. After more silence, she said with a broken voice, "Can we go to my room?"

"Okay." Daniel allowed compassion to override his convictions.

She closed the door and sat down on the bed. Pulling three tissues from the box at her bedside, she began to shake. Daniel sat down next to her and tried to comfort her. "What's wrong, my baby?" he asked as carefully as he could.

She sobbed and leaned into his embrace, while he tightened his hold on her. "Remember I said I wasn't ready for you to kiss me?" she said, still crying.

"Mmm…?"

After a long silence Ester tried to speak again, but her throat was raw. She dug her nails into his back and sobbed again. "This is so hard to tell you."

Sensing that whatever happened was too difficult for her to face, he held her tightly against him and rocked her like a child. "It's okay. Just cry. Get it out."

She folded over onto the bed, grabbed her pillow, and smothered the most pained sounds Daniel had ever heard. Tenderly rubbing her back, he felt helpless.

When she finally gained some calm, she lifted her red face and grabbed a few more tissues. She blew her nose and faced him shyly. "I'm sorry."

"It's okay," Daniel said gently. "Can you tell me what happened?"

"When I was sixteen, I had a boyfriend who was always pressuring me to sleep with him. We didn't have sex, but we did many things we weren't supposed to do. He told me I was naive and that I would see it wasn't such a terrible thing. 'Everybody makes such an issue of it, but after you've done it, you won't have a problem.' That's what he said. He was very obsessed. I didn't want it!" she said emphatically. She drew her breath and continued. "He said he loved me...but he didn't. Because one day he just...just...took me. Against my will." As her voice failed, she squeaked out the words: "He used force and he just did it."

Daniel put his arms around her again, but inside his emotions erupted like a volcano: *I will kill that guy! I will crush his skull!*

She clung to him as if her life depended on it. "It was horrible!" she sobbed. "I hated it!"

Hundreds of questions ran through Daniel's mind as he slowly nodded. "I understand," he said with self-control. "You were raped."

She sat up, blew her nose, and began to cry again.

Daniel put the pillow behind him, leaned back, and took a deep breath. Ester blew her nose again, and when she looked around, he motioned for her to put her head on his chest. He folded one arm around her and gently stroked her back with the other. After a time of quiet, he put his hands in her hair and with his mouth close to her ear asked, "What's his name?"

"Nir," she said quietly.

Daniel nodded again.

They stayed like that for a while. She became very calm and cuddled against him. Probably the exhaustion of having spilled her guts made her fall sound asleep.

About half an hour later, Daniel was feeling uncomfortable. Ester's breathing was slow and peaceful, but his was shallow and staggered.

Daniel's heart was beating wildly, and his mouth was dry. *I'm in trouble. How do I get out of this situation?* He finally shifted from underneath her, gently laid her head on the pillow, got up, and went to the bathroom.

When he came back, Daniel found Ester standing in front of the mirror, trying to clean her face. "Why didn't you tell me I looked like this?" She was embarrassed.

"That's nothing. Look at this mess." He pointed at the mascara stains on her pillow.

Walking over, he put both hands on her shoulders and met her eyes in the mirror. "You feeling okay now?" he asked softly.

She looked down and smiled weakly.

He kissed her on the back of her head and asked, "Will you make us some tea?" He squeezed her shoulders. "We need to talk."

No sexy movies
Not to be alone in my room w/door closed.
Told Daniel about Nir. VERY upset.

Too tired to pray...
X G'night, Abba

TWENTY

Motze Shabbat, 23 June 2007

ESTER SLEPT LATE. When the heat of the day made her uncomfortable, she got up and walked to the kitchen. The clock on the wall showed 12h30.

"Aaaargh!" she stretched and yawned. She grabbed a drink of water and took the hummus from the fridge. She spread it on two rice cakes and cut a tomato and a few slices of cucumber. Taking her plate, she walked back to her room. David's door was closed. She heard him come in at six in the morning. *Today's the day,* she thought decisively.

The house was quiet. *Wonder if Eema went to the congregation?*

She put a tomato slice on the rice cake and took a bite. Looking at her teeth marks in the thick hummus, she closed her eyes. *Mmm...my total favorite!*

Ester propped her pillow against the wall and made herself comfortable. She wiped her hand on a tissue, took her Bible, and opened her journal to the last entry.

Not to watch sexy movies.

She thought back to Thursday night. It was very late before Daniel left. First he wanted to hear more about the incident with Nir.

Did she report him to the police? No.

Did she tell her parents? No. Never crossed her mind to do that.

Daniel felt Nir should be punished. Ester felt the event was in her past and that she'd rather forget it and move on.

Then, he wanted her to understand why he was so uncomfortable watching the movie. He said sexual scenes awaken guys in a big way. He said it's like the pictures get burned into your memory and you struggle with unclean thoughts afterward. "The screen becomes like that dirty river from the dragon's mouth," he said.

What did he mean by that?

Also, Daniel didn't want them to close the door when they were alone in a room. Made him want to do things that should only happen in a marriage.

He's such an innocent guy. I've never met anyone like him!

She thought back to his phone call on Friday morning. Just wanted to hear if she felt better after she had cried so much the night before. To be honest, she did feel like a clogged drain had been opened. All of yesterday's memories with Nir had nauseated her again.

Daniel seemed angry.

Why?

She opened her Bible and began to read randomly.

When she heard the toilet flush in the bathroom, she got up and opened her bedroom door. She thought it was David, but it was her mother.

"Hi, Eema. How was the service?"

"It was good. I helped with the children today. Pastor's wife asked about you."

"What did you tell her?"

"I told her you're doing well, that you are finishing army next month—and that there's a love in your life." She pinched Ester on the cheek.

The girl beamed. "What do you think of Daniel, Eema?"

"Let's make tea."

They sat down at the dining table and chitchatted until Ester steered the conversation back to her question.

"Daniel's very nice, my sweetie. He's the first boy I feel safe having you go out with."

Ester slid her finger around the rim of her cup.

"Eema, he's a present from God. You know, it was only two months ago that I seriously asked God for someone."

"I've been praying for twenty years, sweetheart!" Naomi lovingly stroked her daughter's hair. "Okay, maybe not that long."

"Well, he's a direct answer to *my* prayer." Ester looked up at a sound in the hall.

"Hey, buddy, it's about time you got up—*Boker tov!*

David walked past them, barechested and messy-haired. He grunted as he went into the kitchen. Opening the fridge door, he bent in search of something to eat.

Ester leaned over and whispered into Naomi's ear, "Daniel's coming again tonight." Then she got up and walked into the kitchen.

"You need to eat, Dudi. You look like a skeleton." She put her arms around David, hugged him from behind, and planted a kiss between his bony shoulder blades. Before she released her grip—for just a moment—he laid his hand on her arm. It was as if there was only a faint pulse of life left.

Ester had a plan. "When you're done eating, come to my room. I want to play you a song."

Knowing music was sure bait for David, she winked to her mom and walked away.

Daniel arrived at about 21h30 and, because Ester wanted to go out, he knew something was cooking. They walked to the nearest Burger Bar, but the girl could hardly keep her peace.

"He *is* using drugs," Ester said in a low tone as soon as they sat down. "He told me this afternoon."

Daniel nodded. Feeling the pressure of what she needed to release, he let her talk.

"David's been doing it for two years. He says he's tried every drug you can find in Israel, but he smokes mostly hashish. Sometimes about ten or fifteen heads a day! He says when they gave him the first bong, he took a sharp draw and got it right immediately. Everybody thought it was cool. He said he had a high right away."

"How did you get this info out of him?" Daniel asked, surprised at the vivid detail she recounted.

"I acted as if I were impressed. I told you, we're very close. He trusts me." Ester shrugged in a wordless gesture that said, "What do you expect?" She felt more hurt than disgusted. "I can't believe I didn't know about it! Okay, I was in a pit of my own, but still…" She sighed. "I asked him about ecstasy and LSD and coke and heroin."

"What are the effects of those drugs?" Daniel asked.

"Ecstasy, you know, it's what they use at rave parties. Gives you lots of energy. You can dance really hard, but because you dehydrate and don't know it, it's dangerous. I think it gives you a high for about six hours."

"And LSD?"

"David says you see weird things. Like a car with legs. And little dwarfs climbing all over you and whispering into your ears."

"Man, I'm sure the stuff messes up your brain!"

"Exactly!" Ester hit the table so hard that the cutlery jumped. "Sorry!" she apologized to the people at the next table.

Leaning forward, she whispered, "That's what I told him. Hashish burns your brain cells. I asked him, 'Do you want to become a zombie?'" Ester turned her hand next to her head as if unscrewing a light bulb.

"Besides, *look* at him! He weighs about 45kg and he's what—1.75 meters tall?" Ester's brown eyes filled with tears.

Daniel took her hands into both of his. She was very upset.

"It's okay, sweetheart. At least now we know what's wrong with him."

"Yes, but what can we do?!" Her face betrayed her fears.

"God can do something. Do you remember the guy who played the guitar that night at Debra's place? Roni?"

Ester thought a bit and frowned. Then she nodded. "What about him?"

"He was also on drugs. Smoked hashish and other stuff and was into death metal—some really dark music. But God saved him! And now Abba is using Roni to bring others to the faith." Daniel touched her arm and spoke comfort to Ester's heart. "I saw him at Simchat Adon tonight, and he told me nine youth have come to faith recently. About two years ago, when someone was preaching the gospel at *Beresheet*, he was miraculously healed. Daniel put his hands on both sides of her face and said softly, "What we can do for David is pray."

"But I *have* been praying." Tears stung her eyes.

"I know. So from now on, I'll join you and we'll pray harder."

He got up from the table, walked to the counter, and asked for a pen. When he returned, he sat down and took a napkin. He wrote and underlined *David.*

"Okay, this is what you call a 'crafted prayer,'" Daniel said. You know how Yeshua taught His disciples to pray the Lord's Prayer? It was a specific sequence they could say every day. Spontaneous prayer is good. It's the way we usually speak to God. But if you want to fight for a breakthrough, there is a better way to do it."

Ester was interested. "Please teach me how. I want to see answers to my prayers—and not just for my brother."

"It's actually simple. You ask the Lord what *He* has in mind for David, and then all you do is begin to pray His will. And you continue doing that, over and over—until God answers."

Ester thought for a bit and said, "Okay, Yeshua has to heal his heart from my dad's rejection. I'm sure he just uses drugs as a painkiller. When you're on a trip, you can't think."

"Good!" Daniel wrote "Healing."

"What else?"

Ester closed her eyes. "What do *You* want to do for David, Abba?" She waited.

"Freedom from the addiction," she said. "I'm sure demons come in with those drugs."

Daniel wrote "Deliverance."

He looked at Ester and said, "Would you agree that your brother needs an encounter with God?"

"Yes, but he must *want* that."

Daniel wrote "Desire" and then "Encounter with God."

"Great!" he said. "This is enough. Let's go home and write out a prayer we can say for him every day."

They sat down on the bed. Ester wanted to write the prayer in her journal, but Daniel said it was better to use a separate piece of paper.

She opened the top drawer of her bedside table, scratched around, and found some purple cardboard.

"Perfect! Can you halve that so I can have a piece?" Daniel asked.

"It'll be too small," she protested, folding it to tear.

"No, it's supposed to be short and simple—a size that'll fit into your uniform pocket."

"Oh, okay. Then I'll walk and pray on my way to the army base every morning." Esther gave Daniel a peck on his cheek. He smiled and flattened the napkin on his leg.

David

- *Healing*
- *Freedom*
- *Desire*
- *Encounter w/God*

They wove their requests into a prayer and wrote out two copies. Suddenly Ester felt hopeful. "Wow, thank you! This is really helping me." She placed her prayer on the dresser. Then she picked it up again and slid it straight into the top pocket of her uniform that hung in the closet.

She turned around and frowned at Daniel. "By the way, why did you say the movie was like the dragon's river?"

Daniel was lost.

"Remember—Thursday evening?"

"Oh, yes. Where's your Bible?"

She handed it to him and he turned to Revelation. He pointed to chapter 12 and verse 15. "Read it aloud," he said.

The serpent spewed water like a river out of its mouth after the woman, in order to sweep her away in the flood.

Daniel put his finger on the verse and said, "The woman here is the bride of Messiah. The dragon is Satan. The media of this world—like TV, movies, music, and so forth—is like the mouth of the serpent. All the filthy stuff—like sexual impurity and rebellion—is like rotten semen that spills out from the screen. Like a river of bad seeds, it flows into our homes and conceives the fruit of Satan. People watch the stuff and they do the same."

"You're right! I think it's the music David listens to that feeds the rebellion in his heart."

"Then that's another thing we can ask deliverance from—the bondage of bad music." Daniel got up from the bed. "You see, now that you're praying God's will for David, you can easily add to it; but stick to the backbone." He stretched out his hand and pulled Ester to

91

her feet. Daniel put his palms on both her hands and folded his fingers with hers.

"God will catch David." He smiled, "Nobody gets away when someone else is praying." He leaned forward and gave her a kiss on her forehead. "I've got to go."

She walked with him to the front door, where he insisted she stay.

"Thanks a lot for tonight," she said again. "You really lifted my heart!"

"Thanks to God," he said, smiling. "*Laila tov*, sweetheart!"

TWENTY-ONE

Shabbat, 30 June 2007

A MERCIFUL BREEZE blew across the balcony. Outside, the summer sun was glaring, but at least the oppressive heat wave of the previous week had subsided. Daniel's parents had invited him and Ester for a brunch. Besides meeting her at the congregation, this was their first time to entertain the girl who had stolen their son's heart. The twins were on a hike in the north of Galilee.

The table was arrayed with different kinds of rolls, salads, fruits, and fruit juices. There were jellies, date syrup, honey, white cheeses, and chocolate spread.

Ester looked up. "This your *succah?*" The sun shone through the ribbed covering, making thin lines on Hanan's face.

"Yes, when we purchased the apartment, we liked the idea of a permanent *succah.* We love to spend time outside."

Miriam added, "We've seen our neighbors dragging their palm leaves up and down the stairs at *Succoth.* Looked like too much effort to me."

"It's actually fun to build a *succah,* Eema. The more construction going, the greater the challenge."

Hanan laughed. "You can tell it's a man speaking!"

Daniel continued. "The big effort was to get this iron table down the narrow stairs when we moved in." Daniel tapped the glass top. "You remember, Abba? It was too broad to fit it either way, so we had to carry it above our heads."

Hanan nodded. "I remember."

"It's very heavy, and it was so hard to get it through the front door."

"Couldn't you just take it off?" Ester asked.

"You mean the door? No, we have one of those security doors," said Hanan.

"They had to dismantle the table," Miriam said as she got up from her chair. "Excuse me a minute. I need to get something from the oven." She returned with a muffin pan and a delectable aroma. After flipping two steaming goodies onto Hanan and Daniel's plates, she asked Ester, "Would you like a popover, my dear?"

"Ehmm...popover? Only one, thank you."

"It's really good with lemon curd." Miriam pointed to something yellowish in a jar. Ester sat motionless for a while. She reached for the plate of cut fruit that was covered with plastic. The others began to serve themselves. She watched how Hanan tore open his popover. It looked like a hot "shell." A tuft of steam escaped from its hollow middle. He spread it with butter and strawberry jam.

She finally leaned over to Daniel and asked softly. "Cottage, please?"

"Uh-huh," he answered with a mouth full, and passed it to her.

Ester slowly tore open her popover. She broke off a piece and dipped it into the cottage cheese on the side of her plate, as she might do with pita and hummus.

"How did you make these popovers?" Ester tried to identify the taste.

"You use a lot of eggs," said Miriam, "and a little flour, and you bake it quickly at a high temperature. That causes the hollow inside."

"When Mom wants to spoil me, she prepares popovers." Daniel excitedly took two more from the basket.

The conversation flowed easily. They asked about Ester's extended family, and Hanan and Miriam told her about their lives. Every now and then Hanan touched her arm and looked into his wife's eyes. She in turn threw her head back and laughed with abandon as they reminisced their stories. At about 13h30, Hanan excused himself from the company. "I'm going to read a bit. Are you staying till the service tonight, Ester?"

She looked at Daniel for confirmation, then nodded.

"So I'll see you later." Hanan put his hand on Daniel's head and winked at Ester.

Miriam wouldn't let Ester help in the kitchen on her first visit. "You and Daniel can relax. Besides, I just stick the food into the fridge. We'll do the dishes later. I'm also going to take a *Shabbat* rest." After helping clear the table, Ester and Daniel returned to the balcony. Miriam brought a plate with jam-filled cookies, a jug of water, and two glasses on a tray. "There's more juice in the fridge if you want."

Daniel squeezed his mother's arm and looked at her with honest gratefulness.

"Love you, Eema!"

"Yes Miriam, the food was so tasty. Thank you," said Ester.

"You're welcome." She smiled and left.

Daniel poured some water and Ester took a cookie.

When he was certain no one was within hearing range, Daniel looked at Ester with a baffled expression. "You hardly ate anything." She immediately put the bitten cookie down. It wasn't that he had accused her, it's just...

Seeing her respond like a beaten puppy, he quickly apologized. "No, you're totally allowed. I was just wondering if you're okay." His tenderness melted Ester. Her well-kept defense crumbled.

"Actually," she said, looking down, "I was a bit nervous."

"You don't have to be afraid of my parents. I told you they would like you. You made a good impression this morning."

"It's not that! I...ehmm..." Ester fiddled with her hands. "I didn't know what to eat."

Daniel was lost. She fumbled to make herself clearer. "When there are too many choices, I get confused." Seeing that he still did not understand, she sighed.

"Okay." She took a deep breath. "I've had chaos with my eating and I still struggle sometimes."

Daniel nodded slowly. "Do you want to tell me about it?" His invitation held no threat. Ester pulled her legs up to hold herself. Resting her chin on her knees, she began to blow her cover.

"A year ago, I weighed fifteen kilos more than I do now." Daniel didn't bat an eyelid.

"I was seeing a psychiatrist in the army. Before him, my commander referred me to a psychologist. She counseled me for three months. I was throwing up my food and using laxatives to purge." She paused a while. Daniel continued looking at her in a way that encouraged Ester to tell her story.

"I had been battling with food for a long time, but in the army, I totally lost it. There was such a load served to us at mealtimes. I just ate and ate and ate!"

She frowned. "Funny, the psychologist made me believe I was the victim of something. She asked, 'What trauma happened to you? Who is to blame for your disorder?'"

Daniel asked softly, "Do you think that was the right counsel?"

"No! God's Word says differently. We have a choice. I am totally responsible for my actions."

He nodded in agreement. "Actions or reactions, right?"

"Exactly! Okay, Nir did play a role in breaking me down. And my parents' divorce surely didn't help. But while I was modeling, I never felt accepted anyway. If you don't have a certain nose and a certain pose and a certain figure—just what they are looking for—you never get the job. My self-confidence was on the ground because I was constantly thinking about everything that was wrong with me—at least in *their* eyes."

"But you are such a pretty girl! I don't understand." Daniel stroked her cheek with the back of his finger.

She smiled a little. "Thanks. It's a bit crazy." Then she breathed deeply. "Anyway, the thing I began to understand was that I couldn't blame Nir or my dad. I had to forgive them totally. I couldn't even blame the pressure from modeling. I loved food long before that time. Food made me happy. It was my comforter. *That* was the problem. The Holy Spirit is supposed to be our Comforter." She looked at him from the corner of her eye. "Food was the idol in my life."

For a moment she was quiet. Ester thought of how much God had cleaned her up in the past three years. She saw how demanding her desires were and how they clamored to be fulfilled. Instead of running to Him, she would eat when she was lonely. Eat when she was bored. Eat when she craved love. *Exactly like a caterpillar chewing a leaf all day long.*

"Remember the butterfly?"

Daniel frowned.

"The day we first visited at Aroma, I mentioned that I was coming out of a cocoon? It's because I felt like a worm for so long. A caterpillar is a pest in the garden, you know."

"But a butterfly is a blessing."

"Yes!" She smiled and continued. "So when I started to gain weight, I began to exercise. I'd starve myself and then eat too much again. It was a vicious cycle. Binge, purge. Binge, purge." She swung her hand like a pendulum. "And then, by the time I discovered laxatives and the escape of vomiting, things went haywire. Instead of food being the idol, my body became an idol. I wanted to be perfect. Self was smack in the center of my life. I just wanted to make *me* happy at all costs. Hours in front of the mirror, grooming. Just being caught up with me, me, me. I had a hunger that nothing could satisfy. The Bible says greed is idolatry. Oh man, was I greedy for men's eyes!"

Daniel became aware that his mouth was literally hanging open. *Where did she get the courage to reveal these things?*

The more Ester talked, the easier it became. "This was the issue. As long as my counselor helped me blame somebody else, I felt hopeless. If bulimia was a disease, then for me there was no cure."

"So how did you finally get out of the vortex sucking you down?"

"Well, the psychiatrist prescribed some pills. He said they would stabilize my moods and help me lose weight."

Daniel nodded.

"I was extremely depressed at the time. I was tempted to take the pills." Ester sighed as she remembered her lowest point. "I felt like I was the fattest and the ugliest person in the whole world. But that was the spot where God intervened. Now I'm glad I never used those pills, because the glory can only go to Yeshua."

"How did you change? I mean, the..." He showed the pendulum with his finger.

"Had to take responsibility for my addiction. I knew it was my flesh that brought me into this balagan, but my mom felt I also needed deliverance. She took me to a friend who prayed with me. First the Lord showed that when Nir did that *thing* to me, his depression came into me. There's a lot of heaviness in his family. Did you know that with sex, stuff can get transferred?"

Daniel shook his head.

"I didn't know either. Anyway, so I had to repent because even before that incident, I had pushed the boundaries in my relationship with Nir. Thank God He broke the spirit of depression over me. I could feel an immediate difference. Like something snapped!

"I also had to repent of trying to manipulate the attention of people and thinking about myself so obsessively. You know the strangest thing? You feed your ego all the time, but at the same time you hate yourself. I hated my body so much I couldn't look at myself in the mirror. I smashed the mirror. And I cut myself."

Daniel raised his eyebrows. "You cut yourself? Why?"

"Because I was, like, dead inside. Cutting made me feel something."

"Wow! How long did it take?" asked Daniel.

"What? The healing?" Ester looked into his face. "The breakdown happened over a few years, but my restoration is still in process. It's not done yet. The lady who prayed with me taught me how to put on the armor of God every day. That helped a lot." Ester paused and stretched.

"And then there was a time when Debra encouraged me to drink grape juice often and to declare the Word of God. Just to help my faith. I had to see myself delivered from the bondage and protected by the blood of Yeshua. You understand?"

"I understand." Daniel quoted from Revelation: *"They overcame Satan by the blood of the Lamb."*

"That's right," she said. "So God gave me some steps to follow."

"It's amazing that Yeshua brought you this far! I would never have imagined you were so...*oy va'avoy*. You were messed up, girl!"

He filled her glass with water, but she stood up. "First, I need to empty the tank."

"Second door from the kitchen to your right."

"Second door to my right."

"Wow, it was a relief to share with you," said Ester when she returned. "I felt two-faced, and I was really scared that if you heard this side you wouldn't like me so much."

Daniel was pensive. When he finally spoke, his words flowed out with a long sigh. "You know, this is kind of hard for me, but seeing that you opened up, I want to tell you something as well." He put his hands on his eyes for a while. "Strength—or at least, to appear strong—is *very* important to us men. It's not easy for a guy to reveal his weaknesses, so please be patient."

"Mmm." Ester softly encouraged him.

"Okay, this is my weakness. Or one of my weaknesses." Daniel put his spread fingers on one another and leaned forward in his seat. "Since we saw that movie on TV by accident, I've been plagued with scenes of the woman and the guy in bed. It's weeks now, but it flashes into my memory at the most unexpected times. I'm so frustrated, and I don't know how to get rid of it!"

Ester kept quiet. It was her turn to listen.

"So much of what you said applies to guys as well. You said your flesh was the problem and that you just wanted to feed self. It's the same with our sexual desires. It is like a craving with no bottom to it—just like that worm you spoke about. But when you realize that it's lust—another form of greed—and you call it sin, only then can you begin to get victory. I felt I just wanted to bring this into the light with you."

"You okay?" She gently touched his forearm.

He hadn't intended to say more, but Daniel awkwardly cleared his throat and continued. "It was exactly like you said. When people justify their behavior, it brings only a moment of relief. It's almost like your conscience sighs, 'Phew, I'm not guilty!' But at the end of the day, you're more hopeless because it feels like you're stuck in this condition for the rest of your life."

"I know."

"When I was a teenager, I really struggled with masturbation. Even though it gave a moment's rush, I felt lousy afterward. My conscience kept saying it wasn't right. I told God a million times I wouldn't do it, and then…I did it again! The frustration! I also hated myself. Just like you. I felt so unworthy. Eventually I felt so guilty that I didn't even want to speak to Him."

Feeling his embarrassment, Ester looked at the floor. She remembered how her prolonged struggle undermined her confidence with God.

"When I realized that this thing was stronger than me, I just broke. I knew it wasn't what God intended. I so much wanted to be pure and holy in my sexuality. You know? Not like the world sees men. Wild and lawless and…"

"Like stallions," she said.

"Exactly!" His face remained serious. "I wanted to shine in masculine strength. God, I wanted to be pure!" Daniel sighed. "So I started begging

Him, even fasting. I cried and prayed a lot in that season, and step by step God guided me. For one thing, I realized I had to repent immediately. If I didn't, Satan would have a double victory. First, I would fall to the temptation, and second, he would press my face into the failure."

Daniel got a flash memory and clicked his tongue. "Once we had a puppy. When she was very small, she would make heavy artillery in the house. So we'd bring her face really close to the poop and smack her bottom. I felt that's what Satan was doing to me. He would press my face into my mess and smack me. The shame of sin made me miserable for a long time."

"Good picture!" Ester smiled. "I know about puppy training."

Still a bit uncomfortable with his disclosure, Daniel counted the next step by taking hold of his second finger. "Then I learned that I had to replace the wrong behavior with something else. Like you said, we have a choice. You come to a junction and you can go right or left. And if I stopped the process at an earlier stage—before I went too far toward the action—it was easier to win. Like early in the morning I would lie half awake in my bed. Everything felt gray, but it was not. It was black and white. That's where Satan tried to tempt me. I learned to get up and get busy with something else."

Ester nodded.

"The next thing God taught me was to train my eyes not to look at a woman."

Ester frowned. "How did you do that?"

"It's like this. When guys see a girl in clothing that shows too much skin, or wearing something that's too tight, our minds go in one direction. If you don't believe me, just check where the eyes of men go when they look at a woman."

"Please explain as literally as you can."

"What?" said Daniel "You don't know this?"

"Well, girls like it when guys look at them, but I'm not sure we see things the same way you do. What exactly do you mean?"

For a moment, Daniel was bewildered. "Wait." He got up, walked into the house, and got an advertising booklet from the recipe shelf. He grabbed a pen next to the telephone. "My mom kept this because of some coupons." He sounded apologetic.

"I'll show you what I mean." He opened at the middle. "See this woman?" He drew a circle around her breast area, and a circle where her legs came together.

"These are the problem spots." Then he tore out the page and crumpled it.

"But she's wearing nothing bad." Ester was indignant.

"I know, I know. But if her pants are so tight that they are pulling up…" Daniel felt embarrassed.

"Understood!" Ester rescued him.

"And if she wears a top with a low neckline? Man, we're cooked!"

She laughed. "Come on. I'm sure not all men are…like…sex addicts."

"No, I'm serious. The style of exposed bellies, or short shorts?"

Ester nodded.

"It's too seductive, I tell you! God has made us men to be visually stimulated, and when a girl dresses like that, my mind secretes hormones that make my body prepare itself for sex."

Ester's mouth dropped open in disbelief.

"You asked me to be explicit."

"Oof! Then how many times per day does a guy feel he wants to go to bed with a girl?"

The rhetorical question didn't merit an answer, but Daniel replied undaunted, "That's my point. Temptations are everywhere around us."

Ester was shocked speechless.

"Oh yes! That's what I began to say. The first thing I had to learn was to train my eyes where to look."

She nodded slowly, having difficulty processing the new information.

"In the book of Job it is written, *I have made a covenant with my eyes so that I may not sin with a woman.* So I made a covenant with my eyes that I would look only into the eyes of an approaching girl. I found that when I started controlling my eyes, the temptation to masturbate became almost zero. Of course, that applies to magazine racks and movies, 'cause in this area, temptations are also legion."

"I understand," said Ester. "When my eating was totally bad, I felt like I couldn't go anywhere because there was food wherever I turned. The baked goodies, the smells, meals on TV—everything tempted me. It was almost like the food was a magnet attached to the chaos inside of me."

"That's what I also felt. Like the uncleanness that was already in my life kind of connected with the spirit of seduction in the girls. The two things just built a stronghold of lust in my mind. And the moment I yielded to sin in even the slightest way"—Daniel snapped his fingers—"it would drag me down into a place I couldn't get out of. Like the harlot in the Bible."

She frowned again.

"Proverbs 7 speaks about a foolish woman who leads men to ruin. It says that her words are smooth, but she'll bring you to destruction."

"Interesting," Ester said. "That's exactly what some of the chocolate ads on TV make me think of. Those smooth, creamy chocolate mixtures—they lure you just like the sweet words of a woman. But it's lethal!"

Daniel smiled, enjoying her intensity.

"No, really. For me, chocolate is the beginning of the end. It's a trigger. If I eat one, it leads to the next and the next and the next. I cannot stop. I have to avoid it totally."

"That's right." Daniel sighed. "There are certain things that are bad for me. Wisdom says, 'Stay away!'"

Ester also sighed. "Do you think we could pray together?"

"Sure!" Daniel took her hand.

"Abba, thank You that we can be honest with each other," she began. "Thank You that Daniel doesn't think I'm terrible—or do you?" She peeped with one eye.

"No." He smiled, brought her hand to his mouth and kissed it.

"Thank You for Daniel, Abba, that he so much wants a pure heart. Forgive me for the times I dressed like a foolish woman and made men stumble." She opened her eyes. "Crap, do you know what pressure fashion places on us girls?" Just as abruptly she continued. "God, I'm so sorry I didn't realize what a *big* problem I was creating." Daniel squeezed her hand, which was still against his mouth. "Abba, Your Word says that when You arise, fire goes out and burns up Your enemies. I pray that You will arise over Daniel's mind and burn all those pictures from the movie. We are sorry we ever watched it, God. Please help him to...please make his memory screen clean again. As if he never saw it."

Daniel kissed her hand again.

"Abba, every time Esti speaks to You, I'm blown away. She is like a child with You. Thank You that she's an overcomer. Thank You that she didn't stop fighting, even when she had to crawl through a tunnel of mud. Thank You that she held on to You in her darkest night. You are the best Counselor, Yeshua."

"Yes, You are!" agreed Ester.

"Please help her to know how much You love her and how beautiful she is in Your eyes. Please help us both to become more than conquerors in Yeshua, *Ha Mashiach.*"

He was quiet for a while, then prayed, "And thank You for the Holy Spirit, who gives us the power to break with sin. We love You so much, Abba! Amen."

Ester looked at him with bright eyes. "There's a scripture I am meditating on at the moment that kind of fits with what we spoke about. It's 1 Corinthians 10:13 *No temptation has seized you beyond what people normally experience, but God can be trusted not to allow you to be tempted beyond what you can bear. On the contrary, along with the temptation he will also provide the way out, so that you will be able to endure.*"

"Wow, that's stunning!" said Daniel, meaning both the Word and her flawless recitation.

She smiled and said with excitement, "I got a picture of the first part. When a temptation comes, it feels so big and it pressures me so strongly. It's as if the temptations around me are as many as the grains of sand on the seashore. What's that word you used? Lee…?"

"Legion."

"Yes. There are legions surrounding us, but they are not beyond what people normally experience. They are not extraordinary, or monstrous, you know?" She gestured widely. Like, I experience them—outsized! But they are just like the grains of sand. Ordinary. Common." She rubbed her fingers as if there were something very small between them. "But then I saw a beautiful diamond lying on the sand."

"And what does it symbolize?"

"That's the next part of the verse: *But God can be trusted!* Of course! That's what I want to pick up. The diamond. My trust in God!"

"*Amen!*" said Daniel with emphasis.

"I don't have any revelation on the rest of the scripture yet, but I'm asking Yeshua to help me get it."

"Will you tell me when you get it?"

"No way!" Ester smiled a playful smile. "Diamonds are for girls. You can ask God to explain it to you in a way you can understand."

Daniel got up, put both hands in her thick dark brown hair, and rubbed it into a mess. "Go get ready. It's almost time to leave."

TWENTY-TWO

Monday, 2 July 2007

TWO DAYS AFTER the brunch, Ester called her "big sister." Besides being a spiritual resource, Debra studied nutrition, and Ester was determined to draw from her wisdom.

"Hey, Debush! How are you?"

"Excellent! Where are you?"

"Office. Having tea break."

"And…howzit going?"

"Okayish. Just need to talk to you a bit."

"What's wrong?"

"Nothing. I just…well, do you know we went to Daniel's parents on *Shabbat*?"

"Didn't know, but when I saw you together at Simchat Adon, I thought he must have taken you home."

"Uh-huh. I told him about my eating."

"What did he say?"

"He was kind…didn't make me feel bad."

"That guy's amazing!"

"You're right." Ester smiled.

"So what's up?"

"I'm struggling a bit. You said you eat only twice a day, and I simply cannot get it right. I feel hungry all the time."

"Then you have to eat smaller portions, but more regularly. I think you have a fast metabolism, so you need to eat a midmorning snack and a mid-afternoon snack besides your three main meals."

"That sounds like too much. Won't I add a lot of weight if I eat so many times?"

"No, actually, people who eat in that way don't gain much weight. Their bodies need the slow but constant fuel."

"It just doesn't sound right. What do you think I should eat?"

"Are you avoiding trigger foods?"

"Yes, chocolate. As far as possible."

"Good. Which meals do you eat at HaQirya?"

"Only lunch."

"Let me guess: They serve meat, potatoes, rice, veggies…"

Ester laughed. "And lots of it." She felt less stressed about the army's food than a year ago. The quality was good, just the volume was huge. She was relieved that Debra had been through it as well.

"What do you usually choose to eat?"

"Only meat and salad. When I eat starches, I feel lethargic and I can't work in the afternoon."

"Yes, it's the serotonin."

"What?"

"Serotonin. Starches trigger the secretion of serotonin in your brain and that makes you sleepy. Serotonin is the chemical that makes us feel well and causes good sound sleep."

"Oh?"

"You said you don't have energy when you eat your carbs in the afternoons."

"I guess!"

"Does your mom cook in the evenings?"

"Yes. It's our main meal—for Dudi's sake. At night I usually eat vegetables and, like, a small potato."

"Good. And for breakfast?"

"Don't do breakfast."

"Not good! If you eat only at lunchtime, I'm not surprised that you feel hungry. You need something in the mornings. Even if it's only a slice of toast. Or muesli and yogurt."

"I'm not hungry so early."

"By what time do you get hungry?"

"About ten."

"Then take your muesli to work. Or make a sandwich. Maybe you can eat a banana or an apple when you leave home."

"But that means eating four times a day."

"Don't panic, Esush. This is just an experiment. Try it for a week and see how you feel. The Bible says, *Work out your own salvation.* So you are going to draft a plan in which your body can function at its best. It's not about losing weight. Remember, it's about eating healthy and being self-controlled."

"Thought you were going to say 'being balanced.'"

"I've been thinking about that assumption. You know we naturally have seasons of feasting and seasons of fasting. But the largest chunk is just normal life in between. If you try to keep one diet rigidly, you may think you have balance, but you can come into bondage again. The main thing is to be controlled by the Spirit."

"I hear you."

"Anyway, back to common sense. It sounds to me as if your carbohydrate intake is too low. You exercise twice a day, right?"

"What? How do you mean?"

"Didn't you say that you walk to and from the base?"

"Yes."

"I think your body burns more energy than what you are consuming at the moment. You may need to eat something every two hours."

"Every two hours?"

"Relax, my dear! I don't mean a whole plate of food. Only like a handful of almonds or two dried fruits. A small portion."

"But nuts make you fat."

"Not really. If we eat only a few nuts a day, it helps our metabolism. Eventually we burn fat quicker."

"Wow!"

"Yes, a nut is one of the best sources of essential fatty acids. That's the fuel for your thyroid. Without EFAs, you won't burn *any* fat. Plus, almonds are a very good source of calcium, which is what we all need as women."

Ester thought for a moment. "Okay, I believe you. I'll try what you suggested first."

"Let me know how it goes."

"Thanks a lot, Debs."

"Pleasure Es."

"Mmwha!"

TWENTY-THREE

Thursday, 26 July 2007

ESTER AND FOUR FRIENDS had graduated from the same high school and stayed in touch throughout their army years. When Ester left the south and was stationed in HaQirya, Ma'ayan became her new buddy. She and Ma'ayan and three more girls had long planned to celebrate their release from the army by going to Eilat on the shore of the Red Sea. They booked a reasonable hotel and took a bus south. Sleeping late, snorkeling—and eating, of course—constituted their daily routine.

Ester decided to stay on a plan of small, healthy meals in spite of her friends' indulgence in junk food. It was tough going, but the availability of a green grocer nearby gave her access to fresh fruit. She hadn't kept to her plan perfectly, but at least she had been able to withstand having ice cream twice a day.

On Thursday, after being in the sun all morning, they returned to their chalet with glowing cheeks, sunburned shoulders, and stringy hair. Ester noticed that Ma'ayan was quiet—too quiet. She'd been that way since their arrival on Sunday, but now she exited the bathroom with a frown.

"Everything okay?"

Ma'ayan motioned with her head for Ester to accompany her outside. The other three girls didn't notice their departure. One was in the shower, another passed out on the bed, and the third was digging in a pile of dirty clothes in the corner.

The scorching air—as if from an open oven—blazed into their faces when they walked out of the chalet. The heat wave that came in from the east had been with them since they arrived. The palm fronds overhead stood motionless. It was hot! They walked to a bench about five meters away,

Ma'ayan rubbed her eyes when they sat down. She said, "I think I'm pregnant."

Ma'ayan's words hit Ester head-on, and her eyes widened. "Oh, no!"

"My period was supposed to come a week ago," explained Ma'ayan. "Nothing yet."

"But you use contraceptives, don't you?"

"Yes, that's why I don't understand."

Ester looked at her friend with concern. "Whatcha gonna do? I mean, *if* you're pregs?"

"Don't know." Ma'ayan bit her lip. "I vowed I'd never have another abortion."

"What? When?" Ester was shocked.

"Two years ago. Middle of grade twelve. Ya'acov arranged it."

"Oh, Ma'ayan."

"Uh-huh." Her face was expressionless. "It was a nightmare. He took me to a private clinic when I was six weeks. The doctor gave me three pills that made me sick to my stomach. Yuck! I felt exhausted after taking them. Two days later I had to go back for more pills. Gave me terrible cramps. A few hours later I started bleeding. Too much! This little grayish mass and a bunch of blood clots came out. The thing is, I started crying and I couldn't stop. The doctor told me I was lucky I came in early, because after seven weeks you can't take pills to do an abortion. You need surgery. Sure didn't *feel* lucky! He said that an abortion with pills was very simple and that I'd bleed just like a normal period. But it wasn't true! I bled *so* much, and the pain was excruciating."

"What did your parents say?"

"They didn't know. Still don't. I'd moved in with Ya'acov at that time, and I stayed only one night in the hospital."

"Do your folks know that you...ehmm..."

"Have sex? Of course! My mom just said I had to make sure we don't get into trouble."

Ester shook her head in disbelief.

Ma'ayan sighed. "Ya'acov paid for the abortion."

"Wasn't it scary?"

"Oh, my goodness! I was losing so much blood. I thought I was going to die."

Ester put her hand on Ma'ayan's arm. "Thank God you didn't!" Her honest caring brought tears to Ma'ayan's eyes.

"It didn't end with the abortion. Almost wrecked Ya'acov's and my relationship."

"Did he understand what you were going through?"

Ma'ayan looked cynical. "I don't think so. He was really afraid when I had to go to the hospital. The bleeding scared him to death. At that time he was very nice toward me. The crisis lasted about forty-eight hours. He hoped I would bounce back immediately, but this was a big thing for my body. And my heart! *Oy va'avoy*, it wasn't just nothing!" She sighed. "When I was still crying after two months, he told me to get over it."

"*Did* you get over it?"

"Thought I was fine...until now."

"Those pills the doctor gave you. How do they work?"

"I read up on it online. It's called Mefogine—RU486. Cuts off the nutrients to the baby and it shrivels up. It's disgusting. Your body excretes the fetus after a few weeks, supposedly like a heavy period. Like a miscarriage. Except if you have complications."

"Which is what you had, right?"

"Yes. They say a third of all women who have abortions have infertility issues afterward. And many of them struggle with emotional problems." Ma'ayan rubbed her eyes again. "I just can't be pregnant. It's impossible!"

"Do you think Ya'acov will want you to have another abortion?"

Ma'ayan nodded. "For sure. If I was still in the army, they would pay."

"But you just said you vowed never to have another."

"So, what can I do? Keep the baby and have it mess up my whole life? What do you think? You know I was so much looking forward to my release from the army and a long tour in India. And now this!"

Ester lowered her voice. "It's a *person* you are talking about, Ma'ayan."

"So what? I will not have this 'person' interfere with my future." Suddenly there was harshness in her demeanor.

Ester gently persisted. "Look, Ma'ayan, I don't know how things will work with a child at this stage of your life, but you cannot kill this baby."

"You're crazy. I'm not killing anybody!" She jumped up and her eyes sparked with anger.

"Shhh!" Ester tried to calm her. "All I know is that abortion is not the way to go."

"You think you are better than me!" Ma'ayan shouted. "I should never have told you!"

"That is *not* true, Ma'ayan," Ester almost whispered. "I know where I come from and what I've done. If it wasn't for God's grace, I could be in your shoes."

Ma'ayan sat down again, took a stone, and scratched on the pavement.

Ester continued. "There's a story about a time when people threw a woman who had been caught in adultery at the feet of Yeshua. I'm not accusing you," she said when Ma'ayan looked at her skeptically. "Just hear what I have to say. Yeshua told the people who judged this woman, 'Anyone of you who is without sin, pick up the first rock and stone her.'" Ma'ayan sat upright and looked at Ester, resolute to fight.

"But no one lifted a finger, because each of them had their own issues. Yeshua spoke to the woman and said, 'I don't condemn you either. Go and sin no more.'"

The grace in Ester's voice made the truth easier to swallow. She put her hand on Ma'ayan's shoulder and said, "Let me grab my purse and we'll get a testing kit at Super Pharm. You've got to know for sure."

Ester waited, reading the information sheet of the box in her hand. Rather than going back to their room, they slipped into the public restroom in the foyer of the hotel. When Ma'ayan came out of the toilet, she put the tester down and washed her shaking hands. She hardly breathed as she looked at her own poker-faced expression in the mirror.

"I'm nervous," she said. Ester put the control next to the tester, and Ma'ayan looked down unwillingly. She slowly shook her head and sighed as if the world rested on her shoulders.

"I don't believe it!" Ester could see confusion and panic rush into her friend's eyes. Putting her arms around Ma'ayan, she tenderly held her. Her usual self-confidence had caved in and her body was stiff with shock.

As Ma'ayan stood shivering in Ester's embrace, Ester stroked her friend's long hair. "Don't be afraid, sweetie."

"Can't help it," Ma'ayan whimpered.

"You're not alone. I will do whatever I can to help you."

TWENTY-FOUR

Sunday, 29 July 2007

"HEY, MA'AYANI, IT'S ESTER."

"Where are you?"

"At home. You were so much on my mind in the weekend."

"Oh." Ma'ayan's voice sounded oppressed.

"How you feeling?"

"Nauseous. That's a sure sign."

"Have you told anyone else?"

"No. I'm still hoping it's not true."

"Ehhm...I phoned Debra to ask her advice; hope you don't mind. There's an organization in Jerusalem that deals specifically with women in crisis pregnancies. Maybe you should call their hotline."

"My head's a mess. Don't know what to do."

"Just phone them and discuss your options with one of the counselors."

"I don't know..."

"Ma'ayan, they will not pressure you into anything. They are very understanding because they deal with this kind of thing every day. It won't hurt to phone them."

"Okay, what's their number?"

"Will you call them?"

"I'll see."

"Promise me you'll phone them."

"Give me the number. No promises."

Ester's voice became gentler. "Ma'ayan, remember that I care very, very much about you. That's why I phoned Debra—'cause I want to help you."

"Okay." Ma'ayan was suddenly teary.

Hearing her soften, Ester's compassion was aroused. "I love you, Ma'ayani." Ester heard a sniff and added with tender courage, "And I care about your baby."

"I don't *want* to have a baby now." Ma'ayan's voice was almost inaudible.

When she closed her phone, Ester allowed her overfull heart to spill out to the Father. Her throat felt choked with emotion. "Abba, please give her courage to phone Be'Ad Chaim. This is *Your* baby. Please let Ma'ayan phone them before she takes any steps toward abortion. Have mercy, Abba!"

Later that same day, Ester got a text message from Ma'ayan:

CALLD. ULTRA SOUND NXT WK.

TWENTY-FIVE

9 August 2007

I'm so excited!!! Went with Ma'ayan for the ultrasound today. She's in the seventh week. Was amazing to see that little heart beating. Wow, Abba! It is a child developing in there...This is SO cool!!! Sandy said that between six and eight weeks the baby's organs are formed. The face, mouth, and tongue are developed, and at only eight weeks the baby has fingers and toes. Even the fingerprints he'll have for the rest of his life. Awesome!

She said that doctors determine life by two signs: a heartbeat and brainwaves. The baby growing inside of Ma'ayan already has brainwaves and a strong, fast heartbeat. I could SEE it! Yay!!!

When we had coffee afterward, Ma'ayan said she didn't realize "IT" was a human being until today. And then she said the most wonderful thing: She wants to keep the baby!!! THANK YOU, THANK YOU, ABBA! xxx

Sandy said that Be'ad Chaim wants to help her see beyond her fears. They will provide counsel and encouragement throughout the pregnancy and a birth coach. And...WHATEVER supplies she needs for her baby's first year! Imagine that! They'll even go with her to tell her parents about the pregnancy...if M. wants.

117

Abba, please do not let Ya'acov or her parents pressure Ma'ayan for an abortion. Protect this little one in the safe nest of her womb.

Awesome to think—there's a blueprint for that cluster of cells we saw on the screen. The DNA has all the instructions to make a brain, lungs, eyes, ears, and limbs. Wow! Every organ—a specialized group of cells that do a specific function. Displaying a WONDER of God! It's so awesome! We are more beautiful than mountains and rivers. More valuable than all the gems in the rocks. Much more developed than plants...than any flower or fruit. More intelligent than the smartest animals. Psalm 8 says, "EVEN MORE GLORIOUS THAN THE STARS IN THE UNIVERSE." No wonder man is the crown of God's creation! I heard there's no computer as complex as the human eye, connected to the brain. Wow, God!!!

FOR YOU CREATED MY INMOST BEING; YOU KNIT ME TOGETHER IN MY MOTHER'S WOMB. I PRAISE YOU BECAUSE I AM FEARFULLY AND WONDERFULLY MADE; YOUR WORKS ARE WONDERFUL, I KNOW THAT FULL WELL. MY FRAME WAS NOT HIDDEN FROM YOU WHEN I WAS MADE IN THE SECRET PLACE. WHEN I WAS WOVEN TOGETHER IN THE DEPTHS OF THE EARTH, YOUR EYES SAW MY UNFORMED BODY. ALL THE DAYS ORDAINED FOR ME WERE WRITTEN IN YOUR BOOK BEFORE ONE OF THEM CAME TO BE. Psalm 139:13-16

Abba, Your works are AWESOME!

TWENTY-SIX

Shabbat, **11 August 2007**

E STER HAD A PICNIC packed when Daniel arrived in floral shorts and flip-flops. It was eleven o'clock. She was dressed and ready for a day on the beach. Because they could visit each other only on weekends, they planned longer stretches of time together. Today was special, as they were celebrating her release from the army.

Daniel slung the heavy backpack over his shoulder, while she took the juice and fruit from the fridge and put them into the small cooler. "Let me take that one as well," he said as soon as she had the lid secured.

"But you're already carrying…" she protested.

"It's okay, you can take my daypack—it's light. Put your towel in with mine. Don't want so many loose things. Take the sunscreen too." He pointed to the table.

"And my camera?"

"Yep, in the front zip pocket."

Ester wore knee-length shorts and a T-shirt over her swimsuit. She slipped into her Crocs and grabbed her sunglasses. "Where's my phone?"

"Please leave it at home." Daniel put a strand of her hair behind her ear." I want all your attention."

"I cannot function without it." Ester frowned into his eyes.

"Yonatan, my brother, always says he pays the account, so the phone is his servant and not his boss."

"Meaning?" She was not convinced.

"He's not a slave to his phone. Over weekends, when he wants to have time with his family, he turns his cell phone off completely."

"What happens when your parents want to reach him?"

"Oh, there's a landline. But the guys from work and clients can't bug him."

"Okay. Well, would you call my number so I can find my phone and turn it off?" Ester knew Daniel could not go without his phone, because he was on standby. She watched him pull it out of his pocket and flip it open. A few seconds later, she heard her phone ringing and ran to her bedroom.

On the way to the beach, Ester shared about Ma'ayan and the ultrasound experience. Daniel could hear that she was still awestruck.

When they arrived at the seaside, the sun was glaring. They walked over the burning sand in search of some unoccupied shade. The municipality had erected wooden canopies, which provided a good shadow against the high heat of summer. Ester and Daniel passed a bunch of young people with *nargilas*. The sweet smell of weird tobacco hung around them. By the look, the gang had smoked more than innocent stuff.

"There's one!" Ester pointed to a canopy ahead.

They walked faster, but coming closer, they noticed the shoes and gear of a family with little children. Sure enough, right in front, a toddler and a naked baby played at the edge of the water. The mother sat in her wet clothes where the small waves rolled out, keeping a watchful eye.

They looked around. There was not a spot of unused shade anywhere.

"If we wait, they may leave," suggested Ester. "Doesn't look as if they brought lunch along."

"Yes, and hopefully the baby can't be in the sun much longer."

They put their bags down. Ester pulled her towel out and spread it for them to sit in the edge of the shade.

"Wow, you could fry an egg on this sand!" Daniel quickly pulled his legs up and out of the sun.

The next moment a guy and a girl wearing a skimpy bikini strolled past. His hand was around her middle and her thumb was hooked into the back of his Speedo. Ester covered Daniel's sunglasses.

"Thanks." He smiled. "Keep it there."

"Okay, look at me instead." She took him by the chin and turned his face toward hers. "You wanted all my attention."

"Eyes for you only." He lowered his head and smiled into her eyes over his sunglasses.

"I wanted a bikini when I was a teenager. With all my heart! My friends were all wearing them, but my mom wouldn't buy me one. She said I had to wear a full swimsuit."

"I agree with your mom."

For a moment the wind went out of her sails. She thought guys wanted girls to wear teeny-weeny little things.

He continued. "Even when girls wear a white T-shirt over their suits, as soon as they get into the water, you can see their beautiful curves and *voila*! No imagination needed."

Ester remembered her embarrassment when Daniel showed her the advertisement picture and circled the areas of a woman's body to which men's eyes gravitate.

"When I was in grade three, the boys were very excited about the girls beginning to develop breasts. You know?"

"I know!" Daniel seemed embarrassed.

"So they would chase us and try to touch us. Only, they didn't catch Riki and me. I told them, 'You come near me and I'll break your arm!'"

He laughed, relieved. "Well done!"

"Yes," she said, "I was a real tomboy."

"So, did you wear a bikini?"

121

"Yep, I bought myself one. I wish I could say that I was a good girl, but I was such a rebel. In the evenings before I went out, my mom would say, 'No strapless tops,' so I would cover myself until I left the house. Then I'd take off my jacket. I looked like a…I don't even want to tell you how I dressed. My pants sat like a second skin, my neckline was dangerous. All the things you said make problems for men. I was such a fool."

"But you were ignorant."

"Yep, *and* I wasn't saved."

"So, what do you expect? We're blind when we don't know Yeshua."

Daniel's comment comforted her. Just then, the couple with the little ones walked up, took towels, and wrapped their children. "You can have our place; we're leaving," said the man.

"Thanks a lot!" Ester got up and stepped into the full shade.

"You must be boiling in the sun," said the mother as she put the baby on her wet hip and picked up the beach bag.

"Phew, yes!" Ester wiped her forehead.

The toddler had wriggled himself out of the towel and was running down to the water again. His dad ran after, grabbed the little boy, and swept him into the air. The child's laughter pealed like a bell.

Daniel began to collect their plastic spades and buckets, shaking off the sand. When the couple was gone, Daniel and Ester cleaned the two white lounge chairs and put their stuff down.

"How about a swim?" suggested Daniel.

"*Sabbaba!*"

He grabbed his T-shirt at the back and pulled it over his head. Taking his phone out of his pocket, he rolled his shirt around it.

Ester decided to go into the water fully dressed. She squeezed a bit of sunscreen into her palm and put it on her face and neck, rubbing it thoroughly into her skin.

"Want some?"

"Please." Daniel took the bottle. "Would you do my back?"

She squirted a large blob onto his shoulders as he turned around, and began to rub it down to the elastic of his island shorts. She liked the feeling of his arm muscles gliding under her palms.

"Hateech!" She smiled.

His ears and neck turned redder than they already were. At that moment she found his attraction irresistible. She put her arms around him and hugged him with her face against his back. Daniel purred. She came around and wiped a little sunscreen from his nose and his ear.

"Aren't you…?" Daniel pointed to her clothes.

"I'll take my example from the mother who was here. I will have more confidence in front of you later," she said, smiling. "You think our stuff is safe?"

In Israel it is not unusual to see the ultra-orthodox in their full religious garb in the water. It would take some time for Ester—being a little compulsive—to gain some balance in processing all the new information about clothing Daniel had revealed to her.

After asking their neighbors to keep an eye on their belongings, they walked to the water. When the first waves splashed against their legs, Daniel started running and shouted for her to follow. He dove into the water. She stood for a moment, pulling her hair into a thick bunch behind her head and tying it with the rubber band that was around her wrist. Then she dove into the water and swam toward Daniel.

They laughed and played until all the cares of the world were washed out of them.

"You know what the sea makes me think of?" She wiped the salt water from her eyes.

"What?"

"The grace of God. It's all around you and there's always more."

"Amen! An ocean full."

Ester nodded. "But sometimes I take only a bucketful to my castle. And when I pour, it's immediately gone—into the sand."

"Right! I want to live in this place!" Daniel shouted with his arms outstretched.

"In the sea of His grace!" shouted Ester and splashed into the air.

Daniel dove into the next wave. Ester simply held her nose and put her head under as it rolled out. They swam until hunger pangs drove them back to the beach.

Unpacking the food on one chair, they sat next to one another on the other chair. Ester put out two plastic plates and two sets of cutlery rolled in paper towels. She sliced a tomato and found the saltshaker. She took a carrot and a cucumber stick and dipped them together into hummus. She licked her lips and kissed his upper arm as Daniel stretched across her to take a piece of cold chicken.

They opened the leftover halva, gherkins, and olives. From the cooler came apples and ice-cold juice.

Daniel shook a wet wipe from its plastic bag and began to wash his hands.

She smiled and lifted a cup. "Juice or water?"

Once they finished eating, a lazy *Shabbat* rest overpowered them. Daniel started putting the leftovers into the backpack and discovered a bottle at the bottom.

"Hey, here's wine!"

"That was supposed to be a surprise."

"Now we'll have to stay till the sun sets." He drew her face closer and kissed Ester on the forehead.

They both put the backs of their chairs down, and as soon as his body was horizontal, Daniel fell asleep. Ester rolled her towel to support her head and turned on her side. She studied his masculine form until his chest began to heave peacefully. Everything became hazy as she drifted into lazy land.

About an hour and a half later, the angle of the sun had changed, and the shade was behind them. The sun's rays felt warm and soothing on their skin.

"Sweetheart," he whispered. Daniel lay on his stomach and looked at Ester next to him. She had loosened her hair, and the humid sea air had turned it into a cascade of curls around her face. She was beautiful. Longing to caress her, he noticed how the sun had kissed her cheeks. He took some sand and poured it gently on her arm. "Sleeping Beauty?"

Her eyelids moved. "Mmm...?" Her voice was warm and mellow.

More than anything, he wanted to embrace her. Instead, he continued pouring sand on her arm.

"You awake?"

"Mmm..."

"Shall we go for a walk?"

She turned onto her back and stretched herself out, arms above her head.

"Will you carry me?" She smiled, her eyes still closed.

"I'd love to."

She sleepily blinked a few times and yawned.

Daniel brought the back of his chair upright.

She stretched another time, swung her legs off the chair, and sat up. "My hair is all wild," she said, trying to gather it.

"I love it."

"You do?" She laughed, surprised.

"It's like a flock of goats coming from Mount Gilead."

"What? Of course! Now I know exactly what you mean."

He jumped up and put his spread fingers deep into her hair. "I love *everything* about you." He kissed her on the crown of her head.

They took their belongings and began to walk in the direction of the harbor. The sun was low, and the reflection on the wet sand where the water pulled back shone brightly in their eyes. They walked as if on a mirror. Daniel turned around and looked back. "Can you see any of our footprints?"

"No."

"Grace wiped them."

"Hallelujah!" She pointed to her right, a few meters higher. "Look. The people's tracks remain up there."

"Got to keep walking in grace."

After about ten minutes' leisurely stroll, they came to the marina. The boats on the shore made it impossible to continue walking in the edge of the water. They decided to sit down and watch the sunset. Ester handed Daniel a corkscrew to open the wine. She carefully unwrapped two glasses and put them on a red checked cloth.

"Where did you hide those?"

"They were in here." She showed him the side pocket opposite the water bottle. "I wrapped them in a dish towel so they wouldn't break."

Daniel poured wine into the glasses.

"Hevi'ani el beit hayain," Ester sang. "He brought me into the house of wine."

"The night I met you, we sang that song. Remember?"

"I only remember how beautiful you were."

Ester was surprised. "How do you mean?"

"It felt like lightning hit me when I saw you in the kitchen."

Her mouth dropped open.

Daniel continued. "Yep, you took my breath away. You were wearing a pink top and your hair was down. I couldn't take my eyes off you that evening. And when you spoke about the blood of Yeshua making us clean, clean, clean—you took my heart."

"Are you serious?" She was dumbstruck.

"Yep, you've given me many sleepless nights since that evening, sweetheart."

She was delighted to hear, but she couldn't help but remember her own inner battle. "The night after Simchat Adon you messed up *my* brain. You said I could ride with you the 'next time.' Remember?"

"No."

"I couldn't figure out what you meant. But I couldn't get you out of my mind either. For days…actually weeks!"

"But at the soldier's conference, you didn't even look in my direction." It was Daniel's turn to be puzzled.

"I know." She smiled. "I was trying to avoid you."

"Why?"

"Because I was afraid you would look in my eyes and see what was going on in my heart."

"When I came outside, Nadav was talking to you. He's my friend, but I was…"

Ester didn't seem to hear what he was saying. "I don't know how to describe it. I was very excited to see you there—but I was really scared. I also didn't sleep."

Daniel understood the fear she was talking about. "Did you hope something would happen for us?"

"Oh my goodness! I hoped…I wished…I prayed like crazy!"

Daniel shook his head. "I also prayed—like crazy!" He laughed. "I knew I wanted you, and I was afraid someone else would take you."

Daniel gave her a glass of wine and lifted his own. She clinked his glass and said, "God's grace."

"God's grace!" He rejoiced and took a sip.

The sun kindled two glowing lights in their wine. She leaned against his chest as they drank in the spectacular horizon.

"Where's my camera?" She suddenly remembered. He propped his glass up in the sand, unzipped a pocket, and handed it to her.

She handed her glass over and switched on her digital. As soon as she saw splendor on her screen, she sang again.

"*Ve'diglo alai ahava…* And His banner over me is love…"

TWENTY-SEVEN

2 September 2007

At 4 A.M. Eema got a phone call from the police saying she had to come to the hospital. David and Gur had been in an accident and his friend didn't make it. I went with her. Dudi's okay now—just cuts and bruises. His one eye is black and he has a gash on his forehead. Three stitches.

His face is a bit swollen, but looks okay. Doctor says he x-rayed—no broken bones. He may have whiplash and his body will be stiff and sore later.

David was allowed to come home with us, but he's still in shock.

When I saw him in the emergency room, he looked so pathetic. I put my arms around him and I couldn't help crying. He was pale and thin. And scared! God, please help him! He saw his best friend dying and he couldn't do anything.

Eema still doesn't know David's on drugs. Should I tell her? Won't it break her heart? God, what must I do?

Abba, please hold my brother.

I want my Abba to hold him!!!

TWENTY-EIGHT

Wednesday, 12 September 2007

THEY TRAVELED IN TWO CARS from Tel Aviv. Daniel, Ester, and David in front, Naomi following. The Cohens had invited Ester's family (including Debra) for Rosh Hashanah at their home. The Rosh Hashanah feast happens over two days, so there would be no school or public transport during that time. David was scheduled for a game with his friends the next day, and Naomi agreed to take him back to Tel Aviv while Daniel and Ester stayed overnight. David was withdrawn and insecure at the prospect of meeting strangers.

It was dusk by the time they entered Jerusalem. The streets were quiet as families prepared to enjoy the feast together. The ten days leading up to Yom Kippur are kind of solemn for some people, but the time after that? That's what most kids look forward to for the whole year! They can hardly wait to gather palm branches, build a *succah,* and decorate it. Mostly the dads and sons do the construction; the moms, girls, and smaller kids decorate. For many children this is their favorite family week. An atmosphere of great excitement fills the nation!

Arriving in Malcha, they parked the two cars across the street from the Cohens' apartment. Ester carried a big bowl of fruit salad, and David brought the cooler with juices and wine. Daniel took their two backpacks and locked the car. As they walked down the steps, Naomi rubbed her arms. "It's getting nippy in Jerusalem."

"Yes." Ester clicked her tongue. "I should have told you to bring something warm."

"One gets spoiled with the weather at the coast." Daniel opened the front door. "*Shalo-o-om!*" Immediately members of his family appeared. He introduced his parents and the twins to Naomi and David. Miriam dried her hands on her apron and kissed Ester on the cheek. She greeted Naomi warmly. "Welcome. We are so glad you could come."

Daniel asked, "Is Yoni here yet...and Debra?"

"Yes," Hanan said. "All on the balcony."

Daniel grabbed David around the shoulders. "Come, meet my oldest brother." They walked outside to find a bunch of kids at play. Yonatan had a two-year-old on his hip and Debra was throwing a ball with a girl of about four. Three more boys were playing in the sand.

Debra was glad to see Naomi and hugged her older sister warmly. Then, she affectionately pinched David's cheek. "Wow! You have grown so tall!"

Everybody helped with introductions. Roi put his hands on the heads of Levi and Shmu'el, who were sitting on the rim of the plastic sandpit. "This one is almost nine, and he is seven and a half."

"I'm thikth," said a cute redhead with freckles.

"And his name is David," said Miriam.

"I'm also David." David smiled and held his hand for the little one to shake. Soon his feelings of self-consciousness began to thaw. The atmosphere in this family was warm and permeated with acceptance.

"We have another son—Li'or," said Miriam. "He and his wife, Ruth, are with her parents for the feast. They have a new baby and they live in Galilee."

As the adults walked into the house, Ester asked Miriam for a light sweater to cover Naomi's shoulders. Joining the bunch on the balcony again, she saw the boys explaining their war games. The young men stood in a semicircle and watched with keen interest as they arranged their tanks and soldiers.

"You need to secure your airport," said Yonatan to the boys. A whole discussion followed as everyone was drawn into the game.

"Yoni was in the special forces—*Shaldag*," Ido confided to David, who stood with his arms crossed. It was obvious that he was very proud of his big brother.

Ester looked at Daniel, and he winked. They had prayed for David every day for three months. The recent accident shook him up a lot, and they'd been extremely concerned for him, but in the last few days he seemed better. They took courage that God was at work.

Indeed, it was not so much what Ido said, but something in Yonatan's involvement with his children that clicked with David's heart. He looked at the gentle strength of this father holding his diapered baby and David decided, *I like you!*

Hanan called them into the house for dinner. The long white table in the dining room was laid beautifully with silver cutlery and bone-white plates. Gold napkins were tucked in the wine glasses. In the middle of the table was a fruit arrangement in a crystal bowl with shiny-cheeked pomegranates. Yellow dates on their stalks, figs, and black grapes created a delight for the eyes. At two places on the table were platters with apple wedges laid in a circle and a little bowl of honey set in the middle. These were foods unique to the feast they were celebrating tonight. The fruit species that ripen at this time of the year reminded them that when Israel came into the Promised Land, God gave them harvests of crops they had not planted. Daniel leaned over and took a few pomegranate pips peeled out of the skin from a porcelain bowl.

Miriam invited everyone to be seated and positioned Levi next to his abba at the one end of the table. "I've laid places for the younger ones," she said as she pointed to the square plastic table next to Rachel's place.

"Shmu'el, Granny wants you to watch things here, okay?"

The oldest grandchild nodded his head profusely.

The aroma of roasted meat and vegetables filled the house. Everybody was keen to eat except Levi. "Aren't we going to blow the *shofars*, Grampa?"

"Yes, yes, yes!" A chorus of voices arose from the small table.

"Let's do it afterward. I don't want Granny's food to get cold," Hanan said gently. He winked at Rachel, who was about to quiet her son. "I told him that the Bible calls this feast *Yom Tru'ah*—the Day of the Blast."

"Sitting here makes me feel like I'm at a king's table tonight," said Naomi.

"The King is coming!" shouted little Yardena at the top of her voice. Rachel instinctively put her hand over the girl's mouth, but everybody burst out laughing.

"She's right," said Daniel. "At Yom Tru'ah the trumpets are blown to announce that a King *is* coming!"

"So we are all royalty. You are the King's daughter, Naomi." Miriam smiled graciously.

"I read a scripture that expresses my feeling whenever I come into your home," Debra said. "*The godly people in the land, they are true nobility. My greatest joy is to be with them!* That's in Psalm 16."

"Thank you, Debra. Shall we pray?" Hanan reached for Miriam, and everyone else took hands, as was the family's custom. He thanked the Lord for the food and for the people present. He mentioned everybody in the room, as well as the guests, by name.

"Wow!" said David under his breath when Hanan concluded. Looking at Yonatan next to him, he whispered, "How does he remember?"

Yonatan smiled. "His mind is sharp, and in addition to that, he prays for us every day, so he has us well memorized."

Hanan initiated the Rosh Hashanah ritual, and everybody else followed suit: the kids dipped their apple slices into honey and fed one another. "May yo' year be thweet!" said little David, honey dribbling all over their table as he aimed for Levi's mouth.

When Miriam went to the kitchen, Ido and Roi got up to bring in the food. The steaming roast was placed in front of Hanan. Baked potatoes, fragrant rice, sweet cinnamon vegetables, and a crumbed eggplant dish. Rachel made space for an apple salad with nuts, as well as a jellied carrot ring.

When everything was on the table, everyone dished up and got on with the meal.

"Mmm...tasty!" said Yonatan.

"Mmm...tasty!" the kids imitated.

"I wish my family could gather like this," said Naomi.

"What do you mean?" asked Miriam tenderly.

"We do get together, but I can never share with them about the things in my heart. We're from two different worlds—except for Debra, of course."

"They don't know Yeshua?" Miriam asked.

"Well, I've shared with them about my faith, but they're orthodox Jews, so they prefer that I don't."

Debra nodded. It was clear that the lack of common faith in their family was painful for her as well.

Hanan looked reassuringly at Naomi. "God often starts with one member, but He wants to see the whole family saved."

"Right," said Yonatan. His daughter had crawled onto his lap. "Think of the history of the Bible. First God's plan for Adam—he was one man. Then Noah, they were a family. And then Abraham—God wanted the whole nation in relationship with Him."

"Uh-huh," said Roi with a mouthful, "and when Yeshua came, He had the whole world in mind."

"Exactly," said Hanan. "A royal priesthood from every tongue, tribe, people, and nation."

"I know that when we decide to follow Yeshua, we often lose some support of our family members," said Miriam, understanding all too well.

"And our friends," said Roi, remembering what happened when he made his faith known at school.

"My father was a rabbi," said Miriam. "When he heard that I had become a believer in Yeshua, it crushed him. He told me he couldn't give me any inheritance. We couldn't even speak—for years!"

Naomi asked with concern, "Did he pass away without knowing the Lord?"

"No, and that's the best part!" Miriam's face exuded joy. "When Hanan got saved, we both started praying for my dad, and after many years, the relationship between my father and me was restored. He admitted that Yeshua was the Messiah on his deathbed."

"Wow! That's wonderful!" said Naomi. "I also spoke to my abba about Yeshua, but I'm not sure if he accepted Him."

"Eema, you did?" asked Ester, surprised. "I *also* spoke to Grandpa about Yeshua before he died."

"Well, then you all did what you could, and the matter is in God's hands," said Hanan.

"What's so wonderful," said Miriam, "is that God gave me other fathers in those years when I forfeited the relationship with my dad. It is written that we do not sacrifice anything for the sake of Yeshua that we will not receive in a hundredfold in return. I have learned so much by reading the books of seasoned men of faith."

"Yes! God just gave us other friends," said Roi.

"Right," said Ido. "A whole swarm of brothers and sisters in the congregation. I never feel like I'm in my own bubble anymore."

"Yeah," added Roi. "This year we even had another believer in our class!"

This was a huge thing for Roi and Ido, who had been the only messianic kids in their school for years.

"Naomi, if you pray for your family, it's just a matter of time before they also will come into the kingdom," said Rachel.

Ester put her hand under the table and gave Daniel's leg a squeeze. "Just a matter of time," she whispered.

He smiled.

"More food, anybody?" Miriam encouraged her sons even though they had already taken second helpings. When all responded with compliments and said how satisfied they felt, Hanan took the opportunity.

"Ido, Roi, please remove the plates. There's something I want to share," Hanan said. Daniel and Rachel helped clear the table, while Miriam gathered the little children to sit with the adults.

Ester leaned over to Naomi and said, "Now it's family devotions."

Hanan got up and took his Bible from the low table next to his armchair. When everybody was seated again, he looked up, took off his glasses, and for a while he focused on the children.

"Now, who knows the story of Joseph?"

The hands of the three oldest boys shot up. Shmu'el poked Yardena. "It's the boy with the pretty jacket in your Bible book." Yardena's face lit up and she stuck her little forefinger in the air.

"Good...so tell us." Hanan looked at Levi.

"Once, there was a man named Jacob who had twelve sons. There was one son he loved more than the others, so he made him a special cloak with many colors."

"I want to tell," said Yardena with a tearful voice.

"Okay, what happened then?" Grandfather invited her to speak. "Dey frow him in a da-a-ak hole," she said, spreading her fingers and putting her hands above her head. The boys knew she was showing the picture in the Bible of how Joseph fell into the pit.

"No-o-o!" said little David, who was sitting with Miriam. "They took hith..." He looked to his mother.

"Cloak," said Rachel.

"They took hith cloak and...and...and, uhm...broke it! And..." Little David swallowed and opened his mouth to continue.

Shmu'el jumped into the gap. "And they put blood on it."

"I want to thay that." David was virtually in tears.

135

"It's okay, Davie," comforted Yonatan. "Tell us some more."

The kids construed the story of how Joseph went from pit to Potiphar to jail. The adults delighted in listening to their account. Even David could not help smiling.

When they came to the part where Joseph became a ruler, Hanan asked another question: "So, how do you boys think he looked at that time?" The baby had fallen asleep, and little Yardena was wilting fast.

"I think he had a red mantle like a king." Shmu'el was impressed with his own answer.

"No-o-o!" said Davie. "In the movie he didn't haf any cloveth on." He referred to the *Prince of Egypt*.

"Right," said Levi, "only like a white skirt." He patted his hipbone. "But I think he also had one of those head...head things like the pharaoh."

"Yes," said David, now very excited, "Yes, with a *thnake* here!" He pointed to his forehead.

"And with black eye paint!" said Shmu'el.

"Quite perceptive," said Daniel, smiling.

Hanan agreed. "I also think Joseph was wearing the Egyptian headgear and makeup. So when his brothers came, they didn't recognize him."

"Mmm." Some voices at the table sounded like this was a revelation.

"What do you think?" Hanan looked at Ido and Roi. "Can the Jewish people recognize Yeshua when he looks like the Gentiles' king? The sad pale face and His long hair?"

Both slowly shook their heads from side to side, knowing their father was on to something.

"Right," said Daniel. "Jewish people think He's only the God of the Christians."

Seeing some of the kids' faces looking sad and the adults frowning, Hanan broke the good news. "*But!* The Bible says Joseph revealed himself to his brothers. So let's read from Genesis 45 where he did that."

After conveying the long account with suspense and emotion, Hanan peeped over the rim of his glasses. "So, if Joseph *did* have that funny headdress, I'm sure he took it off." Hanan made a dramatic move with his hand over his head. "And then his brothers recognized him. They fell on one another's shoulders and cried!"

Instead of applause as expected, Shmu'el, who was fully into the dramatic moment, shouted "Oh, *eeechs*! His face became all black from the paint!"

The others erupted in laughter. Ester and Rachel wiped at their eyes with napkins to show how their own mascara had run.

"Exactly!" said Hanan. "Their sadness turned to joy!"

When it became quiet, Miriam said softly, "There's something I've been wondering about. Joseph's true identity was made known when Benjamin was brought in. Maybe our next prime minister will be Bibi. Benjamin Netanyahu. What if Yeshua shows Himself to His Jewish brothers if Bibi comes into office?"

"Well, I don't know when He will do it," said Hanan, "but God will lift the veil from their eyes." He put his hand flat on the Bible. "That's a promise!"

"It's just a matter of time," said Yonatan.

Miriam got up and brought the fruit salad and ice cream to the table. Little David clapped his hands.

"Grampa, can we ple-e-ase blow the *shofar* now?" Levi begged again.

"Yes, let's do it while Granny dishes up dessert."

The boys jumped up from their chairs. One chair was knocked over in their enthusiasm and fell with a loud noise. Daniel grabbed it like lightning and put it gently on its feet again. Everybody knew how the neighbors downstairs felt about such a racket. The kids almost tiptoed out to the balcony. As for the shofars, the neighbors would tolerate that because it was part of the music of Rosh Hashanah. In the distance they had heard many blasts throughout the evening.

Daniel, Ido, and Roi joined them. Hanan took four short rams' horns from the mantelpiece and handed them to the boys. The young ones tried to blow first. Little David pressed his lips to the opening and blew with bulging cheeks until his face was redder than his hair. Only a squeak slipped out. Levi had more success, but Shmu'el seemed to get the trick. Davie ran inside and, jumping next to Yonatan's chair, eagerly begged, "Abba, come help me, quick!"

"How do you ask?"

"*Pleathe*, Abba."

Yonatan got up and gave the baby to Rachel. He and big David joined the cacophony outside. At some point Hanan suggested, "Okay, now let your uncles blow."

Yonatan, Daniel, and the twins each took a shofar and positioned themselves away from the dining room. Hanan took the long kudu horn and brought it to his lips. It was clear that they had done this many times before. Yonatan counted. The sound of the five together was so loud that Levi put his hands over his ears. They did the full round of four blasts. A long unbroken one, three broken blasts, and nine short staccato notes. They ended with a blast as long as their breath lasted. Their next-door neighbors clapped and shouted, "*Hol HaKavod!* Good job! Well done!" without making an appearance.

The boys' admiration was sky-high. "Wow, wow, wow!" they shrieked. The men handed the *shofars* back to them to make another effort, and walked into the house for dessert.

Little Davie was charged. He jumped up and down and shouted, "Pleathe, pleathe, Abba! Thow me again!"

TWENTY-NINE

Thursday, 13 September 2007

HAVING TWO DAYS FREE from the army was a blessing for most. The authorities knew that soldiers spending time with their families did a lot to promote good morale. Plus, a break from the rigid time structure in the forces granted them much needed rest.

Daniel and Ester did just that. They slept late and leisurely hung out with Daniel's parents and the twins. All shops were closed, so instead of going to the mall for coffee, they opted for Rachel and Yonatan's invitation. A coffee and honey-cake afternoon sounded like the right thing to do on Rosh Hashanah.

It was around 15h45 when they got into the car. "When Yoni invited David over last night, my brother was in a conflict to give up the thing with his friends," said Ester. "I know him. I could see he liked your big brother. A lot."

"Then it's good that Yoni told him to come any time."

Daniel took the back road from Malcha to Arnona. Past the mall, the train station, and the industrial neighborhood, down Hebron Road. They went up Ein Gedi Street and turned right on Efrata.

"This is a beautiful neighborhood." Ester noticed all the trees.

"Wait till you see the park behind their apartment. It is a gift from God!"

"I bet that's where the kids play most of the time."

"Yes, I think that's where they'll be this afternoon. Rachel can watch them from her kitchen window. Of course, she doesn't let the baby go from her sight yet, but when Yardena goes with the boys, she'll swing for hours—they take turns watching her."

Inside the apartment, things were minimal. *Child friendly*, thought Ester while Rachel showed her around. In the bedrooms, toys were in baskets and plastic boxes; in the bathroom, face cloths and toothbrushes hung in a row. Throughout the house valuable ornaments were placed above toddler level.

"Rachellie, I am impressed at the order in your home," Ester commented. "With five children, I was expecting a balagan."

Rachel smiled. "That's Yoni's firm hand. He disciplines them from a young age. They can play with all their hearts, but they have to tidy up afterward. And he doesn't speak twice. He doesn't allow disobedience at all."

"I've noticed that your children are all well behaved. It's really a pleasure to have them around. How did you train them that they speak with such respect to grownups?"

"Thank you! We try to instil the fear of the Lord into our children. If they don't learn to respect our authority, they will also rebel against God. You know how it goes when a child is brought up without discipline."

"I know. You should see the kids at the nursery school where my eema works! Sometimes I don't know how she survives the day."

"If you don't command them (by the way—the Bible says that God knew Abraham would *command* his children), and if you do not *demand* instant obedience from them, they'll wear you out. And when a parent or a teacher gets desperate, who knows what they're capable of."

"Exactly!"

"Yoni said we won't give rebellion an inch in our home. So he never raises his voice. He never loses his temper, but the rod works."

140

"You mean you spank the children?" Ester was surprised. "I thought corporal punishment is forbidden in Israel."

"Yes, we spank them," Rachel answered quietly. "The book of Proverbs says that hitting them with a rod won't kill them. It only removes the foolishness from their hearts."

"You're not scared someone will report you to the police?"

"No," Rachel said humbly. "We fear God more, and He helps us discipline them with restraint. Yoni and I are accountable to one another to keep our attitudes right. We never spank them while we're angry."

"I guess if you obey His Word, God will honor you," Ester said, thinking aloud.

"You're right. Nothing compares to the reward of children who have been pruned."

"That's a good word—*pruned.* From my experience I know that even though I grew up like a wild bush—doing just what I wanted, didn't make me a happy child. I mean, *really* happy."

"I believe you. In this house we deal with those wild shoots. That's the secret of having pleasant children." Rachel smiled at Ester and walked ahead to join the men on the balcony.

"Yoni is telling me about a book he read recently. On the airlift from Ethiopia in '91," said Daniel. "Imagine bringing those 14,500 Ethiopian Jews home to Israel in thirty-six hours!"

"Yes," said Yonatan. "With...le' me see...I think it was thirty-four planes, including IAF C-130s and EL AL cargos."

"I didn't have history at school, but I love reading about the rescue missions of the IDF," said Ester.

"You can Google this one. It was 'Operation Solomon.' Actually, it is phenomenal how God worked to bring about the different waves of *aliyah.* It was like a divine hand was moving on the hearts of the Jewish people, and from all over the world they started emigrating back to Israel." Yonatan sat back in his chair.

"Tell Ester what you said about Mark Twain." Daniel was enjoying his eldest brother.

Yonatan repeated himself. "In the late 1800s, Mark Twain was traveling in Israel. He walked from Mount Tabor to the Sea of Galilee and he wrote in his diary about an 'unshaded lake' where there were no trees. He saw no birds, or dew or grass. He saw a flock of goats and wondered if they ate rocks, for there was nothing else in that barren land."

"Wow! I can understand that he refers to the many rocks; there are so many of them here. But barren land? Impossible!" said Ester. "Especially that area of the Galilee he was describing—it's one of the most fruitful regions in all of Israel."

"Right," said Daniel. "But remember, before the Jewish people returned, there were none of those mango orchards or banana plantations."

"Or oranges."

"Now my mouth is watering." Rachel got up. She asked what each one would like to drink and went to the kitchen.

Yonatan continued. "Yes, this country was a wasteland before the prophecies came into fulfillment."

"Which prophecies are you referring to?" asked Ester.

"The Bible says that the mountains of Israel will produce food for its people. I'm sure you've read that passage that says God will bring the people of Israel back from the nations into which He had scattered them. Then He will sprinkle clean water on them, take out their hearts of stone, and give them a heart of flesh."

"No, I actually don't know what you're referring to."

Rachel returned and placed the tray on a low table in the middle of everyone.

"It's in Ezekiel 36. The next chapter says God will bring the dry bones together and make them a great army. You remember? Ezekiel 37."

"Yep. *That* passage always makes me think of the Holocaust," said Ester. "In pictures of the Jews of Europe, you just see bones and more bones."

Rachel sent the platter with cake and halva around while the discussion proceeded. "Anyway, there are many prophesies that promise God was going to bring the people of Israel back to the land that He covenanted to Abraham, Isaac, and Jacob. And then there are chapters 31 and 33 of Jeremiah." Yonatan put a second square of halva into his mouth, enjoying its rich melting flavour. "God also promised to make a new covenant with Israel."

"Sweet! And He'll do them more good than in the beginning," Rachel said, biting into her piece of honey cake. "I *love* to read those prophecies. Every time I walk through Mahane Yehuda market and I see all the fresh produce, I think, *Those words are being fulfilled before my eyes!*"

"And the land doesn't only produce enough for us. Quite a lot of fruit and veggies are exported, right?" Daniel slurped his hot coffee.

"Did you know that Israel is the third largest exporter of flowers in the world?" Rachel spoke over her shoulder as she got up to fetch the baby, who had awakened.

The next moment the door slammed open and children's voices poured into the house. They were all sweaty and loud and excited about their visitors. After letting them greet the adults, Rachel chased the boys to the shower. Ester volunteered to bathe Yardena.

They visited until the sun set. Then at 18h30 Daniel stood to leave.

"We want to attend the international prayer conference at Ramat Rachel Hotel tonight," he explained and peeked into the bathroom, motioning for Ester to come.

"It was so fun visiting you!" Ester got up from her knees and dried her arms.

Rachel kissed her on the cheek. "Please come again. It was wonderful to have you."

Three boys wearing pajamas and shining faces, and a little girl with a wet head wrapped in a pink towel pleaded with them to stay longer.

"We'll come again," promised Daniel.

They hugged and kissed the clean bundles, said goodbye to Yonatan and Rachel, and slipped out the door.

The hall was packed when they walked in. Ester and Daniel opted for a place at the back.

After the singing, the chairman of events went to the lectern.

"The history of Jews believing in Yeshua started with Yeshua's disciples. But shortly after the outpouring of the Holy Spirit, God allowed the believers to be dispersed, and the seed of those carrying the Good News was scattered into the nations. The Romans destroyed Jerusalem, adding to the Assyrian and Babylonian exiles, and many Jews were dispersed into the Diaspora. The Jewish people were away from their homeland for almost two thousand years. But the prophets wrote that God would bring His people back one final time, never to be uprooted again. The spiritual condition of the Jewish people who returned was much like the deserted land. Those who fled the Holocaust were bankrupt in more than one way. As you know, the State of Israel was birthed in 1948, but long before that time, the covenant-keeping God of Abraham, Isaac, and Jacob started to bring them back."

Ester leaned her chin on Daniel's shoulder and whispered, "Exactly what we spoke about this afternoon."

"Tonight we have as a speaker Shmu'el Ben-Tzion and his son-in-law, Michael Maor," said the chairman. "Shmu'el has fought in all of Israel's wars but one, since 1967. Like David in the Bible, he is not only a warrior but also a worshiper. He is a classically trained musician and played in the Jerusalem Symphony Orchestra for seven years. In April this year, Shmu'el conducted Handel's *Messiah* in Hebrew for the first time in Israel.

"At the moment he works as a tour guide. He loves making the Bible come alive as he takes people around to sites in the land. Even more remarkable is the fact that since his father—a Bulgarian aristocrat—came to Israel, theirs became one of the longest family lines of messianic believers in Israel."

A middle-aged man with friendly eyes and a gray beard took the podium. Shmu'el began by telling the story of his father.

"At twenty-three years of age, my dad—Yosef Ben-Tzion—had finished his studies in astronomy and philosophy in Bulgaria. He felt disappointed by everything he had studied. Nobody in his all-Jewish family was religious or even remotely interested, but he was seeking for God even from the time he was a little child.

"One day in his room, he heard the music of trombones and trumpets in the street. He rushed outside to find a brass band of musicians approaching. Something in their eyes and faces drew him. Maybe they were playing this?" Shmu'el walked to the keyboard and started the song "Onward Christian Soldiers."

"My father later found out that it was the Salvation Army. Once outside, someone put a tract into his pocket. It was a booklet with the Sermon on the Mount. He went back to his room and began to read it. My father spoke ten languages. He read endless books in all those languages, but he had never encountered a sentence starting with these words: 'Amen, amen, I tell you…' It cut like a laser through his heart and he couldn't stop reading. He exclaimed, 'This is the Messiah!' and fell to his knees by the bed. Even though he didn't know how to pray, he said, 'Heavenly Father, if this is the Messiah of Israel, then I'm vowing now that I want to discover Him and make Him known to your people.'"

Shmu'el took a sip of water from the glass on the lectern and continued. "This was 1927—eighty years ago. God has fulfilled the prayer and the heart's desire of my father!"

A younger man came onto the stage.

"This is my father-in-law," the younger man said. He put his arm around Shmu'el's shoulder. "I am married to Rachel, Shmu'el's daughter, and my name is Michael Maor. I'm a lawyer."

He continued the story of Yosef Ben-Tzion, the father of Shmu'el. "When Yosef told his family that he was a believer in Yeshua, they totally rejected him. They held a funeral for him and said, 'You are no longer our son.' The Lord showed Yosef he should move to Israel. He registered for Bible school in Bethlehem and lived in a hut behind the school. He went from being part of one of the wealthiest families in Bulgaria—a family that literally owned neighborhoods—to living in a hut. At one point in his studies, he received the message that his father had passed away. His brothers contacted him and said, 'If you will come back and help run the family business, we will give you your inheritance.' The amount was several million dollars at the time. Yosef did not return. He gave up his whole inheritance.

"In 1948, people knew that a war was coming. The believers were connected to Christians outside the land that offered to evacuate them. It was called Operation Mercy. Yosef said, 'I'm not leaving, even if I have to give my life to share God's love.'"

Michael Maor was an excellent speaker and the facts were at his fingertips. "Historically, there were only twenty-three believers left on the evening of the War of Independence, and nine of them were from his family: the mother, father, and seven children. In sixty years, God has built a house—a sanctuary in this land. There are about fifteen thousand believers in Israel today.

"It is said that in 1978 there were about two hundred believers. Fifteen years ago, there were about fifteen hundred to eighteen hundred believers. Within fifteen years, the number has grown ten times. There is an acceleration in the process of the restoration of our people. Jesus said, '*I will build my church and the gates of hell shall not prevail against it!*'"

Michael inspired the young people in his audience. "When we moved here, we heard many evil reports. Like the spies who brought slanderous feedback about the Promised Land. I want to say that although there are giants on the horizon, they are going to be our breakfast! Giants are the breakfast of champions. The Bible says they are going to be your bread!

"Fifteen years ago, when I moved to Israel, I thought I was coming here to be part of a family ministry, and we've done that. We've started a meeting in the home of my parents, and the Lord blessed our work. We were exactly seven people. Today we have a congregation of about two hundred people in the center of Jerusalem."

Michael continued to give a testimony of God's remarkable favor on his own career. "The Lord led me to study law and He blessed my studies. When I finished, He opened the door for me to become an intern in one of the more prestigious law firms of Israel. The man who started the law firm sixty years ago was the attorney general of the state of Israel. He was a member of Knesset and the state prosecutor in the Eichmann trials. He is not only the best-known lawyer in Israel—they've made movies about his life—but he is famous for the saying in the Eichmann trials, 'I stand before you—the court—in the name of six million people.' He was successful in that trial. Since that time, his law firm has been connected to the government. We still represent the government in many projects, like with the Ministry of Environmental Affairs, the Ministry of Housing, the Ministry of Finance, and so forth. The Lord blessed my work.

"When I finished my internship there, the firm asked me to stay on and work for them. There are about sixty-five lawyers in this law firm, with fifteen partners. After my first year, I was asked to be a partner. It was just the Lord's favor and blessing! I was the youngest partner ever.

"I was aware that there was a problem regarding civil rights for Jews who believe in Yeshua, but I really didn't want to have anything to do with it. I was working in commercial law, and I thought that representing believers would not be an easy way to make a living."

He smiled. "I chose not to be a messianic Robin Hood who would live out in the forest with the discriminated community. But at that time the government systematically began to revoke the citizenship of more high-profile believers in the land. Then they ended up coming after my parents, trying to revoke their citizenship. You know, sometimes you are aware of a problem, but you don't really want to get involved until it hits home. So I stepped in and represented my favorite clients. And God gave me success in my parents' case."

Michael continued to share how God led him to make some noise about the discrimination against messianic Jews in Israel. He hired a campaigning agency, went to the newspapers, and was interviewed on television several times. This placed tremendous pressure on the government to change the procedures of injustice in the Ministry of Interior, which handles visas and citizenship, and which is governed by the Ministry of Religious affairs. Eventually, one of the religious parties in the government invited him to a meeting and asked, "What do we have to do to shut you up?"

As a response, Michael immediately contacted the messianic congregations and followed up on about forty cases. He presented, in his words, "cases screaming with injustice," and the Lord gave him success.

The Lord used Michael to expose

1. The fact that within a democratic country, it is "legal" to believe Yeshua is the Messiah;
2. The upstanding nature of messianic believers in the land:
    They pay taxes (which some other citizens don't do),
    They go into the army (which other citizens don't do), and
    They teach their children upright Jewish ethics such as "love your neighbor as yourself";
3. He exposed the fringe group of ultra-orthodox religious people who persecute the community of believers; and
4. He said that unfortunately as a result, the government discriminates against the rights of messianic believers.

Daniel whispered to Ester, "This guy has so much courage!"

Michael brought his message to an end. "People often compare my life with that of Daniel, who was used in government and in politics."

Ester squeezed Daniel's leg.

"But the story of Daniel, Joseph, and Esther isn't really about Daniel, Esther, and Joseph. It's about God wanting to save a nation. To have a Babylonian king decree that the God of Daniel is the true God and He is to be worshiped."

"Cool," said Ester when Michael stepped down from the platform. She leaned her chin on Daniel's shoulder again and whispered into his ear, "I'm praying the Lord makes you like him, so all your commanders will see that you have a different spirit."

Daniel turned his head and kissed her on the nose.

Ester put her arms around him and pressed her lips long against his cheek. "I'm praying that even the general will know that about you."

THIRTY

25 September

David's birthday. Eighteen today, but he's very sad. Asking why Gur had to die...why not him?

THANK YOU ABBA, that You protected David's life! Looks like Gur lost control of the car. It went off the road and into a concrete wall. Took the hit on Gur's side.

Interesting: Just before the accident happened, Dudi heard a voice saying to him, "PUT ON YOUR SEATBELT." He says it had so much authority that he couldn't do anything else. I think it was God who warned him!

Mom asked him if they had alcohol. David told her they had taken drugs. She said to me that she's suspected this for months. She was only praying for a good opportunity to confront him. Eema also said that the night before it happened, she couldn't sleep. She just prayed and prayed for David.

Three days ago Daniel and I spoke with him. I told David how Yeshua changed my life. He listened. He's not so dead anymore. I know he's sad, but it seems like the darkness that hung around him like a blanket is gone. It's as if the brokenness of his heart pierced a way for the truth. Thank You, Abba!

Daniel spoke straight. He asked him where he thinks Gur went—heaven or hell? Told him that one day we'll all stand before the Judge after we die, to give an account of our lives. Only the blood of the Lamb can cover our sins.

It's Yom Kippur today...
Yeshua, please have mercy on David!
AMEN

THIRTY-ONE

Friday, 28 September 2007

Hey, Es!

How was the Succoth dinner with Granny and the family last night?

You asked me to tell about opening night of the Feast at Ein Gedi. I thought to write rather than phone. It was such a full-on experience!

It was organized by the ICEJ (International Christian Embassy Jerusalem), which started in 1980 as an initiative from the Christian world to show support to Israel's government. It was the time when all the other countries' embassies moved to Tel Aviv when a statement was released that Jerusalem is the eternal undivided capital of Israel. The international core was offended, so they upped and went. But there was a small group of people who felt God wanted them to comfort his people according to Isaiah 40:1.

Teddy Kollek, who was the mayor of Jerusalem at the time, was very much in favor of this. He was the first one to call this group an "embassy." The support of the Christians has been a huge comfort to the land since then. Both to the Jews and the Arabs. It's now... what? Twenty-eight years!

Actually, the idea of the feast was birthed the year before that when believers from the nations came together to celebrate Succoth with song and dance. Their vision was also from Isaiah: MY HOUSE WILL BE CALLED A HOUSE OF PRAYER FOR ALL PEOPLES.

Do you remember the big event in the Jerusalem conference center that you and your mom attended last year? That was the Israeli night of the feast, which the Christian Embassy arranged.

Usually the visitors also join the Jerusalem march in the same week. It's quite a sight to see all the national flags and costumes of the people who come! Christians come from all over the world and carry banners with scriptures and encouragement. I love the march—go every year. You really should join me some time! It's like a river of joy that flows through the city when they come....One year there was a group of Native Americans with a massive banner made of leather. It read, "From the First Nations of America, to the First Among the Nations." It was awesome to see them parade in their traditional costumes. One guy had a huge headdress with eagle feathers! I tell you, that whole week when the Christians are here you can feel the lift of their love and their positive spirit.

Anyways, last night, we went by bus, arrived about five o'clock. It was hot-hot-hot in the desert, but when the sun went behind the mountain, it cooled off a bit. There were hundreds of buses!

You know where the Ein Gedi Spa is? When you look toward the Dead Sea, it's just on the left. An area had been fenced off for the event. Hanna and I prebooked our tickets. Thank you, God, because there were very long lines at the entrance. The kibbutz nearby had prepared the food—a nice Israeli meal. They were quite efficient pushing about five or six thousand people through for dinner!

The stage was set up and the chairs ready. Someone who led worship thanked the people for coming and supporting Israel. That was nice! There was dancing with beautiful costumes. Also, there was a choir of little kids from Uganda—orphans. Watoto children's choir. They were adorable! Wish I could take one of those kids home. ☺

153

The evening was fun! Enjoyed the worship and the program. The vibe was great! It's a blessing to feel the excitement and to know that those people pray for Israel. They blew the shofars all the time. Sounded a bit crazy.

We know there is a spiritual war over Israel and Jerusalem. But last night made me feel we are not alone. Hallelujah! I definitely want to do this Ein Gedi thing again. Next year you must come, okay? If God wills! ☺

Love u!

Deb xxx

THIRTY-TWO

Monday, 1 October 2007

IT WAS THE FOURTH DAY of Beresheet. David, Gur, and Natan had attended the New Age festival for the past three years. This year David and Natan were on their own. Soon they found some friends from the year before and pitched their tents nearby. They loved camping by the Sea of Galilee—it was the most favorite place on earth for many Israelis. About three thousand locals do the Beresheet thing every year. Some of the hardcore hippies attended the Shantipi festival at the time of Shavuot as well as Boombamella at Passover. The gang went to visit some friends during the Boombamella festival the year before, but it took them hours to find their tent among the forty thousand people who were camping on the beach.

This year the boys hoped to spend the Feast of Succoth in their "temporary shelters," enjoying the good weather and the water. Camping in tents near the lake, they just wanted to chill. The culture of the event was to make music, make love, and to smoke stuff. Free from the "system," there was no pressure. Peace was what they came for, and they tried many ways to attain it—mostly eastern ideas.

Eating out of tins and making open fires gave the boys an extra high. Roughing it! (That is, when they were sober enough to know what was happening around them.) This year, though, nothing gave David the lift he had before. Not the girls. Not the trips. Not his friends. Not even jamming together. Maybe it was because of Gur's recent death that he felt so forlorn. Yesterday he began looking for the chai tent they discovered last year. At least they could eat there. *The atmosphere in that place was kind of nice*, he remembered. But it was an inner hunger that propelled him. For the first time in his life he was haunted by a fear of death, and by what he had seen in Gur's eyes before he died. He shook his head like crazy, wishing he could get rid of the nightmarish memory of his friend suffocating in his own blood as he gasped for air. He remembered the wild panic in Gur's face—his desperate, voiceless pleadings as a monstrous dread seemed to swallow him. He remembered his own fear and the intense helplessness. It sucked! Maybe the guys at the chai tent would have some hope to sell.

Yesterday, David and Natan asked around, but they couldn't find the big blue-roofed canopy. What they didn't know was that this year several messianic congregations had grouped together to staff an outreach and service to the festival goers at Beresheet. They had set up a small stage, and there was an abundance of sponsored food and drink available. David and Natan went back to their own camp in the evening, and David half-heartedly smoked a joint, trying to soothe his disappointment at not finding the place they wanted.

By midmorning David and Natan emerged and decided to resume their search. The two walked in the opposite direction than the one they'd taken the day before. They chatted with people they met, asked around, and hung loose. David was even more determined not to go home unless he found something. What? Hope? Peace? He didn't know. Some relief! Desperation drove him. They met some girls who were preparing a simple lunch—*pitas* and tuna fish. Begging, mixed with flattery, got their gnawing stomachs filled. After about an hour they got up and continued looking for the tent of hope. At some point, when they were about ready to quit, they heard a cool reggae song coming over some loudspeakers nearby.

Come-
and magnify the Lord with me-
His praise shall continually be in my mouth!

They walked in the direction of the sound and immediately recognized the blue roof of the chai tent. A guy with a banjo and a girl with a guitar were singing. The boys walked over and promptly sat down on the mats. A peace overwhelmed David to the point that he almost wanted to cry. He felt as if they'd journeyed though a waterless land and at last reached an oasis.

A friendly guy walked up and asked if he could serve them something to drink. They ordered coffee and laid back to rest. The chap returned with two steaming cups and some cookies and sat down beside them. Without being overbearing, he began to chat and ask where they were from. They learned his name was Dor. He wasn't in a hurry. He, in turn, answered their questions. David looked at the guy and remembered what drew him to the believers the year before. It was the joy these people seem to have. Unplastered joy! And the fact that they gave him food!

"You giving food again?"

"Yes," said Dor.

"What time?" asked Natan.

"Uhmm... This set will end at 4:30." Dor pointed to the couple making the music. Then Stevenson will tell his story, and dinner will be about 6:00. You're invited."

David made up his mind to stay, even if Natan didn't.

"Stevenson. Who's that?"

"It's a guy who was dead and came back to life. He has an amazing testimony!"

"Aah, please! What's he smoking?" Natan didn't bite.

But David was as wide awake as a hangover headache would allow. He sat upright and asked with curiosity, "Tell me."

"No! You'll have to wait. He's talking in"—Dor looked at his cell phone— "five minutes."

"Is there a toilet close?" David suddenly realized he needed to relieve himself.

"About five hundred meters that way," Dor said, pointing. Calculating that it was too far and his need too urgent, David jumped up, went outside, walked away a bit, and made light artillery against a tree behind someone's tent.

After a few minutes he came back, weaving his way through other people sitting on the floor mats, and joined Dor and Natan. At that moment the translator, whom he remembered from the previous year, took the microphone. He thanked the artists and introduced a black guy.

"Stevenson comes from the Caribbean Islands."

And his face beams like an angel's, thought David. *What makes all these people shine like...like they've swallowed a lightbulb?*

"I was born in the Caribbean, as you heard." Stevenson smiled a broad, beautiful smile. His words were translated. "When I was thirteen years old, something happened to me that makes it impossible for me not to believe in Jesus. My friends and I used to play a game in which we would see who could stay underwater the longest. This day, I was by myself, but I wanted to see if I could improve my own record of three laps in a twenty-meter pool without coming up for air.

"I wanted to do five laps, so I concentrated really hard and started swimming. Three were easy. I pressed through four. By the fifth lap I didn't even feel the need for oxygen. I believed I was a fish. I didn't need to breathe anymore." He smiled for a second and then his face turned serious.

"I cannot tell you the moment I died, but I appeared in a place where I could see my life on a screen like a video. Everything I had done since my childhood played like a movie before my eyes. I was experiencing it all again.

"At the right-hand side on top of me there was an intense, bright light. I was feeling His power, peace, joy, and strong love. But below me, there were strange-looking people. They were decomposing. I could see worms in them, and their clothes were rotting. As they spoke to me, their words sapped my strength.

"Words like *fear*, *hatred*, and *anger* became personified and started coming into me. I became those things. It was as if there was a 'factory' of death inside of me, and I too began to decompose and rot. I don't know how to describe it. These negative things...they were in my cells. In my blood. It was horrible. I was being consumed!"

"Was he in hell?" asked Natan, but got no reply to the question.

Stevenson closed his eyes and shook his head. "I don't have the words. Imagine your worst fear, then multiply it three thousand times. It's a monster that totally devours you."

That's it! David thought, as his eyes fixed on Stevenson. *That's what I saw in Gur. It was a bigger fear than I've ever seen.*

Stevenson came into focus again. "Your mind and your emotions are sharper than I can explain, and you are aware of past, present, and future at the same time. The intensity of the pain you feel is beyond my capacity to describe. By now I was almost paralyzed, and my life on the movie screen was nearing the end. Suddenly I knew that life, just breathing, is the greatest gift there is. However, I was dead. At this point I knew I was dead.

"While I watched the last moments of my life on the screen, I saw my aunt. She always told me to call on the name of Jesus with all my heart and I would be saved. At that moment her words took all of my attention."

David's thoughts trailed off for a moment. He thought of how his mother and sister spoke to him about Yeshua and told him the same thing. He hadn't wanted to hear. *But it was only after Gur died...*

When David zoomed in again, Stevenson said, "When I opened my eyes, I jumped up and the people started to run away!"

"What?" David asked so loudly that the other people jerked their heads around.

"What happened?" he asked again.

"Shhh!" The people quieted him impatiently.

"What happened?" He grabbed Natan's arm, but his fixated friend shrugged him off with a *"Shhheket!"*

"I was so glad to be alive again, I told the lady who was holding me, 'If you only knew where I've been!'" Stevenson's voice was laden with emotion. "I began to cry, and I squeezed this woman so hard, chlorine and water squirted out of my eyes. She said to me, 'Stevenson, everything is okay. You are with us now.' I realized I was back on earth. As I started to calm down, I heard what had happened while I was in the other place.

"I had drowned, and after lying at the bottom of the pool (don't know how long it was, but for sure more than twenty minutes), someone saw my bloated body float to the surface. Someone else swam in and pulled my body out, but it was already blue and hard. I must have been under water for a long time. They tried resuscitation, but nothing helped.

"A boy ran to tell my mother that I was dead, and people could hear her screaming from far away. Before the ambulance came, about two hundred people were standing around my body. They all knew I was dead. That's why it scared them so much when I jumped up. After so much time under water, a person becomes brain damaged because of a lack of oxygen. God did a double miracle on me. Jesus not only saved me, but He healed me perfectly. My brain and my body are working fine...as you can see!" Stevenson shook his arms and laughed.

"But hell is for real. Make sure you don't end up in the wrong place." Stevenson concluded, "And Jesus is the *only* way to heaven. Thank you, guys."

As he walked off the stage, people clapped. Several who heard him on the loudspeakers remained standing on the periphery of the tent. David jumped up to speak to Stevenson, but seeing the crowd swarming around the speaker, he gave up.

"So what happened that he came back to life?" David plunked himself down again and looked at Natan and Dor.

"What was the last thing you heard?" asked Dor.

"His aunt told him to call on the name of Yeshua."

"Okay, so he wanted to call on the name of Yeshua," began Dor, "but there was very much resistance in him. He said he had to fight to be able to even say the name of Yeshua."

"Also, because he was so dead—he felt paralyzed," added Natan.

"Right," said Dor.

Natan was enthusiastic. "He said it felt as if he had to travel down to the bottom of his heart, but that's when he realized how deep we are as human beings. And how much is inside of us—it's like an eternity! He said it felt like he had to travel the distance from here to a star, right?" Natan looked at Dor.

"Exactly," said Dor, and let Natan continue. "So the moment he found the strength to say Yeshu—"

Dor interrupted him. "He said 'Yeshua,' but his voice was so weak, he could just barely get it out. Just a weak, weak 'Yeshua.' He said it with all his heart."

"Right," said Natan. "The moment he whispered that name, a very strong hand reached in and grabbed him, and yanked him out of death!" Natan demonstrated with his fist. "He said it was like the power of lightning snatched him out of the center of the earth."

"And that's when his soul came back into his body and he jumped up!"

"Wow!" David's eyes were big. They continued to discuss the testimony, and Dor could see that David was somehow desperate. He looked around for help and noticed a spunky redhead of about sixty. "Hey, Jan! Please come over here."

She waved back with a huge smile and walked over immediately. "Jan is a mom to us all," said Dor. "Do you mind if she sits in while we talk?" She bent down, put her arms first around David and then around Natan, and hugged them warmly. Love and joy oozed out of her.

David told them about Gur's death and about the fear he'd battled with since.

Jan looked lovingly into David's eyes and said quietly, "Death was an enemy from the time when Adam and Eve first sinned. But we have all sinned and fallen short of God's glory. That's why we are afraid—because our hearts condemn us. But God loves us and wants to restore us to a right relationship with Him. So His plan was to give His Son Yeshua as the ultimate and final sacrifice to take away our sins. When we believe Yeshua was that innocent Lamb slaughtered for us, we can be cleansed."

David nodded in understanding.

"So if you believe Yeshua was killed on that tree in your place, and that He rose from death after three days, and if you repent of your sin…" David was eager.

"Then God is willing to forgive your sins and wash you white as snow," Jan added. "That's written in Isaiah 1:18. Isn't God's love for us just great?"

David could not help the tears coming to his eyes. All the things his mom had told him through the years made sense, yet all of a sudden, he felt confused and helpless. "How do I do this? I want the joy you all have."

Jan hugged him. "You have to believe that Yeshua died in your place and call on His name and you will be saved. Like Stevenson did."

David wiped his eyes on his sleeve.

"The Bible says, *Whoever calls on the name of the Lord shall be saved.* You are weeping because the One who made you is touching your heart. This is such a blessing."

David could not stand it anymore. He sensed the love of God, but he also felt the weight of all the things he had done wrong.

"My life is such a mess! How do I get right with Him? I want to go to heaven." The walls of his heart began to cave in.

"You just pour it all out to God," said Jan. "Tell Him everything you have done. Say that you are sorry and ask Him to forgive you."

David bowed his head.

"God, I've told many, many lies," he began. "I am really sorry. Please forgive me." He cried quietly. Surprisingly, Natan blurted out after him, "God, I have also been lying. Please forgive me. And make me clean."

"I have stolen things, God," David's voice broke. He croaked, "Forgive me, God."

Natan confessed the same.

After David finished recounting his sexual sins before the Lord, Jan looked up and asked him straight out, "Was your father unfaithful to your mother?"

He nodded and looked down.

"This is a generational sin." She kept quiet for a moment, as if she were listening and then said, "Did someone mess with you when you were around thirteen years old? A man—a young guy?"

He looked up and frowned. *How does she know these things—is she psychic or what?*

"Mmmm, so there are open doors." As if she could read his mind, she said, "The Holy Spirit is showing me these things, and you don't have to fear. He loves you very much."

She remained silent, and David's tears began to stream. She could see that he was deeply wounded by some of the stuff that was coming into the light. Whispering, embarrassed that the others would hear, he laid his broken heart bare in the presence of the Most High. Jan knelt with her ear right by his mouth. When he became peaceful, she took a bottle of anointing oil from her pants pocket, put a drop on her finger, and asked David's permission to anoint him. "This is not magic, David. The Bible says when someone needs healing, we must anoint him with oil and pray for him so he can be healed."

She touched his forehead. "Heavenly Father," she prayed, "thank You for showing us what opened David's life to so much darkness and hurt. Thank You that through the power of your Spirit these open doors can be closed now. I thank You for delivering David from the sins of his fathers. I rebuke the lying spirits and the spirits of sexual perversion and command them to go now in the mighty name of Jesus from Nazareth, who came in the flesh!"

Daniel felt a powerful sensation in his stomach. For a moment he was nauseous and wanted to throw up.

Jan kept her eyes open and watched closely how God was dealing with David. After a while she continued. "Lord, I ask that You fill him with Your Holy Spirit—with Your light and Your love. I declare that by Your stripes, David is healed—his heart, his mind, his body.

"I thank You, Yeshua, for Your blood that cleanses us from all our sins and unrighteousness. In the name of Yeshua, the Messiah, amen."

Jan hugged David as he wept and laughed at the same time. "How do you feel?"

David shook his head and smiled, wiping his nose on his sleeve again. He was overwhelmed by the moment.

"I feel"—he put his hand on his heart as if to test its condition—"peace. A huge peace." He shook his head, amazed.

"And you?" Jan put her hand on Natan's shoulder.

He nodded and smiled. "I feel good."

"Do you want me to pray for you also?" asked Jan.

"No. No, I'm okay."

Jan enthusiastically jumped up and gave praise to God. "Hey, let's get you baptized in the Sea of Galilee!"

"Right now?" asked David.

"Why not?" she said. "It's just a sign that Yeshua has washed away all your sins."

"Why not?" David looked at his friend. He recalled Ester's baptism and the excitement that filled his mother that day.

"Wait...what are we doing?" asked Natan.

"It's like a *mikve*," said David.

"Exactly," explained Jan. "When you become a new man in Yeshua, you symbolically go under the water as if you are going into a grave. The old person is dead and must be buried. Then you come up again because you have been raised to a new life. You come out of the grave with Yeshua. Basically it's making a statement of what you believe."

"No, I don't want to," said Natan immediately. "I need to think first."

"It's okay," said Jan. "No one's forcing you." Looking to David, she asked, "How about you?"

He nodded. "I'm ready."

"Great! Hey, Dor, let's go dunk him!" She playfully grabbed him around the neck.

The four of them walked about a hundred meters to the lake. Strangely enough, neither Dor nor Jan baptized David. After explaining to him that the first believers were immersed in the name of the Father, the Son, and the Holy Spirit, they invited him to go under the water voluntarily—on his own. Jan asked David what he believed, and after his public confession, she said, "Now you can go under as many times as you like, because this day marks a brand-new beginning in your life. It's totally between you and God!"

THIRTY-THREE

Tuesday, 2 October 2007

THE SUN MADE A BRIGHT STREAK on the roof of his tent. David had slept like a baby. The heat drove him out of his sleeping bag, but he lay down on top of it again, thinking, *It's the first time in years that I don't have a headache upon waking. Why? Because I didn't smoke last night?* He was pleasantly puzzled. Was it the cleanness he felt since he got out of the water? He couldn't pinpoint it, but something had changed. A huge load of guilt and heaviness had rolled off his shoulders.

He dug through his stuff and found a very creased T-shirt. He pressed it against his nose to discern if it was fresh and pulled it over his head. Then he found his toothbrush and crawled out of the tent—rear end first. David squinted at the position of the sun. *Must be early 'cause the whole camp seems asleep and Natan's tent is zipped.* He walked to the nearest wash-up area and splashed his face. Standing legs spread like a giraffe, he positioned his awkward height to see his face in the mirror. He tried to organize his matted hair and brushed his teeth. "Man, something's different. I feel light, the colours are bright, something's cool with me!" he said to himself, bending to drink water from the tap.

David decided to walk to the messianic tent to see what was happening. The air was crisp, and the first beams laid straight shafts of light through the trees. For some reason, everything was beautiful around him. When he approached the blue canopy, people were sitting in small groups. By the aroma of coffee and scrambled eggs, he thought they would be eating, but it seemed they were…what…praying?

Someone noticed David approaching and got up to greet him. *"Boker tov!"* The stranger grabbed his hand. "Had a good night?"

"Yes, really good. Slept in peace."

"We'll eat in a little while. The guys are just praying for the day ahead. You can hang around till breakfast."

"Thanks!" David rubbed his tummy, feeling hunger beginning to register.

The next moment, he saw a person he knew among the other men in a small group. Their heads were all bowed.

"Hey," David said to the stranger, "is that guy's name Yonatan?" He pointed him out.

"Yep, he's a friend of Haim, our leader. Came in this morning."

"I know him!" said David with excitement. "His brother is going steady with my sister."

When the people formed a line for breakfast, David walked over to Yonatan. Haim stretched out his hand first and greeted him warmly. "You got baptized yesterday, right?"

David smiled, but before he could respond, Yonatan grabbed him and hugged him.

"David, what? You were baptized? How come? Tell me about it!" Yonatan exclaimed loudly.

"What are you doing here?" asked David, ignoring his questions.

"Haim is my buddy, and I just came in to be with him this morning. Rachel and the kids are camping."

"Where?"

"At Kibbutz Ma'agan."

"Uh-huh, over on that side of the lake?" David pointed.

Yonatan smiled at David and commented, "You look great! Okay, now…I want to hear what happened. Did you really get baptized yesterday?"

David started telling Yonatan about the day before while Haim became occupied with other things. Somebody gave them plastic plates when their line reached the food serving table.

After dishing up, the two sat down on a mattress. They clearly had a good connection.

By the time Haim joined them again, the same couple who sang the reggae song the afternoon before were once more on the stage.

"They're cool!" David pointed his thumb over his shoulder.

"Uh-huh," said Haim, nodding while he gulped down a bite of his sandwich with coffee. "Where are you from?"

"Me? Tel Aviv." David put his hand on his chest.

"We need to connect you with a congregation in your area. Would you give me your number so we can be in touch?" Haim gave his coffee cup to Yonatan and took a pen and a small notebook from his pocket.

David called out his number while Haim wrote.

"Would you guys also like to have some coffee?" Haim offered.

"Actually, I'm going to skip that one." Yonatan put his finger on his watch. "I told Rachel I'd be back by nine."

Haim looked at the time and raised his eyebrows. "Yep, you'd better be going."

Yonatan smiled. "I'll call her the minute I'm in the car. She'll be glad to hear that I saw David here." He put his arm around the young man's neck and gave him a hard squeeze. "Did I tell you we're like family?" Yonatan said to Haim with David still in his grip. He turned him loose and lifted his hand to slap a high five. "You've got to visit us!"

"How long will your family be camping?" asked David.

"Till the end of Succoth."

"Which is…?"

"Thursday. Two more days," said Yonatan.

"I'll come," said David.

"Rachel and the kids would love that. Can I tell her about your new experience?"

David smiled. "Sure!"

Yonatan gave him another hug. He also embraced Haim and said, "Hey, buddy! God bless you!"

"Thanks for coming, Yoni. It was great to pray with you."

Yonatan affectionately slapped Haim on the back and turned to David. "*Sabbaba!* See you at the kibbutz. Come anytime!"

As soon as Yonatan pulled away, he called his wife. Then he phoned Daniel to share the good news. Daniel promptly phoned Ester…who phoned her mother…who phoned Debra.

THIRTY-FOUR

Shabbat, 20 October 2007

H E DIDN'T KNOW who was more excited—the boys or himself. Daniel had promised to bring his family to the air force base and show them around. He parked his car under a tree at the entrance while he and David waited for the others to arrive.

The excitement stirred memories of his graduation, when all his extended family had attended. *That was one of the biggest days of my life—when I finally got my wings!* He remembered how it felt to dress in his formal pilot's uniform for the first time. How all his relatives admired him in his light blue shirt with navy pants and cap, as if he were being decorated for some heroic act. *Wish Ester could have attended the ceremony that day...she would have been so proud!*

Daniel snapped back to reality when his family arrived. His dad had suggested an all-men's outing, so Miriam, Rachel, and Ruth agreed to look after the babies. Ido, Levi, and Shmu'el jumped out of the van, ran to Daniel's car, and piled into the backseat. Daniel drove ahead, showing his ID card at the checkpoint. He explained that the vehicle behind them was following him. They passed the airfield and arrived at the operational building. After parking the cars, Daniel asked them to wait while he got final clearance for their visit.

In the meantime, David greeted Daniel's family. This time, they felt like his brothers. All of them hugged him and expressed their joy at seeing him again. The special bond between them had grown because of several phone calls since he had visited with Yonatan's family in the Galilee.

When Daniel returned, he took the entourage into the building—straight to the pilots' dressing room. The little boys were over the moon about everything.

"Cool!" Levi pointed at the helmets hanging in a row. Daniel showed them the vest he wore whenever he flew. He explained the equipment tucked into the pockets and allowed David and his brothers to feel its weight. The little boys each got an opportunity to put on Daniel's helmet. Looking at their dwarfed faces, Yonatan wished he were allowed to take pictures.

"These helmets are made to fit each pilot's head exactly." Daniel put his hands on his head. "When they measure you, they place a mould around your head and then pour hot stuff into it." He pulled a pained face. "It burns your brains out!"

"What if you need a new helmet?" Little David was mischievous.

"I hope I never do." Daniel pinched him on the cheek as he started leading them out of the room.

Hanan looked at his son when they came to the door. "Make sure your head never grows." He gave Daniel's shoulder a playful squeeze. The young pilot smiled and nodded in agreement.

Looking to make sure everybody was outside, he pulled the door shut and activated the alarm system. Next, he took them into the OPS room.

"It's like the movies!" shouted Shmu'el.

"Yes, a small theater," said Daniel.

"And how do you know that?" asked his uncle Li'or, sitting down in the padded seats of the first row. "The movies" were not a place the boys visited habitually.

"My friend had a birthday and we went to see *Finding Nemo*. In a…a place just like this!" answered Shmu'el. Yonatan and Lior smiled.

"A theater," their abba offered.

Daniel walked to the front. "Every time our commanders want to speak to us, we come in here."

"Yes, before a war," announced Levi.

Yonatan gently corrected the boy while rubbing his head. "Even when there isn't a war. They come every time before and after they fly."

Daniel told them a little bit about the IAF. He asked Ido and Roi if they learned in history about the time when Israel destroyed Egypt's air force on the ground.

"In 1967?" asked Ido.

"Yes," answered Daniel, switching on the DVD player.

"And in '73 they hijacked their radar," added Ido, quite sharp on dates.

"Right," said Li'or, "but wasn't the equipment too heavy for the helicopter?"

"Almost." Daniel prepared to educate his family. "Okay," he said, bending down to check the settings, "I am going to show you a DVD about helicopters."

Little David shifted himself deeply into his seat and exclaimed, "Thith ith cool!"

"The first part is like a flight simulator."

"What's that?" asked Levi.

His dad answered under his breath, trying not to interrupt Daniel's lesson. "As if you are sitting in the cockpit yourself—it shows all the controls and the view out the window through the pilot's goggles."

"Cool!" said Levi.

"Flying an attack helicopter at high speed and low altitude in a hostile environment is difficult and risky," said the voice of the narrator over the sound system. "The cockpit is highly automated to simplify the tasks of the pilot and allow him or her to concentrate on the battlefield."

Daniel pressed the pause button and the scene froze. He brought their attention to certain sounds, beeps, and tones on the DVD. "If you are flying too low, or if your tail is not rightly set for landing, these alarms will warn you. Also, you cannot shoot unless you are at a certain speed or altitude. A computer controls everything."

The narration continued. "The helicopter's speed and maneuverability make it an ideal vehicle for scouting and reconnaissance. They usually go out in front of armored divisions to look for enemy forces. Ironically, their slow speed is one of their main advantages. They can spot small targets easier than jet aircraft can, so they are precise enough to attack enemy positions close to friendly forces. Often they are part of the ground force rather than the air force."

When the DVD ended, Daniel asked the boys, "Did you see the paratroopers?"

They all nodded. "If there is a war, do you think it is best to jump from an airplane or a helicopter?"

Each gave their opinion.

"So, what about picking up the paratroopers from the ground?"

Again, the boys came up with fantasy answers.

"And if there is no place for a plane to land? Then the paratroopers have to fight their way out, right?"

Daniel let the question hang in the air a while, stimulating their thoughts.

"Can't the helicopter pick you up?" asked Levi uncertainly.

"Yes," said Daniel. "A helicopter can land almost anywhere. Even in a small space, because it doesn't need a long runway. It lifts up like this." He demonstrated by raising his hand vertically.

"But they don't drop paratroops anymore because they are too easy a target. And it's the job of a rescue helicopter to carry the troops," said Roi, who had been quiet until now. "You are a snake pilot."

"Right," answered Daniel.

"Wha that?" asked little David, his face all scrunched.

"Roi means that Daniel flies a Cobra, and that's an attack helicopter. It doesn't carry more than two people," explained Yonatan.

The men continued to discuss things with the boys as they walked up the stairs of the OPS room and out. Daniel punched in the security code after closing the door.

They walked to the line, where two of the helicopters were positioned on the edge of the runway. Daniel pointed and said, "These are on standby, which means that within a few minutes they could be ready for lift-off."

"Is there always a pilot on standby?" asked Roi.

"Yes, also engineers and other personnel. That's why I cannot come home on the weekends when I'm on duty."

"Or when you're with Ester," added Yonatan and winked at Ester's brother.

When they came to the helicopter, Levi pointed to the sticker on the Cobra. "Hey, that's why you're a snake...uhm..."

"Snake pilot," said Ido helpfully.

Daniel pointed to the cockpit. "Usually I sit at the back and the gunner sits in the front. Or the other way around."

"I want to be the gunner!" shouted Davie.

When the boys saw all the controls, they got loud. "Wow! Cool!" they yelled over and over.

Hanan held his hands behind his back and peeped through the window. He shook his head and asked, "Do you know what all these meters are for, my son?"

Daniel sensed his dad's admiration. "Yes, Abba," he said without acclaim.

Li'or asked the next question. "Do you go only by instruments, or do you sometimes look out the window?"

"I look out the window. It's only in clouds or bad weather that we fly by instruments alone."

"What are the most basic things they teach you?" asked Roi.

174

"To take off...to hover...and to land. They also teach us forced landings. Like the instructor would cut the power at a moment when you don't expect it."

"Oh my!" Hanan looked worried.

"Yes, you learn to react instinctively. Usually the IP will do that when everything else is going wrong."

"You must have nerves of steel," said Hanan.

Daniel lowered his head. "Look at my gray hairs! Abba, did you know they say all the pilots of Israel have white hair at forty-five? That's before they retire."

"Seriously?" asked Roi.

"The stress," commented Li'or.

"I tell you," Daniel shook his head, "just drafting the flight schedule for our squadron makes me gray."

"So, if those you mentioned were the basic maneuvers, what are considered advanced?" asked Yonatan.

"Well..." Daniel thought back. "We also learned tactical flying and navigation. In ground school we learned aerodynamics, maintenance of the aircraft, and about the weather. Also night flying, but I think it's mainly the assaults in the air and on the ground that require specialized skills."

"Tell us about the weapons your ship carries." Ido was the one for technical stuff.

"Nearly any kind of helicopter can carry guns. Capabilities depend on their lift. The more lift, the more ammunition it can hold. Because of the tandem configuration of an attack helicopter, it's much more streamlined and also much lighter than the average helicopter. The weapons are numerous. There's a standard array of machine guns. The Cobra has one on its nose." Daniel walked to the front and touched the barrel.

"Wow, cool!" the boys sang out in unison.

"Are these missiles?" asked Ido, pointing to the rocket pods on the sides of the helicopter.

"We do carry anti-tank missiles." Daniel navigated carefully around his brother's questions.

"I know—they're called hellfire," said Ido before inquiring about another detail. "Are your missiles heat guided or laser guided?"

Daniel laughed. "Ido, you know that some of the info about the IAF is classified, right? You've studied their website on the Internet. That should give you all facts you need to know."

"Hey, Daniel, what is this?" Shmu'el shouted behind them.

Daniel swung around. Shmu'el was pointing to the nose of the aircraft at a device that looked like a combination of lenses, mirrors, and small glass windows. "Oh! That's the helicopter's eyes. It helps the pilot see where he flies at night," answered Daniel.

"PNVS?" asked Yonatan.

"Right. The Pilot's Night Vision System. It also guides you right onto the target where the helicopter has to shoot."

"Cool!" Levi and Shmu'el exclaimed simultaneously.

"Did you never mith?" Little David looked up at Daniel with eyes squinting in the sun.

Daniel hunched down and faced him squarely. "The instruments are very good, buddy, and I always do my best, but sometimes things work out differently."

Davie nodded, making big eyes.

They hung around the helicopter a while longer and exhausted Daniel with questions.

When they began to walk away, David came side by side with Daniel. Until now he was the only one who hadn't said a word.

"What's the purpose of war?" he asked. A heavy sigh escaped with the question.

Daniel, whose whole morning had been about technical detail, quoted from his textbook: "Warfare is a fighting philosophy that seeks to shatter the enemy's cohesion. Through a series of rapid, violent, and unexpected actions, a turbulent and deteriorating situation is created, with which the enemy cannot cope."

Yonatan realized that his brother's answer didn't intersect with the real problem.

"David." His voice was comforting. "War is dreadful. Always will be. You know that Israel would much rather live in peace with her neighbors than fight them. The Bible says that war happens when people do not get what they want. In the case of Islamic terrorism, this is 100 percent true. They fight because they want this land for Allah. All of it."

Yonatan put his hand on David's shoulder as they walked. "Israel has a defense force. God expects us to defend the land He entrusted to us, and also protect the people who cannot defend themselves. Do you agree that children, women, and old people are vulnerable?"

David nodded.

"So that's the reason why I was in Special Forces, why Li'or was a paratrooper, and why Daniel's in the air force. We want to give our best to make sure those we love are safe."

"Abba, I also want to be in *Shaldag*, like you!" Yonatan took Shmu'el's hand, who had come to walk next to him.

"That's great, buddy, but it's tough. You'll have to become very fit."

"I do pushups, Abba. Look at my muscles!" He tapped on his upper arm.

His dad pressed the hard muscle. "Feels good!"

Suddenly Shmu'el's broad grin changed to a serious face. "If I become strong, I won't die, right, Abba?"

Yonatan put his hand on his son's head. "All men will die one day, my boy."

There was a moment of silence before Ido, who followed the conversation from behind, commented, "Shakespeare said, 'a coward dies a thousand deaths, but the valiant dies only once.'"

Yonatan met his nine-year-old's eyes as Shmu'el looked up questioningly. "That means it can feel like your heart stops beating when you are afraid," and then in a lighter tone, "but if you are brave…"

Little David caught only the last word. "I'm brave!" he shouted at the top of his lungs and lifted both fists in the air. The others delighted in the moment.

Yonatan looked at Shmu'el again. "Yeshua said the test for love is if you are willing to lay down your life for a friend. That's when you're really brave."

David nodded, and Yonatan sensed that a paradigm shift might be taking place. Not wanting to add any more weight to the young man's narrow shoulders, he gave him a squeeze on the neck.

"Defending people is an expression of love, David." Yonatan's voice was reassuring. "And love is stronger than hatred and stronger than war. Even than death!"

THIRTY-FIVE

Thursday, 1 November 2007

ESTER DREW A HEART in the foam of her cappuccino. Her own heart was beating in her throat with longing and expectation. Looking out the window, she pulled her sleeves over her hands and clasped the cup tightly to soak up its heat. A cold wind was driving the rain outside. "Any minute now…" She looked at her cell phone. It was 21h35.

They had agreed to meet at the Aroma at the beach. Daniel had served in the settlements for the past week. Everybody in the Permanent Force must do this special duty once a year. The next moment the door of the coffee shop swung open and the handsome officer walked in. Ester felt the blood rushing to her face as she got up to greet Daniel. He kissed her on the forehead and folded his arms around her. Unaware of the people, she melted into his chest. His army jacket was cold and sprinkled with raindrops, but his embrace was warm. She clung until the rush in her ears quieted.

As soon as they sat, she grabbed both his hands and kissed them on the knuckles. "I'm so glad you're back safely." Her eyes were radiating.

He lifted his hands and cradled her face. Leaning forward, he whispered, "I missed you."

"I missed you too. How was your time?"

"Oh, it was wonderful just to be a simple soldier and stand guard for the whole week. I enjoyed it very much."

"I was a bit worried about you."

"You didn't need to be. I was totally stress free."

"I prayed for you."

"Thank you. Maybe that's why it felt like I was on holiday." He unfolded her fingers and kissed her palm.

"Why do you say 'stress free'? Just because there were no incidents?"

"Honey, if you knew the pressure that I—we—live under daily, you'd understand that this was time off."

"Explain?" Her eyes searched his for understanding.

"Sometimes I think, here I am—twenty-four years old. I'm supposed to be excited about my future. In America, people my age think about their studies. Many of them are in college or university. They do things young people do—like play soccer on the beach." Daniel sighed. "But I'm part of a setup that plans and strategizes the survival or death of people. It's crazy! To have this threat of destruction looming over our nation all the time. Our best years are spent in such seriousness."

"I know." Ester's voice was soothing.

"The time off was good, because for one whole week I saw life again. Families. Children at play. Settlers with their kids. Love. But when I go to the office, get into the helicopter, train, and do missions here and there, it's such a huge responsibility, it's like I lose my soul." Daniel's voice sounded raw and his eyes burned with emotion that rarely came to the surface. "That's why you are so important in my life. You help me feel. I don't want to be a machine."

She put her velvet-soft hand on the side of his face. *"Ahuv shelee,"* she said tenderly. "One can become a machine in any setup. Just living day by day, being too busy."

"You're right." Daniel moved her hand over his mouth and kissed her palm again.

"I'm sure there are students, even mothers, who also experience what you do. It's a kind of burnout when there's too much work and constant pressure."

He nodded. "I know."

"While you were away, I read in the Bible how Yeshua said to His disciples, *Come apart and rest a while.*"

Daniel drank in her words like a thirsty deer.

"I think that's why Abba took you away for this time. He knew how much you needed the break."

Her gentleness melted his heart. He put both his hands over his eyes and sat like that for a while. Finally, he took two napkins from the dispenser on the table, put them together, and wiped his nose. Looking up, his eyes were bloodshot. Tears formed in Ester's eyes as well.

They looked into the naked depths of one another's souls.

"I love you," he whispered, barely audible.

Sweetness like honey…how she had longed to hear him say those words! She kissed his knuckles with her eyes closed. The tears began to run down her cheeks, wetting his hands. With the back of his finger, he softly wiped her eyes. She looked at him for another long while before getting the words out. "And I admire you *so* much!"

Daniel's heart beat so hard he could feel it pounding in his chest.

Ester also took two napkins and blew her nose.

Then she perked up and said, "I have a gift for you." Bending down, she dug in her sling bag. She placed a rectangular tin box in front of him. There was an old-styled pilot with round goggles, wearing a leather helmet in the picture and a double-winged airplane in the background. He picked it up and studied it.

"Inside." She pulled her sleeves over her hands again. With only her index finger peeping out, she pointed.

He carefully opened the lid and found a few seashells with a letter rolled into a tiny scroll. He unpacked the shells on the table one by one.

"I collected them when I was thinking about you."

He smiled.

Ester tapped her finger on the letter.

He removed the golden ribbon, flattened in on the table, and began to read softly.

Prince!
I love your eyes. They are sharp like an eagle's.
Few people perceive things the way you do!

He looked up and smiled.

Your face is SO handsome. Your form SO masculine.
Your character is upright.
I ADORE your strong arms. I feel safe in your protection.
I trust the way you lead.
I admire your shoulders. You carry your responsibilities with excellence.

I respect you very much!
I look up to you...
Kisses promised,
Yours Only

At the end were two oval circles, one inside the other, with a *shin* in the middle.

"And this?" he asked.

"It's supposed to be the seal of a royal signet ring," she said, a bit embarrassed.

"Why the letter *shin*?"

"Don't know. Just because we've have always believed that *shin* is for *Shaddai* and for *Shekinah*—God's presence. That's why it's on the *mezuzah* of every Jewish door."

"Why here?"

"Because this letter is official," she smiled shyly.

Daniel took her hand and gently kissed every fingertip.

"Thanks," he said tenderly. It felt like his heart was going to burst.

Then he stretched out his leg and reached deep into his pocket. He held his fist closed over her open palm. "And here's something for you as well." A smooth stone dropped into her hand. It was almost the perfect shape of a heart.

She turned it around and read the carved letters: *Ani ohev otach*

Folding her fingers over it, she kissed her own fist.

"I love you too," she whispered and motioned a kiss.

"I made it 'cause I had you on my mind...all the time!"

THIRTY-SIX

Thursday 8 November 2007

A MONTH AFTER she started working as a receptionist at a business in Ra'ananna, Ester "accidentally" discovered a *Jerusalem Post* write-up on the Internet about abortion. "Actually, I know this was not a coincidence," she told Debra on the phone after work. "It was God who made me see it."

Ruthie Blum did an interview with Sandy Shoshani and packed it with facts about abortion in Israel and her heart for the work of Be'ad Chaim. "I simply love children," said Sandy, who was herself a mother of seven. Ester was so excited that she forwarded the link to Ma'ayan, Debra, and her mother. Then she purchased a *Post* at Steimatzki, and when she came home she thoroughly read the article again.

> The Jewish position is that it's not a human being until the head comes out, but it is a *potential life*.

Ester underlined the words with her orange highlighter. Sandy said,

I've read in the commentaries that the rabbis say we don't have the right to destroy even a potential life.

Ester felt that she was no longer just contending for the life of Ma'ayan's baby. Suddenly she was gaining understanding for a whole sector of the Israeli female population who had experienced another kind of grief besides the trauma of terrorism—the loss of a child.

Daydreaming for a moment, she remembered the words of a mother she had read about. *"The decision to have a child is to have your heart forever walk outside your body."* But what about a girl who regrets that she aborted her baby? Ester asked herself. *Where is her heart?*

She tried to get her thoughts focused to read the article in front of her.

A secondary consideration for an abortion may be...

Ester took her pen and highlighted,

...a problem with the baby. But then I ask: "Who are we to decide whether or not *that* baby with *that* defect has a right to live? What defect has the right to live and what defect does not?" Furthermore, people who have handicapped children say they would never have aborted them.

A third point has to do with *motive.* Hitler began abortions in Germany when he wanted to clean out the psychiatric hospitals. He said, "These people don't have a right to life. We're going to abort all their babies."

Ester was shocked at the callous approach, and her mind reverted to something she'd heard on the day of Ma'ayan's ultrasound. A doctor in Israel typically watches the ultrasound screen as he begins an abortion procedure, locating the moving baby and monitoring his beating heart. As he surgically removes the "contents" of the womb, he can see and hear that same heart stop beating. Ester teared up. *How could anyone be so heartless? Ruthless?*

185

Her thoughts went back to one of the testimonies she had read in one of the organization's newsletters. She quickly found its address in her mailbox, opened the email, and scanned though the facts.

> Hadassah is four months pregnant and is very determined to continue her pregnancy despite financial and social constraints. As she put it: "I had a lot of fun for one night, and now I ended up pregnant, but I'll shoulder the cost." She isn't in touch with her "one-night-stand" and he isn't aware of the pregnancy. When Hadassah's parents divorced in her youth, her mother left the family. Hadassah felt responsible for her two younger sisters. She's now only twenty-five, but has had a number of successful jobs. Currently she is unemployed because it's hard to find a job when pregnant, so she lives with her ill grandmother.

Ester found her story particularly interesting because it shed light on the abortion industry in Israel. Horrible word, but that's what it had become—an industry!

Early in her pregnancy, Hadassah called a doctor to see how she could have an abortion. Over the phone, he asked her a few questions and concluded she was a fit candidate for an abortion. She was told to make an appointment for the abortion committee of which he was a member. The committee would okay her abortion and then she could come directly into his office so he could remove the baby.

Her research on the topic caused Ester to know that legally the abortion committee is supposed to decide whether a woman is eligible for an abortion according to certain criteria. These criteria include age (under seventeen, over forty), endangered health of the mother or baby, rape, incest, or adultery. Though seemingly restrictive, in reality "endangered health" is a catch-all category for any woman who is upset, poor, or unsettled in her marriage—entitling her to a free abortion. Soldiers are given two free abortions during their two year service. Ester struggled to digest this fact. *What a stain on the name of our people!*

She knew that the abortion was supposed to take place in certain government clinics. Yet, in the case of Hadassah, the abortionist himself was on the committee and did the abortion in a private clinic. Publically financed abortions account for nearly twenty thousand abortions yearly, but there are at least another twenty thousand to thirty thousand more illegal and unregulated abortions done in the private sector. Through additional research, Ester learned that doctors and social workers in government hospitals actually make a commission on every abortion they approve. Nearly every woman who applies for an abortion through national health insurance is confirmed. Many choose, because it's more "convenient," to have a private abortion, unaware that it's illegal. Ester folded the newspaper to another page and searched for Sandy's answers to Ruthi's interview.

Ruthi: Do you hold demonstrations, like the right-to-life groups in the US? Do you file complaints against doctors who perform illegal abortions?

Sandy: No, we don't do that sort of thing. We are here to educate and help—to provide options, not put up a fight. I don't judge anybody who's had an abortion; I just want to let them know that we're giving them a choice.

Again Ester's compassion rose up for women who were scarred by an abortion. She had read stories of girls who made the wrong choice and were plagued by nightmares and feelings of remorse. Some even thought they heard their baby cry at night—when there was no baby in the house. Apparently Be'ad Chaim had acquired a plot of land where people who suffered this trauma could plant a tree for the loss of their unborn child. According to Sandy, a young woman flew to Israel specifically to plant a tree. Having had a chemical abortion some time earlier, she still grieved daily for the loss of her baby. She clung to a piece of cloth covered with bloodstains. She would not part with it. Just before planting a tree, she wept as she shared how she did not want to have an abortion but felt she had no choice. As she planted the small cloth in the ground and tenderly covered it with a sapling and fresh dirt, regret mingled with tears of relief as she embraced God's forgiveness and redemption.

Ester's thoughts turned to her friend again. *Praise God, Ma'ayan accepted the counsel of Be'ad Chaim before it was too late. I know she will be a good mother!* Ester smiled as she thought of how it seemed that all of a sudden her friend knew every baby store in Tel Aviv. If she could, she would buy everything for this child. Because of the constant arguing with her parents, Ma'ayan decided to move out of their house. She found a temporary job and a one-bedroom apartment downtown. Her salary covered the rent only just, but at least she had peace. Ester checked on her regularly and told her about God's love for Ma'ayan and the little one in her belly.

She sat back in the office chair and picked up the newspaper again. Sandy handed out flyers at the Central Bus Station every Sunday morning.

That's when there are thousands of soldiers to reach—2.4 percent of them get pregnant during their army service.

One day I'm going to help her hand out flyers, Ester resolved. *And one day too I want to go water those little trees in the Garden of Life.*

THIRTY-SEVEN

Motze Shabbat, **10 November 2007**

L ATE ONE AFTERNOON Daniel, Ester, and David got into the car and headed for Jerusalem. They arrived early enough to find seats in Simchat Adon.

David liked the vibe. He checked out the guy on the drums. A bunch of wild curly hair, moustache, and a beard made him look like a hippie. "Sure knows what he's doing on the set."

"That's Roni," Ester said, pointing to the guy. "He used to do drugs."

"He also met Yeshua at Beresheet," added Daniel, "two years before you did."

"*Viola!*"

David recognized some other faces from the chai tent. They came to greet him and were extremely surprised to learn that he was Ester's brother. After worship, the senior leader of the congregation invited a woman to the microphone to pray for the country. She asked for rain. "Not only in the natural, Abba. We need spiritual rain. Pour out Your Spirit!"

Then another man prayed for the Palestinian people and Israel's neighbors.

In the middle of the meeting, during the break when people socialized, David suddenly heard an exclamation of surprise behind him. The next moment Debra had his arm in a lock, hugging him from behind.

"Hey, Dudi! How are you?" She came round and kissed him on both cheeks. Debra had always been his favorite relative, but now that he knew Yeshua, he understood the source of her warm affection.

Suddenly, another shriek drew his attention.

It was Jan—the red-headed woman who prayed for him at the festival. With all the people making a fuss, he felt really welcome.

The break over, they sat down again. The young speaker looked quite dignified with his black pants and white shirt. David wondered how old he was. Couldn't be more than twenty-five.

He started his message by telling how before his salvation he had been a wild kid. He dropped out of school, but then God intervened.

By grace he was now a different person. Went to study. Got married. But then he started making rules to live by. He read the Bible aloud on his honeymoon. Got up at three o' clock in the morning. Tried to pray three times a day, and so forth. Tried his best to earn God's approval, but couldn't keep it up. He just about burned himself out by trying to keep all the laws he had made, and he ended up having no real relationship with the Father. Finally, he humbled himself, and David was quite amazed at how vulnerable the man became. This guy was not trying to impress the people. It reminded David of how hard he cried when he confessed his sins to Jan at Beresheet.

The speaker went on to read many verses, all beginning with, *"Grace to you, grace to you, grace and shalom to you."* He said that almost all Paul's letters in the New Covenant started and ended with those words.

At the end of a very inspiring message, the senior leader took the microphone. Putting his arm around the young man's shoulders, he spoke like a father. "I am so proud of you!"

His tenderness touched a nerve, and David felt a lump in his throat.

Ido and Roi came to say hi after the service. They ended up riding home with Daniel. Usually they hung out with their friends and came home by bus—but not tonight.

Once home, Miriam made hot chocolate. Hanan preferred fresh mint tea, and Ester joined him in his choice. They visited with Daniel's parents in the lounge, while the twins and David went to the computer.

"Check out this guy, Aviad Cohen. He's quite an online sensation." Roi pulled up the website www.aviadcohen.com.

Ido filled in the details. "Yeah, Jewish guy from New York who found Yeshua. Before that, he was called 'the world's most kosher MC.'"

"Yep—hip-hop artist. Heard of 50 Shekel? It's him. Became famous for the song 'In da Shul.' The religious kids really like him."

Roi pulled up a page where Aviad sang "Hooked on the Truth." His style was fresh and the rhythm funky.

"Amazing words!" David listened with focus.

Ya know times can get really hard
When you decide to walk with the Lord (Yeshua)
Now many people get really angry at me (why)
'Cause I just have a piece a bitty inch of faith

Let me tell you about a story that's called my life
I was a Jew boy and now I came to Christ
Many people thought that I'm a fool
They thought I betrayed them oh how uncool
Whoa they're wrong!
I'm just a man after God's heart
If you know me I'm just playin' the part of that
Wandering Jew maybe someone like you
If you open the Book then maybe baby then you will see
How Jesus is for you like Jesus is for me yeah

191

I came I
I saw I
I opened up that Book
Now look at me I'm hooked on the Truth yeah

Let me tell you about some people that I know
They like to hurt me they like to break me (ignorant)
'Cause I have the Truth
They wanna tell that they're right
They're wrong I know
I've seen the evidence and I know what's True (oh yeah)
What about Zechariah 12:10 what about Psalm 22
What about Isaiah 53 oh rabbi please don't tell me that's not true
I've seen it I felt it I know it what you gonna do
I'm just tryin' to be true Jew yeah

I took my pride and then I threw it out the window
Ya see I said to God I really wanna know you for real
I opened up Matthew and I opened up John
And then I said wait this is so Jewish how could I've been so wrong
Could it be it's true that there's a part two for every Jew
Do you know what I'm talkin' about
Oh my God I can't keep rappin' about this
Ya gotta open up that Book
I said ya gotta open up that Book
And if they're tryin' to tell you don't open up that Book
That means open up that Book yeah.

"He rocks!" said David.

"Wait till you read his bio," said Roi. "He was brought up as a conservative Jew, but became orthodox because he was truly looking for God. At one point he became frustrated with Judaism. He was asking questions that were not getting answered. He was at the rabbi's house one night, and the rab told Aviad that he couldn't leave, because it was Shabbat. That scared him. He was shocked that none of the other guests cared about being held captive in this rabbi's house. He felt kidnapped! So Aviad went to another room and cried out to God. I mean really cried."

"Yeah," said Ido. "After that incident, he realized he was getting no spiritual food at the synagogue. A Jewish lady whom he had met in a chat room witnessed to him, and he began to read the Scriptures online. One day he went into a shop and bought Mel Gibson's *The Passion*. After watching the movie, he sat there with his mouth open. The revelation hit him that Yeshua was the Jewish *Mashiach!*"

"For real?"

"Serious! You heard in the song. He calls himself a 'true Jew.'"

Daniel entered the room and saw the screen the boys were looking at. "Oh, Aviad? Great!" He put his hand on David's shoulder. "We're leaving in five minutes."

"Aaahh," moaned Roi. "Why so soon?"

"I'm flying tomorrow and I've got to be..." Daniel raised his eyebrows as Ido completed his sentence.

"Alert and awake." Obviously he'd heard the line before. "What's the link?"

"It's aviadcohen—one word—dot com."

"Hey, can we chat on Messenger? What's your name?" Roi grabbed a sticky note and scribbled.

David rose to leave. The boys knew that when Daniel got going, you didn't waste time.

"Sabbaba!"

They slapped one another's hands and hugged as they said goodbye.

THIRTY-EIGHT

Motze Shabbat, 24 November 2007

THE BEAMING GROUP of family and friends had agreed to meet at Focaccia after the service. Two girls in the gang were anticipating their birthdays soon, but the big celebration was the eighteenth birthday of Ido and Roi Cohen. For the boys it was more than a festivity. They had recently got their drivers' licenses and would soon be going into the army. Daniel, Ester, and David came for the weekend. The family celebrated the occasion the night before. But as with all rites of passage in Israel, the community wanted to pay respects. This party was for the twins' friends.

Fifteen places had been reserved in the upstairs level of the popular restaurant. Two waitresses showered down menus, and the usual considerations ensued. Even though some dishes were exotic, the guys searched for that which they were most comfortable eating: burgers, pizza, pasta, and the like. The girls knew that the portions would be big and determined to tackle a meal together. All agreed to settle their own bills. Drinks arrived in no time, and Daniel tapped his glass with a knife to quiet the unruly mob. He raised his voice to welcome the guests. "I would like to bless Ido and Roi as well as the two girls, Emily and…"

"Abi," Debra whispered aloud.

"Emily and Abigail—you're turning sixteen, yes?"

"Sweet seventeen tomorrow." Abi smiled with confidence.

"Good. So let's bless them!"

David put his arm over Roi's shoulder, while Daniel rested his hand firmly on Ido's head. The girls hung all over Abi and Emily.

"Abba, thank You for the birthdays in Your family this week." Those praying with open eyes saw the smile on Daniel's uplifted face. "I ask that You will strengthen our brothers and sisters in the coming year. Help them grow in love—for You and for those around them. Plant them in Your Word and make them bold in their testimony. Help them to fear God alone, and never to compromise their faith. Shine Your face on them, Adonai! May their light displace the darkness. May blessings overtake them as they obey You with all their hearts. Thank You for giving them to us. They are so precious! In the name of Yeshua *HaMaschiach,* amen."

A small uproar ensued as the fifteen sprang up from their seats to hug, kiss, and clink their glasses in honor of the celebrated ones. When the food arrived, the hungry crowd wasted no time.

"Hey, Daniel," Avishai said as he took a big bite of his steak burger, "I saw some air strikes in Gaza this week on the news. You involved in any of them?"

Daniel nodded.

"Most of the clashes were around the security fence," noted Debra. "It's like the terrorists look for opportunities to attack the Israelis."

"Why do they hate the Jews so much?" asked Emily, jumping into the conversation with uninformed feet. She was not Jewish.

"Hey, we've have been asking that question for centuries, girl!" said Debra.

"Wait a moment!" Those listening could hear the wheels turning in David's head. "Do you mean why do they hate Israel, or why do they hate us as believers?"

"It applies to both," said Roi, "because the reason's spiritual."

"Explain." David chomped his food.

"When we—Ido and I—were mocked at school for our faith, my mom said we shouldn't take it personally. Some people are rebellious towards God, but because they cannot fight Him, they fight His children. That's us." Roi pointed to his friends around the table.

"Right," said Ido. "It's two opposite spiritual powers at war." He hit his knuckles together.

"Makes me think of the Maccabees' revolt," said Debra.

"What do you mean?" asked Emily, clueless.

Debra took the gap to explain to the newcomer. "When the Greeks invaded the Middle East under Alexander the Great, one of his generals had the assignment to conquer and hold this strip of land. His name was Antiochus Epiphanes."

"Yeah, but the people called him *Epimanies* 'cause the man was crazy." Jake twirled his finger next to his head.

"So the Greeks were saying," Debra continued, "'Why are you Jews so exclusive? Be broadminded and accept Zeus as well! He's just another god in the pantheon.'"

"What?" Ido was indignant. "*Adonai echad!* There's only one God."

"Right," said Debra, "but you know that the Greek mind-set became the humanism of today. 'Be tolerant. Accept all. No absolutes.'"

Everyone was in on the lesson.

"The Jews said exactly what Ido said. 'No! *Adonai Eloheinu, Adonai echad.*' The Lord is our God, the Lord is One.'" Debra translated for Hanna. "So it was two worldviews—basically two kingdoms that clashed." She hit her knuckles together.

"When the Greeks saw they couldn't win the Jews over to their philosophy, they tried to neutralize them," said Avishai.

"Exactly," added Ester. "That's when they burned Torah scrolls and the revolt started."

"Right. It was a priest and his five sons who led the Maccabean Revolt, and they pushed back the Greek invasion," said Debra. "Those brothers were so brave; they were all champions like the mightly men of King David."

"What are you saying?" exclaimed David. "I never made the connection. That's why our national sports champions are called *Maccabees*… because of those guys. Of course!" He turned to Ido, whom he'd discovered was a genius with dates. "Remind me when this happened?"

"Judas the Maccabee rededicated the temple around 165 B.C.—that was before Yeshua was born."

"Wow!" said Daniel. "Maybe that's what Zechariah 9:13 means: *I will rouse your sons, O Zion, against your sons, O Greece, and make you like a warrior's sword.* That verse caught my attention this morning."

Ester was amazed at its relevance. "You even have two kingdoms in one verse. I agree with Roi," she said. "I don't think the physical conflict with the Palestinians is the root problem. There's a spiritual war behind it."

"It's Satan and his demons," said Bibi.

After a thick moment of contemplation, Daniel spoke up. "Actually, I can think of more than one reason why God's people were so persecuted over the centuries."

"For instance?" Avishai was keen to receive his friend's insight.

"Well…like Roi said, people who are in rebellion against God think, 'Wipe out His people and His Book, and then do what you like!'"

"As if you can kill your conscience!" Roi said with his mouth full.

"Look," Daniel said to Emily, "Israel was supposed to be like…how can I say it? Like the representatives of God in this world."

"Exactly!" said Debra. "Isra-*el*. There's God, right in the middle of our name."

"It's not in the middle, it's at the end."

"Okay, Professor!" Debra stuck out her tongue at Avishai.

"So El Al is like—the airline of God," said Emily with a smile.

"You bet!" said Ido, laughing. "It's probably the safest airline in the world."

"Even our flag has the star," quipped Roi.

197

The frowning expressions on some faces caused him to explain.

"There's a prophecy in the *Torah* that a star shall come out of Jacob. That star is the Messiah. In Revelation 22, Yeshua said, *'I am the bright Morning Star.'*"

"People may not understand about the flag and the star," said Jake, "but if our real enemies are spiritual, there's one thing I know for sure—the demons recognize Yeshua!"

"So that's the main reason why people who don't worship the God of Israel would hate Israel," Avishai said, thinking out loud.

"Right!" exclaimed Daniel. "Psalm 2 says the nations rage against God and against His Messiah. This nation brought Yeshua into the world, so what do you expect?"

"So…" Emily had connected the dots. "I think you shouldn't take it personally that they hate you. It's a spiritual battle and it is opposite kingdoms."

"Good student!" Debra beamed.

"Good student!" repeated Bibi. He reached across the table to slap Emily a high five and knocked over her glass. Coke ran over the edge of the table and onto her clothes. She jumped up with a squeal.

"*Oy*, sorry…so sorry!" said Bibi.

Debra called a waitress while the others helped to dry the mess with tissues and napkins. At that point the atmosphere lightened up considerably. Laughing, Emily flicked the last drops from her glass at the stammering boy.

"I'm really sorry." Bibi looked sheepish.

"Don't worry about it. But if you're wondering, Hamashbir is the cheapest shop to buy me a new skirt."

THIRTY-NINE

Shabbat, 1 December 2007

"DAN-DAN," Ester began hesitantly, "would you be okay if I...if we press 'pause' on our relationship for a while?"

"What do you mean?"

"Well, since Yeshua saved me, every year I do a...like a time of dedication to Him during the Feast of Hanukkah."

"You mean you want to fast for a week?"

"No, no! I just want to take time to go deep with Him again. Maybe I'll fast from you a bit."

"Hey, I'm suffering rejection here." Daniel smiled and messed up her hair.

"You don't understand. This is a hard sacrifice." Her voice became soft as she leaned her head on his shoulder, "I love you so much, but—I miss Yeshua. He brought me out of a very a deep place. Before you, it was just Him and me. I feel like I've neglected Him."

"I understand, my precious." He spoke with tenderness. Reaching into his pocket, he pulled out a flat roll of toilet paper, unrolled a bit, and blotted the tears swimming in her eyes.

He played brave. "How do you want to do it?"

"I was thinking that you and I can light the first candle on December 4. Then we can pray together, but we mustn't phone until next week—Tuesday. On the last night we can light all the candles—together."

"Okay," said Daniel. "This will be tough, but we can do it."

"I know. I've been thinking about this for weeks. I will so miss you. But I want to give Yeshua something that hurts me. He must have the first place in my heart."

"It's difficult for me not to be selfish and feel jealous." Daniel was honest as he stroked the side of her face with his forefinger.

"Well, you can do the same," said Ester, trying to lighten the matter. "I mean, you can use the time to read your Bible."

"How do you usually do it?" asked Daniel.

"The first year I prayed for one of my friends on each night of Hanukkah."

"Okay," said Daniel with more conviction. "So we'll come together when? Next Tuesday?"

Ester nodded. "I was afraid you'd be upset." She put her arms around him and hugged him tightly.

FORTY

Wednesday, 5 December 2007

Dani, i had amzng day! How yrs?
Nthng special.

E STER PHONED IMMEDIATELY.
"Hey, why did you have a bad day?

"I didn't say it was bad. It was just nothing special. But why are you calling me, sweetheart? I thought you wanted to take a break."

"To text was going to take too long." She bubbled ahead. "I had a wonderful day! I decided to take last week's sermon—you know, the reasons why we are valuable—and meditate on one verse every day. Today's was 'I have value because God loves me.' Hey, it was so wonderful to think on this. I read Jeremiah 31:2, where it says God loved us with an everlasting love, and I realized that He will never stop loving us. He's not like my dad, who walked out. And I thought, you are like Him too, because you love everything about me. Even when I'm a balagan, you don't become angry. Or at least you don't seem to be." She spoke without taking a breath.

201

Daniel laughed. "I'm glad you're so happy, Esti. I didn't really have time to read my Bible this morning and I'm still at the office. It's been a long day."

"Maybe you can read tonight when you get home. Anyway, I wasn't supposed to call you. But I'll pray for you. I'm going to light my candles now. Bye-bye. *Mmmwha!*" She hung up abruptly.

For a moment Daniel smiled at his cell phone. Then he sighed and whispered, "You sure lit up my day, sweetheart."

Ester kindled the servant candle of the little *hanukkia* on her windowsill and blew out the match. She pulled the candle out of its middle socket and used it to light the first two candles on the right. Putting it back, she whispered, "Yeshua, Your love is my flame. You made light for the whole world. Thank You so much for Your everlasting love. This is what gives me value. Thank You so much for Daniel, that he cherishes me too. Please help him with his work and to have a better day tomorrow. I love You, Abba. I love You, Yeshua. You are the best!"

She searched for her journal in the pile of books next to her bed. "Oh, my," she mumbled. "It's been a long time since I have written You a letter!"

FORTY-ONE

Thursday, 6 December 2007

ESTER'S DAY WAS CHAOTIC. She got up too late and rushed to work without breakfast. At ten o'clock she became ravenously hungry and bought a packet of chips and got some coffee. Then she went back to the kiosk and bought pretzels and a chocolate dip. Later a slab of chocolate. Then she became panicky. Her friendship with Daniel had helped to stabilize her extreme food swings. By grace she had maintained a regular exercising schedule. Today it felt as if she was back to square one. She went to the bathroom with the intention of sticking her finger down her throat. Looking at herself in the mirror she thought, *I hate it when you don't have self-discipline.* When she recognized the pattern of self-hatred, she fled behind the toilet stall door and locked herself in. Burying her face in her hands, she began to beg. "Abba, please help me...pleeeze help me! I don't want to fall into the pit again."

I'm not supposed to phone Daniel, she thought. *Who can I phone? Not Debra. She's in class this morning.*

"Abba...Abba...Abba!" She began to whimper softly as she rocked back and forth. Gradually, peace settled on her. She took a strip of toilet paper, folded it, and blew her nose. Then she clenched her jaw and whispered aloud, "You will not have me, Satan! I *shall* overcome. In Yeshua's name!"

She employed the sword of the Spirit—the Word of God. "I decree victory over this giant in my life," she said. "Yeshua in me is the hope of glory. I am more than a conqueror through Him. I will work out my own salvation with fear and trembling. Not by might, nor by power, but by Your Spirit. Oh, God, please help me get a grip on my eating. I need You, Abba!" she pled as warm tears ran down her cheeks.

After she washed her face, she tiptoed back to her desk, hoping no one would see her. Her eyes were red and her heart raw. Taking out her diary, she paged to the current date and checked the time on her cell phone. She circled 14h00, 16h00, 18h00, and 20h00.

She wrote next to 14h00, "Water."

Next to 16h00, "Apple."

She thought a bit, then wrote next to 18h00, "Exercise," and at 20h00, "Eema's dinner."

That evening she wrote in her journal:

I am valuable because God chose me.

GOD CHOOSES THE FOOLISH AND THE WEAK TO CONFOUND THE WISE AND TO DESTROY THE MIGHTY.

—I Cor. 1:27

After closing the book, she slipped into bed, put her head on her pillow, and prayed. "God, I am *so* weak! Debra said I shouldn't meditate on my failures but upon Your grace. You chose me in spite of my foolishness. Thank You that Your blood washed me clean. Please give me a better day tomorrow. And bless Daniel too. Amen."

FORTY-TWO

Tuesday, 11 December 2007

ON THURSDAY Ester sent Daniel another text:

> Hi! won't phone, jst ask - Wht u do on Shbt?
> Go to congrgtn. I miss u!
> Miss u 2! Bad day 4me yest…
> Sori 2 hear! R u ok now? U need 2 tlk?
> No thx, gud now.
> Will be long w/end w/out u!
> Miss u much xxxxx
> U2 my Love xxxxxx

The longing gnawed like hunger on their insides, and they were both relieved that there were only a few days left to be apart. Her mom invited their neighbors over for *Erev Shabbat*. Ester loved to see the children's excitement. Their eyes shone when it was time for the *hanukkia,* and each child wanted a turn to light a candle. They sang two joyful songs and sat down for dinner. Potato fritters, baked zucchini, and salad with fried haloumi cheese. The kids at Naomi's nursery school had made *sufganiot* earlier in the day. Afterward Naomi stayed and fried another batch of the small dough balls in deep oil. At home, Ester helped fill them for dessert. Some with chocolate and some with custard. After dinner Ester played *dreidel* with the kids. The little ones feasted on M&Ms and ate Hanukkah coins until the chocolate framed their sweet mouths.

During the weekend, Ester got a call from her brother, David, who excitedly told her about the conference in Galilee that he was attending. She and Daniel had prayed for the youth camp that was to take place at the Sea of Galilee during Hanukkah. God didn't disappoint them. Things happened that had never featured before. During worship one night, the kids started gathering in groups, praying and encouraging one another. There was a powerful unity. The room was charged with the presence of Yeshua. When Asher Intrater came to the front to bring the message, it was like fire fell from heaven. Some shy guys who had never opened their mouths before were ignited with holy boldness. Suddenly they couldn't stop praising God and testifying about His goodness. David said it was as if they had been lit up like torches.

Tuesday Ester sent Daniel another text:

So-o-o much 2 share! Can u cum early?
Do my best, 18h00 ok?
Sure! Love u more-n-more!
Cant wait 2 c u.

When Daniel walked in at 18h10, Ester ran up and gave him a big, long hug. She was bright-eyed and glowing. She had told Naomi that she and Daniel wanted be alone for a while and asked not to be disturbed.

Ester's room was immaculate. The extra time had allowed her to clean up and organize things. In the middle of her bed was a tray with the *hanukkia,* a lighter, and her Bible. After they'd lit all eight candles, she put them up on the window sill again. Ester's smile was so wide it seemed as if it were hooked behind her ears, and she talked nonstop. "Oh, Dani, this was such a good time! It feels like I'm in love with Yeshua again. The Bible is alive all over and it's like my heart is burning! You know? Like in Song of Songs." She grabbed her Bible and paged quickly to Song of Songs 8:6. *"Set me like a seal upon your heart, like a seal on your arm... The very flame of Yah."*

"The very flame of Yah," she repeated. "That's what I felt when I lit my candles every night. God was kindling my heart with His love. Remember, I was meditating on the reasons I'm valuable? One of them was 'I am valuable because God created me.' You know how I've struggled to accept my body. The day I thought about this concept, I got a picture. Say someone comes to my room, lights a match, and burns my curtains. I would be so upset, right? Because I made these drapes so my room can be pretty and it's *mine!* In the same way, if someone hurts me, God will be furious because He made me and I'm His."

Daniel looked at her and smiled. Their hearts swelled with the joy of being together again.

Finally it was Daniel who spoke with an emotion-laden voice. "Esti, this week was good for me too. I realized that you have become so important to me that I have been trying to draw all my happiness from you. Suddenly, when you were gone, I felt so empty, almost depressed. I had to dig deep to find my fountain in Yeshua again.

"I want to show you some scriptures I found." He took Ester's Bible and, turning to Psalm 36:8, he read aloud: *You give them to drink*

207

from the river of your pleasures. God is the River of Pleasure! Also, Psalm 16:11, *In your presence is fullness of joy; at your right hand are pleasures forevermore.*" Daniel looked up. "My dad told me that our first duty is to make ourselves glad in God. Every day. We should not pray only to fulfill some obligation, but we must drink from the Pleasure River—from God Himself."

"That is beautiful," said Ester, gazing up at him. She had put a pillow on the floor and slid down to sit at his feet.

"Here's another thing. Did you know that what we've done this week is in the Bible?"

"What do you mean?"

Daniel found 1 Corinthians 7:5 and read, "*Do not deprive each other, except for a limited time, by mutual agreement, and then only so as to have extra time for prayer; but afterwards come together again.*

"Okay," Daniel added quickly, "I know it's for married couples, but still…"

Ester smiled. "I'm so glad it was just for a limited time!"

He bent down and put his arms around her. "You bet!" he said and he kissed her on the crown of her head.

Ester told Daniel what happened with the youth at the conference.

"I know. Roi and Ido also went as leaders. They said it looked like God is making the kids bold to stand up for Yeshua. Even to suffer for His name's sake."

"Wow, that's powerful!"

"Aren't you cold on the floor, sweetheart?"

"Not really. You warm me." She smiled into his eyes. "D'you want some hot chocolate?"

He nodded.

In the kitchen Ester presented two big sufganiot she had specially bought to celebrate their reunification. "Which one?"

He picked the caramel doughnut. Cutting the jam-filled one in half, she said, "You're getting a half of this one as well."

"Come here." He put his arms around her waist and drew her tight. "I want *all* of you."

She kissed his chest at his heart and whispered, "You're even sweeter than before."

Putting his mouth right by her ear, Daniel purred, "Hmmm...and you are irresistible!"

FORTY-THREE

Erev Shabbat, 14 December

THEY JABBERED ALL THE WAY to *Yad HaShmona.* The *moshav* outside of Jerusalem had hosted many conferences, but this one was special. Jake was one of the speakers. Jake Martin, their very own eighteen-year-old buddy.

Daniel and Ester were in the front and Ido, Roi, and David at the back of the car. The boys were packed ceiling to sides. At least their tall arms and legs could fold up.

The brochure for the Be'ad Chaim Conference was quite nice. A little child's hand holding on to an old person's finger. "FROM GENERATION TO GENERATION," it read. Sandy Shoshani, who directed the pro-life organization, invited Jake to tell what God had put on his heart. Never before, in the twenty years of their existence, had so many youth attended an anti-abortion conference in Israel.

After Daniel parked the car, they walked down the side of reception to the entrance.

In the foyer there were book tables with free literature and some for sale. They browsed around a while. "That's a good book!" Ester pointed to the one David picked up. *The Purity Principle* by Randy

Alcorn. "Daniel and I read it in August. Gives really good guidance for a physical relationship with the opposite sex."

"And since we've read it," Daniel added, putting his arm around Ester's shoulder, "our connection deepened. Right, my precious?" He kissed her forehead.

"Ah-hah!" Ester smiled. She turned to David again. "If you want it, you can have my copy."

"Even if I don't have a girlfriend?"

Ester spoke as a sister who cared. "It's better to prepare your mind to set the standard high lo-o-ong before you begin a relationship. We made some mistakes we had to rein in later."

"Is that why you guys don't kiss anymore? I mean… really kiss?" As soon as the question escaped his lips David was a little embarrassed.

They nodded in sync and looked at one another, smiling knowingly.

As they continued to browse, David walked over to Roi, who held a neon orange brochure in his hand.

"What's that?" He looked over Roi's shoulder at the drawings of a baby growing in the womb. Roi didn't answer. He was engrossed in the descriptions of the various methods of abortion.

"Eeechs!" David pointed to a knife and the limbs of a baby.

Roi read, "Dilation and curettage. The doctor cuts the baby into pieces in the mother's womb."

"This one is surgical and the other method is with pills."

"How can they cut the baby out without damaging the mother?" David was shocked.

Roi shook his head and continued reading. "You need to know that abortion is murder, not having tonsils removed."

"*Oy va'avoy*, this thing is *so* wrong!" David took a brochure for himself.

Ester and Daniel dawdled in the hall. Onstage, the instruments were set up and the young guys were doing a sound check.

Near starting time, they went in, found seats, and put their stuff down. Jake walked in with Ido and came to greet them. Daniel put his hand on Jake's shoulder. "How're you feeling?"

"A little nervous," he said, smiling, "but I'll be okay."

"We've been praying for you," said Ester. "You're going to do great!"

"All glory to God," said Jake.

Jake brought a powerful message. He started off with a passage in Ezekiel about God looking for someone to stand in the gap, but finding none. He spoke about the blood of the innocent crying out. And the heavens being like bronze because of the sin of the people.

Then he showed a DVD about the "Silent Siege," which they had recently organized. On 29 September, ten young people went to the Knesset, the Israeli government building, to protest against abortion in Israel. It was a silent revolt, so they all had broad red tape over their mouths with the word *Chaim* written on it. "Life." That's what they stood for. Life for the unborn.

On 30 September and 1 October they went to an abortion clinic in Tel Aviv and stood outside the building for three hours. The DVD showed about sixteen youth with red tape over their mouths. Only two of them were allowed to talk. Jake was one of the guys who explained to the passersby what they were doing.

He ended his talk by saying that just like Daniel in the Bible, they all had the responsibility to take the sins of the nation upon their shoulders and intercede. "We need to come in humility before God and repent. He will fight the battle. Something will break and revival will come."

This was a word from God, not just a young man. When Jake stepped off the platform, the chairman of the board took up the challenge. He opened the Bible to Daniel 9:4–5 and began to pray: "*Lord, the great and awesome God, who keeps his covenant of love with all who love him and obey his commands, we have sinned and done wrong. We have been wicked and have rebelled; we have turned away from your commands and laws.*"

212

After the meeting the guys and girls hung out near the refreshments and chatted. "Hey, Jake, repeat what you said about the voices of the babies." Ester pulled her sleeves over her hands to hold the hot mug of tea.

"I said the smaller a human being, the higher the pitch of his voice."

"You bet!" Ido put up his hand. "When my brother's baby screams, it's like..." He searched for words. "It hurts you badly, man."

"I was thinking," said Ester, "if a baby in the womb has a voice and it gets slaughtered so brutally, it must hurt the ears of God."

"Sweetheart, I don't know about that." Daniel was a little sceptical.

"Wait, Daniel. Let's think about it," said Jake. "The Bible does say that blood cries out. That's written more than once. So whether the unborn have a literal voice, or it's their blood crying out, one thing is sure: God hears them."

The discussion took a less serious direction until the evening dwindled into small circles of friends. Some youth stayed overnight, and some returned home.

When they got into the car, David was curious. "Did you see that model of a baby's development? It was at the back of the room."

"You mean when it's in the womb?" asked Ido.

"Yes. You know what I was thinking?"

The others had all seen it and listened with interest.

"Last week I was looking on the Internet at the preservation of wildlife. There are some species in danger of becoming extinct because natives in the jungles kill them, and they don't realize how few of the species are left. Some Olympic athletes gave a short message to say we should protect wildlife."

"Hey, that rocks. Will you send me the link?" said Roi.

"*Shhheket*, Roi, he wanted to say something." Daniel was tired and had difficulty focusing.

In the back of the car David raised his eyebrows in jest and wagged his finger at Roi. "I was thinking that human life is by far the most valuable species there is, and we should protect that the most."

"Right," Ester agreed.

"When I was on drugs, I felt like an animal. My self-image was so low that I felt like…like sub-human. But now I know I was made in the image of God and He loves me—and He loves each one of those little babies." David was embarrassed at the emotion in his voice.

"It sounds like you need to become a fighter for the rights of the unborn," said Roi. "You have the zeal for it."

"Well, if Jake and his team do a silent siege again, I want to go with them," said Ester.

"Me too," said David.

"I wouldn't mind joining, but I don't think I'm allowed to take part in a public campaign," said Daniel.

"Don't worry, we'll stand in the gap for you." There was laughter in Roi's comment. He got a jostle from the others at the back. The boys began to wrestle so that the car became unstable on the road.

"Quit it!" shouted Ester.

"Hey!" It was Daniel's big-brother voice again. "You guys wanna walk home?"

FORTY-FOUR

Tuesday, 25 December 2007

H EY DANI, can we go to Bethlehem tonight?" It was Ester's call.
"Bethlehem? What for?"

"It's Christmas today!"

"So? I don't like Christmas. Besides, it's a Palestinian town. They won't let us in."

"No," she said. "There was an announcement on the news that everybody with an Israeli passport can go in—only today."

"Look, I work till five, no Jew in my office cares for Christmas, and I can't take the time off."

"Please, Dani! I've always wanted to do it."

"Put it out of your mind."

"Oh, Dan-dan, don't be like that."

"Can't talk now. Bye!"

A few minutes later, Ester's phone rang.

"Hello?"

"Esti, it's me. Sorry for being rude."

"Forgiven!"

"It's like this. If you can give me till six, I'll finish here and we can shoot over to Bethlehem. But you'll need to be ready on time, because it's more than an hour's drive. *If* we don't hit traffic, we may be there by eight."

"Thank you, thank you, thank you! I'll be ready!"

When Daniel arrived, he shook his head at Ester. She was wearing a red scarf and a red hat with two earlike tassels. He said, "Never seen you in that outfit before."

"The beanie is David's. Isn't it cute?" She smiled and flopped into the front seat.

"You're the cute one, sweetheart." He gave her a peck on the cheek and turned the key.

On the way, in a lengthy discussion, Daniel unpacked his reasons for disliking Christmas.

"Before we made *aliyah,* we lived in a town in America that made such a fuss. By Thanksgiving people were putting up lights in their gardens. If it was only nativity scenes, it would have been okay, but it was gross."

"What's a nativity scene?"

"It's a model of baby Yeshua with Mary and Joseph and some cows and donkeys."

"Okay…carry on."

"Where was I?"

"You said something was gross."

"Yes! 'Cause besides the nativity scene, people would also have Santa Claus and Rudolph the red-nosed reindeer and plastic snowmen and gingerbread and tin soldiers and…and…whatnot!"

"All this in their garden? Wow, it sounds like a storybook. You didn't like it?"

"Ehhh…it was fun as a kid. Every year we would walk the neighborhood and check out all the new lights. But as I grew up, I asked my dad why our family was not celebrating Christmas. When he explained to me where the festival came from, I lost my taste for it. And, of course, in America it's a joke. The shops are playing carols and 'Rudolph' and 'Jingle Bells' and there's such a buying craze it made me sick."

"Where does Christmas come from? I thought it's Yeshua's birth."

"Don't know the whole story. You'll have to ask my dad. Some pagan feast adopted into the Christian calendar. And then the tree... and Santa Claus. I *hate* that fat little man with his red hat. It's an idol."

"Why are you getting so angry? Shall I take my hat off?" Ester laughed, but Daniel didn't lighten up.

"They drag the kids into believing this 'character' will make all their dreams come true," he said with disdain. "Their parents have them write letters to Santa and request gifts—the kids really believe he'll give them. They even pray about it. It's so stupid. I mean, what does a child of three or four know? For them it's real. The adults defile the faith of the little ones!"

"But I'm sure their parents tell them Santa's just made-up?"

"No, they don't! The kids keep on believing it until one day they figure out the guy with the bell and the stuck-on beard is fake."

It was quiet for a while before Ester spoke. "Maybe you're right. Parents should be careful about what they put into the hearts of little ones. Like you said before, it's like seeds. It grows there." She sighed, "But please, Dani, I don't want this seriousness to ruin our evening."

Again there was an awkward silence.

"I have another question," she said softly. "Please don't get upset with me."

"Sorry." Daniel took her hand.

Ester kissed his hand. "Do you really think Yeshua was born in December? I mean, would they make people travel for a census from Galilee when it could rain?"

Daniel breathed deeply. "No, He wasn't born in December. That much can be understood from the facts of Scripture. If you calculate the time from Zachariah's priestly service through Elizabeth's pregnancy to John's birth, you have the exact timing."

"Which is?"

"Yeshua was born five months after John, so it must have been during Succoth."

"I'm confused now."

"Don't worry. I'll show it to you on paper. Believe me, it was *not* in December. It was either late September or October."

As they pulled into the parking lot at a checkpoint outside Bethlehem, a bus rolled past them. Everybody on it wore red Christmas hats.

"That looks so silly!" Daniel snapped.

"I like it. They look like elves," said Ester, laughing.

They got out of the car and began to walk toward the heavily armed gates. There were long lines of people—the majority looking like tourists. A smile broke on Daniel's face. The crowd with the red hats were comical.

Two young people behind them spoke English, but it took a few minutes for Daniel and Ester to figure out they were also Jewish, but not part of the group. It was a most unusual occasion—Jews coming to a Christian feast. Yet, knowing the general curiosity and desire to learn new things among Israelis, Daniel thought, *Weird, but it makes sense.* He had seen them bring their children to look at the Christmas lights and gigantic tree at the Christian embassy before.

"So, where are you from?" Ester asked the young lady.

"New York."

"And your names?"

"Oh, I'm Tamar and this is Gadi."

"I'm Ester."

Daniel joined in. "Hi! Daniel." He reached out his hand.

"What brings you to Israel?" Ester asked.

"I'm a journalist. I have a press card with *Ha Aretz* newspaper. Gadi is my boyfriend. He has a holiday from school for three weeks."

"What are you studying?" Ester asked Gadi.

"Medicine."

"Mmm, good for you!"

They presented their passports, and suddenly Daniel was grateful that there was no reference to his profession in the document. Israel is so secretive about the identity of her pilots—the border police might have refused his entry. *That* would have popped Ester's balloon.

As they began to walk through the long narrow passage, Gadi spoke. "My goodness, this is quite a fence, hey?" He pointed to the seven-meter-high security wall that seemed to shield Bethlehem from the outside world.

Daniel shook his head. "Pity we had to put it up."

"*Had* to put it up? What do you mean? Surely there are no suicide bombers here. Isn't Bethlehem a Christian town?" asked Gadi.

"Used to be. Not anymore. If you were here in 2002 with the *intifada* you'd understand. We had bus bombings and incidents on the roads almost every day. The wall was first put up along the roads to protect drivers from snipers. Later—when the IDF discovered that many of the bus bombs came from this neighborhood—they put up a fence on the Jerusalem side."

"Have you seen the graffiti of the snake on the inside of the wall?" asked Tamar.

"No. Where?" Ester jerked her head to look behind her.

"Not on this side. It's at the entrance where tour buses come through. There's a massive airbrush of a viper with his mouth open and fangs exposed. In the belly of the snake there is a painting of a child, a goat, and a piece of land."

"Hmph...speaks volumes, alright!" Ester wagged her head.

"Yep, that's exactly how the Palestinians feel about the Jewish people. Israel is the snake that swallowed them," said Tamar.

"I can imagine that they feel hedged in. This wall restrains their free access to Jerusalem quite a lot." Daniel's face showed that it bothered him too.

"Yes, it's very hard for them to get through the checkpoints every day, even if they have a work permit," said Tamar with compassion. "The families really suffer."

"Oof, I can imagine how much resentment and bitterness that breeds!" Ester sounded depressed.

Daniel raised his shoulders and sighed. "What can we do? The wall is not a separatist issue. It's for the safety of our people."

"So that is how they see us...as a viper." Ester thought about that idea.

"Very sad," said Daniel, "when the *actual* poison is the hatred of radical Islam."

"Exactly!" exclaimed Ester.

Tamar seemed to have had more exposure. "The wall never goes all around the Palestinian villages—with this one for example, Bethlehem is completely open on the side. But even so, you would have to be in their shoes to understand how the Palestinians really feel. Life is very hard for them, and many of them are innocent, ordinary people who just want a place in the sun."

Ester was grieved by the thought of their suffering. "The problem is that it's only a small fringe that is so extreme."

"Shall we take a taxi together?" Daniel suggested, pointing to the line where a lot of white cars with yellow signs on their roofs were parked.

"Where're you guys going?" Tamar asked.

"Where everyone's going," chirped Ester.

"Manger Square? There will be thousands of people," said Tamar. Daniel raised his eyebrows, slowly shaking his head.

"Yes!" said Ester quickly. "We'll ride with you!"

A few minutes later, the driver pulled over, collected his money, and dropped them off. No kidding, Manger Square was packed!

Gadi raised his voice over the noise of a blaring sound system. "Shall we split up and meet in an hour?"

"Okay," shouted Daniel. "Nine fifteen then."

"I'm hungry," were his first words as they turned from their company.

"Me too." Ester hooked her arm through his. They looked around for a place to buy food. Noticing a stand with sweet corn boiling in a huge pot, they walked over.

"One or two?" Daniel asked.

"One."

Daniel leaned over and whispered in Ester's ear. "Let's speak English tonight."

"Three please." Digging in his back pocket for a few shekels, he thanked the Arab man and paid.

The corn was steaming hot. Daniel pulled back the husk to sprinkle salt. He gave one to Ester, then put the extra in a plastic bag and hung it on his wrist. He devoured his first one on the spot. Ester ate hers methodically from one side to the other.

"There's stuff in your teeth," she said when Daniel threw the cob in a trash can nearby.

"Can feel it." He nodded and started his second.

"*Eeechs*, my fingers are sticky." Ester wrinkled her nose.

They bought a big bottle of water and used half of it to clean their hands and rinse their mouths. After drinking the rest, they popped the empty into the garbage and moved on. They milled through the crowd walking toward the source of the music. All the while Ester kept her arm hooked like steel through Daniel's. He picked up that she was nervous. Finding themselves in the middle of a crowd of Palestinian people was not quite what she had in mind when she suggested the trip.

"Don't be afraid," said Daniel with his mouth close to her ear. "Everything will be okay."

They stood still a while, watching the singer in her sexy red dress swinging in front of hundreds of men.

"She sounds Spanish, but I'm not sure she's doing Christmas carols." Daniel frowned. "Maybe they've imported her from Mexico." He pulled Ester away. Shoving and bumping their way through the crowd, they saw someone selling rainbow-colored lights. Rings, balls, and sticks that blinked and blinked until you saw double. The next seller had a myriad of party hats for sale. He wore three on his head and one on his nose like a snout. Ester giggled.

Another vendor shouted to advertise his plastic balloons with Santa faces. Someone must have lost his grip, because a bunch of balloons were on their way to heaven.

"Hot air," said Daniel.

"What?" shouted Ester.

"It's all hot air!"

They migrated to the opposite side from the place where they had entered the plaza. Outside a souvenir shop on the far side, there was a life-sized Santa Claus doll. He had a Palestinian flag in his hand and he moved his head down, arms up, head down, arms up....

"Oh, *eeechs!*" said Ester as she viewed him full on.

This time it was Daniel who laughed. "Isn't that ridiculous?" He pointed to a scene below the grotesque image. A baby doll with a golden halo was lying beneath a snow-white tree. Small red Santas dangled from the branches. Nothing here connected with Ester's craving for Yeshua's presence. They hung around a while but had no desire to browse in the souvenir shops.

"This is so boring," she finally blurted out.

"I know." Daniel drew her into his arms to absorb the disappointment.

"Oh, there you are!" They looked up to see the faces of Gadi and Tamar.

"Anything much?'

"Naaah…"

"Look at that one!" Ester pointed toward the caricature of Santa.

"My, my, my, it requires a photo." Tamar reached for her camera with the supersized lens around her neck.

"Can't we go to the stable where Jesus was born?" Ester wanted to know.

"I'm not sure that's what you want to visit. I've been to the place they *say* it is. It's like a cave with many candles and Christian images." Tamar pointed toward the Church of the Nativity. Lights illuminated the roof.

"Oh no, please!" Ester exclaimed. "Daniel thinks Santa is horrible, but I tell you, those saint icons give me the creeps."

"Do you want to go to the Shepherd's Field?" Tamar asked.

"What's that? Where?"

"I'm not sure, but I think it's an area more in the countryside. We can ask a taxi guy to take us there."

"Why not?" said Daniel. "Anything but this place."

They walked around the periphery of the plaza and back to the entrance to find another taxi driver who knew where to go. This time it was a longer ride. The farther from the square he took them, the more relaxed they became.

The taxi stopped at an arched entrance with the words "Shepherd's Field." They got out and paid the man. As they started walking on the stone path, Gadi piped up, "So, what's the actual story?"

"What do you mean?" Daniel tried to understand his question.

"Well…what happened at Christmas?"

"Oh. That's when Christians around the world celebrate the birth of Yeshua."

"I know, but how did it happen?"

Daniel could hardly believe the open question. It's not often that Jews have the confidence to ask straight questions about Yeshua, so he gladly explained. "In the *Tanach*, the prophet Isaiah wrote that a virgin would conceive a child. So about 160 years after the Maccabees, the angel Gabriel appeared to a girl named Miriam from Nazareth. He told her she was going to bring Messiah into the world."

Ester dug in her sling bag, pulled out a small green paperback, kissed it, and handed it to Daniel.

"That a New Testament?" asked Tamar.

"Yes, the story is written here in Luke 2." Flipping through to find the chapter, Daniel said, "Wait. I need better light." He walked toward a lamppost and the others followed. "Okay. The part about the angel Gabriel is in chapter 1. Hmmm, it's rather long."

"Can I tell the story, and then you can read about the shepherds?" Ester's eyes sparkled with excitement.

"Sure, go ahead."

"So after the angel spoke to Miriam, she became pregnant by the Spirit of God. But her fiancé wanted to send her away because he was so shocked. Where did this baby come from? Would anyone believe them? But the angel told Joseph he must marry her, because this baby was of God. So, when she was very pregnant they came to Bethlehem. Traveled all the way from Nazareth to Bethlehem—you know that's about a week's journey, right? When they came here, the poor girl had shaken so much, the baby was about to drop out," Ester said all in one breath.

Tamar laughed.

"Where did you get that one?" Gadi asked "About the baby ready to drop out?"

Ester continued undaunted. "Can you imagine what a hard trip it was for a girl in her ninth month? I mean, you're a doctor. Joseph searched hard for a place to stay, but the town was very full. Finally, someone gave them the cave with all their animals—you know? The smell and the flies…eechs! All unhygienic. That's where Yeshua was born."

Daniel followed right in her slipstream. "Here's the story of the shepherds. Reading from Luke 2:4,

The Birth of Jesus

"In those days Caesar Augustus issued a decree that a census should be taken of the entire Roman world. (This was the first census that took place while Quirinius was governor of Syria.) And everyone went to his own town to register. So Joseph also went up from the town of Nazareth in Galilee to Judea, to Bethlehem the town of David, because he belonged to the house and line of David. He went there to register with Mary, who was pledged to be married to him and was expecting a child. While they were there, the time came

for the baby to be born, and she gave birth to her firstborn, a son. She wrapped him in cloths and placed him in a manger, because there was no room for them in the inn. And there were shepherds living out in the fields near by, keeping watch over their flocks at night. An angel of the Lord appeared to them, and the glory of the Lord shone around them, and they were terrified. But the angel said to them, Do not be afraid. I bring you good news of great joy that will be for all the people. Today in the town of David a Saviour has been born to you; he is Christ the Lord. This will be a sign to you: You will find a baby wrapped in cloths and lying in a manger. Suddenly a great company of the heavenly host appeared with the angel, praising God and saying, Glory to God in the highest, and on earth peace to men on whom his favour rests. When the angels had left them and gone into heaven, the shepherds said to one another, Let's go to Bethlehem and see this thing that has happened, which the Lord has told us about. So they hurried off and found Mary and Joseph, and the baby, who was lying in the manger. When they had seen him, they spread the word concerning what had been told them about this child, and all who heard it were amazed at what the shepherds said to them. But Mary treasured up all these things and pondered them in her heart. The shepherds returned, glorifying and praising God for all the things they had heard and seen, which were just as they had been told.

"Verse 21. *On the eighth day*…wait! This is about his circumcision."

Gadi nodded. "Interesting." And they say this is the place the shepherds were that night?"

"Well, you know how it goes with sites of antiquity," said Daniel. "Only if they discover archaeological proof can we know for sure it's the exact spot. Must have been somewhere in the vicinity."

The corners of Gadi's mouth bent down like he was not convinced.

"How about you guys look around a bit? I see there's a lit-up cave over there, probably with the nativity scene," said Daniel. "Ester and I are going to the trees over there to look at the stars. About ten minutes, okay?" He pulled Ester into a half-run next to his long strides. When they came to an open spot, Daniel put his arms around her from behind and drew her against his chest. Looking up, he said, "Wow, Abba! That was great! Telling them about Yeshua made the whole evening worthwhile."

"Abba," Ester added, "I ask that You will give Tamar and Gadi the desire to know the whole story about Yeshua. Please go after their hearts and draw them to Yourself, Abba. And thank you so much for Daniel." Ester leaned her head on his arm. "Thank You that we could come tonight."

A fleecy cloud moved overhead and began to sift a few drops. Daniel put his hand over Ester's face. "Yes, Abba, let Your kingdom come into their hearts. In Yeshua's name, amen."

They walked back at a brisk pace and joined with Tamar and Gadi. As they returned to the arched entrance, Ester gave Tamar her New Testament. "Here. Since you're a journalist, you need better facts than I could give."

"You sure? Thanks! Been wanting to read the New Covenant for a long time."

The guys walked behind. Suddenly a thought hit Daniel. "You know, that same quote from Isaiah about a virgin getting a child says this about the Messiah: *His name shall be called Wonderful Counselor.* I think that's what our government needs in this crazy situation—a Counselor who can bring about wonders—miracles."

Gadi nodded in contemplation while Daniel continued. "It also says He is the Prince of Peace. We'll never have peace unless the Prince of Peace brings it about."

"And you think Yeshua is this person?"

"Absolutely!"

They reached the street and Daniel waved over a taxi.

FORTY-FIVE

Erev Shabbat, 11 January 2008

B Y THE TIME they sat down for dinner, the aroma of roasted chicken and potatoes filled the house. Naomi looked at her sister and said, "Why do we have to beg you to come and visit?"

Debra shrugged her shoulders. "I'm studying. What can I do?"

"We miss you, sweetheart." Naomi motioned for Ester to light the candles, then smiled at Hanna. "You are very welcome in our home tonight."

"*Baruch Ata Adonai Eloheinu Melech Ha Olam*. Blessed are You, Lord our God, King of the universe." Ester lit the first candle. "Thank You for giving us the Light of the World—Yeshua *Ha Mashiach*." Striking a new match for the second, she continued "and for making us a light to the nations."

Next Daniel took the *hallah*, lifted it, and said the blessing on the bread. Then he broke it, sprinkled it with salt on his plate, and handed everyone a piece.

David took the wine and poured a glass. He prayed in the same way the others did, but so fast that Hanna hardly recognized the words, *borey pri hagafen.* At least she understood that. It means, "You bring forth fruit of the vine."

David passed the cup around. When it returned to him, he downed what was left.

Naomi got up from her seat, placed her hands on David's shoulders, and blessed him. "Thank You for my strong son, Abba. Thank You that he's going to be like King David—a mighty warrior and a sweet singer. Bless his gift of music and prepare him for the army. Help him to study for his matric exams. Thank You for bringing him out of darkness into Your marvelous light." She kissed him on the top of his head.

Then she stepped around and placed her hands on Ester and Daniel's heads. "Abba, thank You for the lives of Your children. Thank You that You brought Esti and Dani together." Naomi smiled gratefully. "Thank you for Daniel's excellent spirit. Please make him excel in everything he does. Help him to solve knotty problems. Give him great wisdom with all his responsibilities."

Naomi was quiet for a moment. "And thank You for Ester, Abba. Thank You that You are making her so beautiful for Yourself. Thank You for helping her to overcome her struggles, step by step. Please bless their relationship and help her to have a good testimony at work. I pray in Yeshua's name."

Daniel leaned over and kissed Ester on the cheek.

"That's nice!" Hanna exclaimed. "Do you do this every Shabbat?"

"You mean blessing my children?" asked Naomi. "Since they were small, yes. Now…only when they are home on *Erev Shabbat.*"

"I want to bless you too." Ester grabbed Debra's hands. "Both of you!"

"Let's all take hands," Daniel suggested.

"*Abba shebashamayim*…Father in heaven…" began Ester in her childlike voice, "thank You for bringing Debra and Hanna to visit us. Please let us be a blessing to them. Help their faith to survive at the university, and use them among the students. Please bless their studies, and let them come again. In the name of Yeshua the Messiah, amen."

She hugged Debra sideways and got up from her seat to give Hanna a squeeze from behind.

Naomi and David went to the kitchen to get the food.

When they began to dish up, Daniel looked at Debra. "How was Bush's visit in Jerusalem this week?"

"Well, you can imagine…security like never before, streets blocked off around King David Hotel. It was quite something!"

"Apparently about ten thousand police and army were deployed," Hanna commented.

"Wow!" exclaimed Ester with a chicken drumstick in one hand. "And I understand that it cost a huge amount of money."

"What's the point?" David chewed open-mouthed.

"Buddy," said Daniel, "Bush is hoping that by the time he leaves office there will be a Palestinian state—side by side with Israel, living in peace."

"I don't get it. Palestinians don't want just a piece of the land, they want all of Israel. It will never work."

"Interesting that you say that," said Debra. "Apparently Itamar Marcus from Palestinian Media Watch did three video clips to prove that what Bush said was translated differently to the Palestinians in Arabic. The last clip was a promo showing the whole map of Israel as a Palestinian state."

"To be quite honest, I don't understand the roadmap deal," said Hanna.

Daniel explained. "Basically, the evacuation of eight thousand Jews from Gaza was the first step. Next, they will try to remove the Jews from their homes in Judea and Samaria." He wiped his mouth with the back of his hand. "Or from the West Bank—as the media calls it."

"What ticks me off is that the Palestinian leadership have not even fulfilled one of their promises to halt the terror." David was aggravated. "I mean, if the Palestinian state is going to become like Gaza, God help us!"

Daniel looked at Hanna. "You realize that Hamas and Hisb'Allah have the same objective, and they are both a long arm of Iran. So if the West Bank becomes a Palestinian state, all of Tel-Aviv, Haifa, and even Jerusalem will be in range of their rockets."

"This is really upsetting," said Ester. "I cannot imagine their controlling all of Judea and Samaria. The Jewish people who live there are already in danger."

Daniel laid his hand reassuringly on Ester's arm. "Don't leave God out of the picture, honey. Those who touch Israel touch the apple of His eye. Remember? That's in the Bible."

"I know, but we'll have to pray so much!" said Ester.

"Talking about a roadmap…" Debra looked to Naomi. "Do you have a piece of paper? I want to show Hanna something."

Naomi got up and brought Debra a clean sheet with a thick marker.

Debra drew a line from one corner to the opposite, and marked off seven dots on the line. "Okay, this is Highway 60 from Be'ersheva. She wrote the name of the city next to the bottom dot and Nazareth beside the top dot. "This is Hebron." She wrote the following town. "Then what?"

"Bethlehem," Ester said.

"Then Jerusalem," said Hanna.

"Right," said Debra. "Then Beit-El, Shilo, and…"

"*Shechem,*" David concluded.

Debra went on to explain to Hanna. She drew a dotted line horizontally through Jerusalem. "The area down here is Judea. Above Jerusalem is Samaria. All of these towns fall in the so-called 'West Bank.'"

"The western bank of Jordan," David filled in.

Debra continued. "But the Bible says these are the 'mountains of Israel.' In Ezekiel 36 you can read how her enemies will take these pasturelands as their own."

"Which is precisely what happened!" David was adamant.

Hanna put her finger on the paper and said with a frown, "But according to the Bible, all these places were, like, important sites in Israel's history."

"Exactly! That's why we call it the biblical heartland," said Debra. "Bethlehem is where Yeshua was born."

"And King David," added David with pride.

"And Hebron is such a hotspot for both Jews and Arabs because that's where the grave of Abraham is. Both groups claim him as the father of their nation," said Daniel.

"Sarah's tomb is also there," commented Naomi.

"And what about Shilo, where the tabernacle stood for...what? Almost four hundred years? And Beit-El, where Jacob saw the ladder?" asked Hanna.

Debra shrugged and put the pen down.

"You know what the real issue is?" David turned the pen and pointed it toward Jerusalem.

"That!"

"You're right. I heard something that helped me put things in perspective." Daniel made a big circle with his arms to explain. "The issue in the world is the Middle East, right?" He shrank the circle a bit. "The issue in the Middle East is Israel. In Israel, the point of contention is Jerusalem." He showed a small circle with his hands. "And the trigger of Jerusalem is the Temple Mount." He put his index finger on the paper. "And the question on the Temple Mount is 'Whom will you worship?'"

For a moment everyone pondered the gravity of what Daniel said.

"That's the whole point!" David exclaimed. "The Dome of the Rock is just a symbol. It sits up there like a...like a throne. But it's the wrong throne. Worshiping Allah is just one type of false religion. It's only when people accept the rule of Yeshua that the chaos in this world will stop."

"Hey, Davie, you are getting strong in your faith!" Daniel slapped him on the shoulder.

David was impressed with himself. "Eema—any dessert?"

231

After they'd all had ice cream—mountains of it for the boys—the conversation turned back to Judea and Samaria.

"What do you all think about those seven settler girls who were jailed last week?" asked Ester.

"What are you talking about?" David was clueless.

"Apparently they were arrested at an outpost and refused to give their names or cooperate in court. They said they do not acknowledge the present government because they do not follow the Torah."

"Man, those kids are brave! They really stand up for what they believe," said Daniel.

"Yes! They take an Israeli flag and go camp in a ruined building and they say, 'This is our land, given by God!'" Debra smiled, remembering one of the billboards the settlers had put up in the past week. It said, "Read your Bible, Mr. Bush!"

"Or these fifteen-, sixteen-year-olds live in tents on the hills. They are convinced they have to protect this land with their lives. I love those guys," said David.

"And when they get chased away by the police, they go back again and again," said Daniel. "They irritate everyone, but they're an example to us believers."

"That reminds me," said Debra pensively. "I had a dream this week that Israel was preparing for war. It was about us who believe in Yeshua and the Jewish youth who believe in God, as well as Arab Christians, all coming together. In the dream we were singing a new song, which I could actually remember when I woke up. The words were 'He is everything, He is everything, He is everything, oh He is the Holy One.'

"Toward the end of the dream I heard the word *warhorse*. It stuck with me."

"Now that's interesting," said Daniel and whispered to Ester, "Please fetch your Bible quickly. Just before Hanukkah, I saw a passage in Zechariah that sparked my attention, so I read all the way from chapter 9 to the end of the book."

When Ester returned, Daniel opened to Zechariah and began to read at 10:4:

"*My anger burns against the shepherds and I will vent it against the leaders of the flock. For Adonai-Tsva'ot will care for His flock, the people of Y'huda; He will make them like His royal war-horse.*"

"Amazing!" said Debra. "I think God is getting His spiritual army ready. It's definitely not the time of Yeshua on a donkey anymore. He will come back on a white horse, and He will judge the nations with fire in His eyes."

"Right," said Daniel. "The Lion of Judah is going to roar. Everywhere in Zechariah you read about God's jealousy for Jerusalem."

"He is Z for Z and J for J," said Hanna. "Zealous for Zion and jealous for Jerusalem."

"I like that!" Ester gave her a high five.

"Man, this is so fascinating! I think I read about chemical war… here somewhere…" Daniel searched for the relevant verse. He gained David's renewed attention.

"Uhmm…in 14:12 *Adonai will strike the peoples who made war against Yerushalayim with a plague in which their flesh rots away while they are standing on their feet, their eyes rot away in their sockets, and their tongues rot away in their mouths.*"

"That's what's going to happen to those who make war against Jerusalem?"

"This is what it says. A plague will make their flesh and eyeballs rot away. It sure looks like the effects of chemical war to me."

"Mr. Ahmadinejad!" David shook his finger in the air. "Your bomb might just nuke your own people!"

"Exactly," Daniel agreed. "With chemical warfare, the weather plays an important role; and we know who is in charge of that. Job says that God stores up snow, hail, lightning, and thunder for days of battle and war. He has a whole arsenal of weapons. The ash of one volcano can shut down all the aviation of Europe for several weeks."

"Great!" Ester banged the table. "What gives me hope is that God has helped Israel in all of their previous wars. If we pray and trust in Him He will defend and protect us again. Adonai-Tsva'ot is a God of covenant and He will be faithful—let's not be fearful." Collecting the dessert bowls, she asked, "Tea or coffee, anybody?"

While the others began to clean up, David went to his room and returned with a red *kipa*.

"Hey, Debs, look. I'm a settler."

"It looks more like a drop of blood on your head, buddy." She laughed and hugged him.

"How did you know? That's exactly why I chose this color!"

FORTY-SIX

24 January, 2008

Yeshua, it's a little hard for me today...

I failed my driver's test. For NO reason! The policeman said I cannot park properly, but what's that got to do with driving?!

I also did not sleep enough this past week and I'm about to collapse.

My head is a balagan, Abba, I have very little patience. I'm sorry for being so short-fused with Daniel!

My room is also a balagan! Since I started working, I have even less time than when I was in the army.

With my new job I'm working all the time!!! I cannot cope anymore.

I know my boss wants to keep me, but I don't know the program on the computer. I feel so stupid with some of the projects he gives me to do! What if he fires me?! The preacher said on Shabbat that God was upset with the ten spies. They were too small in their own eyes—felt like grasshoppers. They thought they couldn't conquer the giants. That's how I feel. I'm scared of that stupid computer!

God, I know this is a long problem. When I was a model, I felt like the dumbest girl in town. Why are there still places in my heart where

I feel...how can I say it? Please speak to me, Abba! I am so fragile and tired tonight.

There was a stampede in Gaza yesterday. The Palestinians broke through the wall on the border with Egypt. That's how I feel. Like too many things stampeded over me. Abba, will You build me up again? Can You rebuild my broken walls?

REMEMBERING A SCRIPTURE to that effect, she took up her Bible and began to search. Suddenly, the note that Rachel had slipped into her hand on Shabbat flew out of the pages. She read:

You have been on a pedestal, a platform, but you have lost that. Satan has attacked your womanhood. He has tried to destroy your mind. But God is restoring it. Not only will He heal you, but rivers of living water will flow from your innermost being. You have a deep compassion for those who are broken—whose hearts have been ripped apart. God will use you to bring healing.

Ester had only glanced over the note before, but now it encouraged her a lot.

Wow! Rachellie doesn't even know me that well. How did she...? Ester stared at the light blue paper. When she slowly continued to page through her Bible, her eye caught a passage she had highlighted:

I have loved you with an everlasting love; this is why in my grace I draw you to Me. Once again I will rebuild you; you will be rebuilt, virgin of Israel.

She looked up from the page and big tears began to roll out of her eyes. "O, Abba!" She closed her Bible and pressed it to her heart. "You are really speaking to me. In spite of what I've done, You call me a virgin!" She rocked herself forward. "And You *will* rebuild my ruins."

A huge weight of guilt rolled away.

"Wow!" she whispered again, amazed by restoring grace. "Thank You, Yeshua." She blew her nose. "Please help me to remember that as long as I obey You, I am the head and not the tail. You will help me at work. I am above and not beneath the rubble of my collapsed ideals. I love You, Abba."

She wrote Jeremiah 31:3&4 in her journal and stuck the note underneath it. After brushing her teeth she changed for bed. When the bedside lamp was off, she searched for the Bassett dog Daniel had given her. With the soft toy firmly tucked into her arm, she smiled in the dark. "Your Word is awesome, Yeshua. Thanks for a kiss from Your mouth!"

FORTY-SEVEN

Wednesday, 30 January 2008

SINCE THE BE'AD CHAIM CONFERENCE, David and Roi had become big buddies. They chatted on MSN messenger almost every day. Today adventure fever ran high.

hi roi! howz d snow?
dave bro! cool. all white
how much in jslm?
abt 20cm by us.
no school?
nope! no busses
cud u go out?
yes. built snoman acrss street
how big?
small. 1 mtr.
ido and i hd sno-fight w/neighbrs
in park?
no, balcny
fun!

huge!
cold?
not bad
temp?
what?
temperature?
- 2 C
brrr...
heat's on
good!
saw old man w/only sweater. worried abt hm
in snow?
no, last night bfr sno startd
where?
on bus
think abt holocaust survivrs. cold's bad
congrgtion bought blankts t/help
good. what abt street pple?
how u mean?
Is thr sheltr fr drug-adcts/street ppl in jslm?
cn find out. why?
jst wnt 2 kno. feel f/them
wil ask dov
who?
dov and bro. they know street kids
what?
hang out @ cat sqr @ night
tell more
they wnt to build scate prk for str youth
ice scate?
ha-ha. no, scatebrd
cool. u w/them?

yes
cn i join?
sure. will intro u
good. until when sno?
thurs noon
grt! i mst comelook
s'bba! why not come for w/end?
wil let u kno. gottago
cool!
c u
bye bro!

FORTY-EIGHT

Sunday, 3 February 2008

18h00.

D ANIEL ANSWERED his cell phone. "Hey, sweetheart. I've just started the helicopter. Will call you when I'm back, okay?"

"Good. Fly safely! Love you."

She thought back to Tuesday when Daniel had to do an assassination mission. He left before dawn. She had never seen him so wiped out as when he returned that evening. He was like a zombie. His target was a group of terrorists who had launched a Qassam rocket, and they were about to launch another. For three days he couldn't really talk, it was so bad for him, but last night he opened up. A bit. Even then, his neck muscles were strung and his face tense. He told Ester how every minute, every second, was calculated, from the time he heard the air force siren to the moment he got into the Cobra. He had only a few minutes to get dressed, his boots on, get to the line, and sprint to the helicopter. The missiles had been loaded by the time he got his helmet on. The target was close to S'derot. From Palmachim to Gaza—five minutes. Often they would only fire warning shots and destroy the launcher, but this time headquarters said they had to take out all four men.

Daniel said he tried not to think that he was killing someone; rather, that he was keeping other people from being killed. He envisioned an Israeli home being blown up by a rocket. But what about the families of the Palestinian men in his aim? Some of their brothers or cousins might become terrorists of revenge. Who knew? But on Tuesday, Daniel had to stop them because…because that's what he had to do.

Daniel said they had a heat-sensitive targeting system and people presented like black spots on the screen. The trees and buildings were gray and white, but heat-radiating objects showed a black dot. And when that dot no longer moved, you knew you'd hit it. He said his heart was pounding so hard, he could almost hear it beating. His adrenaline went crazy before he fired.

They actually hit only three of the men. One escaped. He felt like he failed. But also, the thought that he had killed three people was horrible. Ester tried to put herself in his shoes. Back at the squadron, Daniel looked at the video again and again. When the black dots went down, it was not a nice feeling, he said.

Ester stared into space. She remembered how awkward she felt when he told her. *Strange that death always leaves one speechless.* She didn't know how to comfort Daniel. But she made up her mind to pray for him much, much more.

After dinner she went to her room and opened the Psalms. This is where the Jews always read when someone died. Yet she found no relief. *How do I square this incident with God's love for all people? Surely the Father cares when one bird drops to the ground—how can He not feel the grief of the Palestinians?*

When Daniel phoned at ten that night, she had showered and was tucked in bed. She was feeling mellow.

"Where did you train tonight?" Ester yawned.

"Mount Hermon. The snow was beautiful!"

"Did you go right to the top?"

"No, that's on the Syrian side, but we landed in other places."

"Did you actually set the helicopter down?"

"Yes. One of the skills we learn is to recognize a spot where the helicopter can land in safety. So that's what I practiced today—in the snow."

"Was it cold?"

"Not too much. We stayed in the helicopter."

"Can you fly anywhere you want, at any time?"

Daniel laughed. "No, my sweetie. Each air force base has a 'zone,' an airspace they guard. Our flights have to be scheduled well in advance."

"But Israel is so small and there are so many military airports. How do you do it?"

"It's not simple! When all the pilots have to train and fulfill their missions, you can imagine it gets pretty busy up there."

"Do they have 'roads' to travel in the air so they don't collide with one another?"

Daniel smiled and explained patiently, "Yes, there are fixed flight paths that secure the flow of the traffic."

"I see."

"That's besides the flight paths of all the birds that migrate through our country."

"Do you have to navigate through that as well?"

"You know that if a stork hits a fighter jet, it's fifty million dollars that comes down."

"Just a bird can bring an F-15 down?"

"Yes, my love." Daniel could hear that she was tired, so he changed the subject and promised to tell Ester more about it another time. "What did you do today?"

"Worked. Afterward, went shopping with Ma'ayan. We looked for jeans. She's bursting out of her clothes."

"How does she feel?"

Ester shared about her friend's difficulties in planning for the coming baby. Eventually, she yawned a third time.

"You tired?" he asked.

"Hmmm. And you?"

"Kind of. The snow made the training exciting, but I'm ready for bed."

"Okay, *ahuvi*." She yawned again.

He smiled. "Sleep well, my precious. Speak to you tomorrow."

FORTY-NINE

Thursday Night, 21 February 2008

IT WAS AROUND midnight when they entered his parents' home. They were surprised to see lights on as they walked through the door. Around the corner in the lounge, Hanan sat under the lamp, reading.

"Hi, Abba. Glad you're still awake." Daniel put his hand on his father's shoulder and kissed him on the forehead.

"I waited up for you, my son."

Hanan looked over the rim of his glasses.

"*Shalom,* Ester. How are you?"

She bent down and kissed Daniel's father on the cheek.

"Bless the Name, Hanan—I'm well."

He put his book aside and invited them to sit down. "Are you coming from Tel Aviv now?" He removed his specs.

"No, Abba, we were visiting with Joy and Adam. Actually only with Adam. Joy went to bed earlier."

"She has twin babies, right?"

"Yes. Have you heard about his experience in the war of Lebanon?"

"Not sure what you are referring to."

"Adam told us about a Hizb'Allah terrorist firing a grenade so close to him that he could see the bright flash of its launch. But nothing happened. It didn't hit him."

Hanan thought back. "I remember. We were praying very much for Adam at that time. It was in July 2006, yes?"

"Correct." Daniel took Ester's hand and cleared his throat. "Abba, I've meant to ask you…"

Hanan could hear that something was weighing on his boy's heart.

"You know last week I had to…uhm…kill some people," he began.

"Mmm…?" His dad's voice encouraged him to speak.

"I know we discussed it so many times, Abba." Daniel sounded heavy. "But now it has actually happened. Can you please explain to me how you see it? I'm struggling."

"Dani, do you know that the commanders of the IDF and the air force also wrestle with that question?"

Daniel nodded. Ester wanted to hear more.

"I remember on September 6, 2003, there was an incident that involved all of Israel's leaders—the top military commander, the air force chief, the head of intelligence, as well as the minister of defense," explained Daniel's dad. "Even the prime minister was phoned for guidance at some point. These men knew that eight Hamas leaders were gathering in Gaza to plan an attack. This was a rare moment, because these terrorists were senior bomb makers, strategists, and rocket developers. They were all on the IDF's wanted list—all with blood on their hands. They had surrounded themselves with civilians. Lived in cellars, moved only at night. They had stopped using cars and telephones. Information from intelligence said they were going to gather in a private home. But this was in a neighborhood where a big strike could mean many casualties."

Daniel sat forward and put his fingers on one another.

Hanan continued. "The leaders were in conflict about what they should do. Should they try to target these leaders or not? Ya'alon felt that to 'kill someone before he kills you,' which comes from the Talmud, conflicted with the biblical commandment 'Thou shalt not kill.'

"Dichter, on the other hand, said, 'It's not an eye for an eye; it's having him for lunch before he has you for dinner.'"

Ester made a face and looked away. "Awful!"

Daniel took her hand again.

"So all day long, there was a debate among the leaders. Should they bomb or should they not? The issue was that there were women and children in that building. Time was running out because the terrorists would meet for only so long."

"So, did they bomb?" Ester's voice was thin, betraying her tension.

"Yes, an F-16 dropped a quarter-ton bomb, but it destroyed only the third floor of the house, and the men were on the first," said Hanan. "They all escaped."

"*Oy va'avoy!*" Ester exhaled loudly.

Daniel sank back into the couch. "Between the time you fire and the time you hit the target, you can hardly breathe. You just hope no innocent people come into your crosshairs. Another gunner told me that when he's done, usually his whole body down to his underwear is soaked with sweat." Daniel shook his head. "It's never a good feeling. Even if the mission was successful."

"I understand," his father said tenderly. "But your commanders don't tell you to kill out of vengeance, Dani. Don't forget that! Whenever there has been an attack, such as a suicide bombing, Israel just targets the next name on their list."

"I know. Targeted killing is the most precise weapon we have," Daniel said with intensity. As he leaned forward again, Ester could see a sheen of moisture on his brown forearms. "Our commanders have notebooks with all the details about the lives of those marked men."

"And those terrorists are extremely dangerous, my son. I don't have to tell you that! When your conscience bothers you, remember that if they are let loose, they will kill many others. The Bible teaches that one of the duties of a government is to punish those who do evil."

"And one of our duties is to obey our leaders," Ester said, thinking aloud. "So you're just following instructions when you shoot. The final decision is not your responsibility."

In a weird way, her words comforted Daniel.

Hanan rubbed his forehead. "Let me ask you a question, my son. Ahmadinejad: do you think he should be stopped, or allowed to continue with his plans to annihilate Israel?"

"Stopped, of course!" Daniel didn't hesitate.

"What is the stated aim of the Arab world?"

"In '65, Nasser, the president of Egypt, said, 'We aim at the destruction of the State of Israel.'" Daniel cited what he had been taught.

"And the president of Iraq said in 1967 that the state of Israel was a mistake that needed to be rectified," added Hanan. "Their goal was clear: to wipe Israel off the map. Many Arab nations embrace this rhetoric, right?"

"Sounds just like the words written on the Shihab-3 missiles of Iran!" Daniel sounded indignant.

"Of course that comes straight from the Scriptures." Hanan pointed to the sideboard. "Pass my Bible, please."

Daniel got up and handed it to his father. Putting his glasses on his nose, Hanan turned to Psalm 83. "Here—verses 4 through 6:

"They say: Come let's wipe them out as a nation; let the name of Isra'el be remembered no more. With one mind they plot their schemes; the covenant they have made is against You."

"Exactly!" Ester's emotions were getting a bit worked up. "God made a covenant with the people of Israel, but these nations are making a covenant *against* God."

Hanan smiled. "Malcolm Hedding from the International Christian Embassy says Ahmadinejad will have to remove God from His throne before he can remove Israel from the map."

Daniel's face showed relief.

"Something else I was thinking about," said Ester. "King David was a man after God's heart and he killed people. He said to Goliath"—she pointed her forefinger in the air and said with a stern voice—"You are challenging the God of the armies of Israel!"

Hanan nodded. "Right. David killed many, many of God's enemies."

"But aren't we supposed to love our enemies?" Daniel sounded confused.

"You're right, and that's why we not only pray for Israel in Simchat Adon, but also for our Arab neighbors. Because we know that if they do not turn to the God of Abraham, Isaac, and Jacob, they will come under His judgment."

Hanan lowered his glasses onto his nose and looked at the passage again. He put his finger on the last verse and spoke to Daniel and Ester. "This psalm is a prayer for God to deal with enemies of Israel, but right at the end you can see His intention. He doesn't just want their destruction."

Then he read verse 19: "*Let them know that you alone, whose name is Adonai, are the most High over all the earth.*

"In other words, *save them, God!* Let them know that the God of Israel is the true and only God."

The room was filled with silence as the words sank in.

Ester's face turned serious. "About two weeks ago, when that suicide bomber blew himself up in Dimona, I felt a bit guilty."

Daniel was puzzled. "Why?"

"When I heard that someone had shot the second bomber in the head before he could detonate, I was so glad." Her face turned deep red, while tears came to her eyes. "Later, I felt so sad for the terrorists who died 'cause I don't think they went to heaven."

Understanding her conflict, Daniel gently pulled her head onto his shoulder. "If they hadn't taken him out, he would have killed more people than the first guy, my love."

Hanan breathed deeply. Looking at his son, he said with kindness, "The next time you feel the way you did tonight, remember what you said just now. If you don't deal with these terrorists, they will kill more people." Then he looked at Ester and said, "Actually, Ester, we can say that God has 'mixed feelings' too."

She kept her head on Daniel's shoulder, listening to Hanan and taking in the information.

"John Piper wrote that God looks at things through two lenses. In His narrow lens, He sees individuals and single incidents. Human tragedy saddens God. He doesn't want anyone to perish. It grieves Him that people rape and hurt one another.

"But in His wide-angled lens He sees the big picture. He sees how everything is going to work out in the end. How it will all fit into His eternal plan. And that makes Him a God who is always in control."

Ester slowly nodded.

Hanan sat forward in his chair, folded his hands, and said in a quiet voice, "Why don't we pray together?"

"Please, Abba," said Daniel. Like so many times before, his father's rock-solid relationship with God became the safe haven where Daniel found healing. As he listened to the peaceful stream of his dad's prayer, Daniel's heart melted. It felt like the pain locked inside was punctured and began to trickle out. The relief was sweet.

When Hanan was done, Ester had fallen asleep. He winked at his son and whispered, "Take her to Li'or's room."

Daniel kissed her forehead tenderly. "Come, my baby—time for bed." Then he gently picked her up and carried her to the spare bedroom.

FIFTY

Friday, 22 February 2008

AFTER BREAKFAST, Daniel and Ester parked in front of the computer to read the letter Adam had promised to forward after their visit on the night before.

"This wasn't written recently, right?"

"No, he wrote the report in 2006, shortly after he came back from Lebanon. But I asked him to send it to me because I want to know how he processed the difficult moments of the war."

Ester snuggled up to Daniel as he began to read.

Hello, dear friends, I want to thank you all for your prayers, for your phone calls and emails, for visiting and helping Joy and the kids while I was away.

Looking at the length of the letter, Daniel decided to read selectively. His eyes began to search.

It was the night of Saturday, July 29th. We had just celebrated my son's third birthday that day and at 12:30 I received a phone call telling me through a computerized calling service that I need to report for duty at 7:00 the next morning. I became sombre and began to prepare myself, both physically and emotionally, for what I had to do. I packed my clothes and got to the meeting point as early as possible. I was actually the first person there, a half hour early. I spent my time reading the Word and praying. And in praying, I decided to "roll" my family, our business, and our band onto the Lord and this is how I treated those matters for the rest of my service. It is in God's hands completely. All of a sudden, I wasn't concerned about finances, about upcoming projects, or any other needs. I was full of joy! After the three days of training, we drove up to the northern border in buses.

During this time, we became very close as fellow soldiers—though many were fresh out of mandatory service and meeting the reservist troop for the first time. Many others were also familiar faces from my past five years of reserve duty, and we became closer than ever before. We arrived at a northern military base at night, and we were told to prepare our gear because we needed to go into Lebanon that same night. This was an experience unlike anything I ever felt. Everyone was rushed and active and we didn't know what to expect. We didn't know what was going to happen to us. A religious man was walking among us, asking if we wanted to buy letters in a torah scroll. This felt very disturbing—like we were being asked to do one more "mitzvah" before we went off to war, and for the first time it felt like we might not survive.

Daniel skipped to another paragraph.

We were told that we would be going into the southern Lebanese town of Ayta A Shayeb, approximately one to two kilometers from the Israeli border. This town is known as a Hizb'Allah stronghold. Our mission was to "clear out" houses in that village (at this point in the war, southern Lebanon was uninhabited by civilians, and Hizb'Allah terrorists would go into homes and shoot anti-tank missiles and mortars from there) and eliminate any terrorists we found. This method of combat required us to move into the village and enter homes at night and remain in those homes during the day, waiting for nightfall to move on again.

We awaited clearance for our entry at the border. The religious soldiers were praying, and I noticed many other soldiers joining in the prayers. I saw such an admiration of God on their faces, it even took me a bit by surprise. After long hours, we finally lined up in our combat formation, as one unit (approximately twenty people in two parallel lines) and entered Lebanon on foot. The units broke down into four-man teams, and within those teams were "iron pairs"—you and the person you are always in contact with. You never separate. My "iron pair" was our staff sergeant, Elad Ram, an engineer from Haifa in his early thirties, married with a ten-month-old daughter. After a night of walking around, up hills, down hills, over rocks, etc., we finally got to the first house we were to enter. It was daybreak, and our entire troop (approximately seventy to eighty people) was lined up outside, rushing to get in, as our unit was still clearing out the rooms. Praise God there were no terrorists in that house.

Day 1: Our presence in the house was quickly made known to the terrorists, probably due to our delay at daybreak in the house's entrance. Soon after we were inside, mortars began falling around us. The mortars got closer and closer. We finally decided to take cover in the basement, aside from those who needed to reside in observation points on the higher floors. We ran in a line down to the basement. Just after I made the turn on the last flight of stairs, a mortar dropped right outside the house and I saw sparks flying behind the legs of the soldier running behind me. By then my hands were shaking as we tried to get situated in an overcrowded, dark, and smelly basement. We began to hear shooting outside and we were sure that Hizb'Allah were attacking the house on foot. You could hear the windows break upstairs as bullets hit the windows. All of a sudden, we saw about thirty of our soldiers get up and point their guns aimlessly around the basement. It looked like we were about to shoot each other out of shock. From where I stood, I could see three small, baseball-sized holes in the wall in front of us and a larger hole in a wall in the adjacent room. We were afraid that the terrorists would try to put a grenade in through one of these holes. I had a sniper rifle and my friend Tal, who was next to me, had a machine gun. We decided we would keep a constant eye on the holes to protect those in the basement. Only later did we learn that due to an unfortunate case of poor communication and mistaken identity, it was another of our troops shooting at us. The shooting stopped, and, praise God, no one was hurt in this incident.

There was also a tank protecting the area we were in. In the middle of the day, we heard the terrible noise of a missile hitting that tank. The four members of the crew escaped the tank unscathed, but the tank itself burned throughout the day.

The day was long and the conditions in the basement worsened. Soldiers were urinating in the corner of the basement (there was no bathroom there) and the air became dustier. One soldier vomited in the corner. It became unbearable. Finally night came, and in the pitch darkness we left for another house deeper inside the village. As our unit left, we ran down the road past the burning tank. Due to the explosives inside it, there was a glowing chemical spill across the road. It smelled terrible, and it stuck to our shoes. We continued to make our way to the next house.

"Wait," said Ester. "With all the running, their bodies must have smelled bad by now." She pointed on the screen to a heading that read "Day 2." "Do you think they could bathe?" The words had scarcely left her lips when she felt convicted about their absurdity, but Daniel, still reading, saw an explanation.

"Look here," he said.

I would like to make it clear that we were unable to remove any clothing to shower or sleep during our time in Lebanon. In most cases we were unable to take off our helmets or our packs and flack jackets. So when I say rest, it basically means leaning up against a wall. We were also low on supplies and food was scarce, though we had little appetite. One of our most veteran soldiers, Yossi, finally decided to check out the kitchen. He lovingly made coffee and found some rice to cook from the limited resources in there. During this time I stood watch by the window of what apparently was the maid's room. This was a very special time for me, as I was able to lift up my family in a wonderful time of prayer. I was close to the kitchen, so I got to eat well! Once again we moved out as nightfall came.

Daniel skipped forward again.

Day 3: Three hours later—at 9 A.M.—we who were dozing off were awakened to these words: "Prepare for an all-out attack on the house." I jumped up and walked back to the window. We were all feeling a bit startled and tired. I looked out the window to see the same apparent four soldiers I saw earlier, running back across the street. This time I decided to mention it to one of our commanders because our forces were not supposed to be moving outside and Hizb'Allah are known to wear IDF uniforms. An older, bearded religious brigade commander of high rank told me that I most likely saw terrorists and I had to prepare to shoot them with my sniper rifle. I instantly felt very guilty for not mentioning what I saw three hours prior, as if I had let those terrorists go unnoticed. I felt very uncomfortable to shoot at these people; for although we had suspicions, we were unsure as to whether these were terrorists or IDF soldiers. There was discussion, due to the distance we were from the house, as to whether I should try to shoot or if we should call in an attack helicopter to take out the building where they were. I was very shook up and was relieved when we were finally notified that those were IDF soldiers. From that point on, I was fragile. To calm things down a bit, the high ranking commander asked me in a friendly manner where I came from in Israel, and I answered while fighting back tears. Any time I was asked a question, I wanted to cry. I went into the kitchen and sat there for a while. The warnings of "all-out attacks" continued, but we were getting used to them and became a bit indifferent. After a nerve-racking day, at about 4 P.M. we heard the first missile. Apparently, Hizb'Allah had discovered our location and they were shooting anti-tank missiles at our houses. The first shot missed us, but more came. After the second blast, we heard on the communications radio that the house next to ours was hit and there were wounded in the house. It was our unit's job to create cover fire so the wounded could be evacuated. We ran out into the street and prepared to descend upon an empty school, which was a central place for Hizb'Allah activity. I remember feeling relieved to be outdoors instead of waiting in the house and not knowing if we were going to be hit or not. We ran across backyards, trying to keep out of sight. We climbed over high fences and walls, jumping off them, falling all over the place and then getting up and running again. Our regiment second in command, a major, admirably let us climb over him to get to some higher places. Another member of our unit, Ran Avni, lay down over a razor-wire fence so we could walk over him. We all stopped when we heard a small explosion. We couldn't figure out what it was, but apparently a piece of some larger explosive device that had been lying around (don't ask me how it got there) blew up between Ran's flak jacket and the ground he was lying on. He was unharmed. Then we ran up a hill that gave us a good position facing the school from above. I remember Tal, our gunner (who carries a heavy machine gun), falling down from exhaustion. Another soldier quickly took the machine gun from him and kept running up the hill. Our unit took position on the hill above the school, shooting with LAW missiles, machine guns, and rifles. It was hard to get a good position and I was trying to find a place where I could use my sniper rifle, as well as dealing with the fear and reluctance of engaging the enemy. Missiles were also being shot from behind us, and one of them hit the hill we were on—just to the left of me. Rocks were blasted into the air and some of them fell on us. As I tried to get into a good position, I almost fell off a high rock wall; someone had to grab my foot and pull me back. I finally found a position and searched the windows of the school with my telescope, looking for terrorists. I did not find any. I was able to create covering fire, which, with the help of others, allowed the wounded to be evacuated from the house they were in. My lieutenant took a position just to my right and his gunshots were very close to my ear—it affected my hearing. At some point, my friend Shai stood up, gunfire all around him, and said something along the lines of "Alright, the training drill's over!" It was evidence that humor is not absent in combat. After a while, we were able to fall back into one of the houses and wait for a helicopter to come and level the school. Our unit piled into one room and we felt extremely relieved—as if the battle was done. The relief allowed us to laugh together a bit and we were processing what had just happened. We were then called on to evacuate the wounded—on foot—to the Israeli border. We trickled out one by one, gave recovery fire to our left, and ran down the street. It was a strange sight, as one wounded soldier was carried on a stretcher and one wounded officer, whose face was lacerated in the explosion, ran in the lead wearing bandages on his head and hand and in his underwear only.

It was during these moments that I ran through an exposed area between two houses and saw a figure standing on a balcony about thirty meters away. There were sparks coming from his weapon as he fired on us. I then saw a larger flash come from under the barrel of his gun, where some guns have grenade launchers attached. I realized that a grenade was being shot at me. I turned to the left to run back and then I turned to the right to run forward, but there was nowhere to take cover. It was weird. I heard no blast and no explosion, so I kept running. I believe that this is God's signature on the whole event, although I can't explain exactly what happened—only what I observed.

"Wow!" said Daniel, shaking his head. "That was a miracle." He began to read lower down.

Our unit was to stay inside Lebanon for further missions. My lieutenant asked me how I was feeling and I resisted his question, for tears were welling up and I didn't want to make a scene. He realized that I was shook up and asked if I could leave the unit to escort the wounded into Israel. I don't know exactly if I was needed or not, because the second we crossed the border, we were met with a division of medics who cared for the two wounded (one of them was now dead) and a handful of others who had slight injuries, including me. Although I had nothing aside from shock and temporary hearing loss, I was taken in an ambulance to the hospital in Nahariya and I remained there for two days. It was like a dream. One minute you're in a battle, the next, you're lying in a hospital bed, trying to process what just happened. My first days back with the troop were spent readjusting, including talking with a military psychiatrist regarding my experience. It was very helpful.

I finally geared up to go on my next mission a few days later, and as I was sitting in the bus on the way to the border, I suddenly got a chill in my body. I had come down with flu. This prevented my going on the mission. I spent a lot of time wondering if my mind was telling my body to get sick so I wouldn't have to go back to Lebanon. Whatever it was, I believe it was God's grace. I returned to our camp and buried myself in my sleeping bag. I felt terrible that I did not go on the mission. I still felt that I wasn't "pulling my own weight" as a member of the troop.

258

Daniel understood. He and Ester read on to learn how Adam came to grips with the tormenting emotions inside him.

I later learned that this behavior of "feeling bad because I wish I could do more" is very destructive. When we feel this way, people usually say things like, "You've done enough and you're being too hard on yourself." The truth is that either you have or you haven't. And you have two options:

1. When we realize that we've done enough, we need to rest and walk in the faith that God is in control.
2. When we realize we haven't done enough, we need to get off our behinds and stop feeling sorry for ourselves. It requires a change of attitude and the intention to take action. In my military experience I chose option 1, and it opened the door for me later on to be able to spend an entire night witnessing to Yaron, another soldier who was slightly wounded. Like me, he did not go on any further missions and was probably processing the same emotions I was. God gave me His perfect peace, and this opened the door to be a light and a witness to someone on a level deeper than I have ever experienced in my reserve military duty. Praise God!

Soon afterward, on the afternoon before the ceasefire was announced, we sat feeling euphoric that the end of the war was near. We began hearing secondhand information of what was happening to those from our troop who were inside Lebanon. We heard reports of injured troops. Some were killed. It was all unclear. We waited anxiously for any official information. The hours went by and I tried to sleep to kill time. Our troops finally did return, and I walked up to my unit as they were putting their gear down. Our unit commander, Guy, was standing there in torn clothes; his left arm and leg were bandaged. They had returned from a battle, but no one knew exactly what had happened—only what they saw through their own eyes. They did not know the condition of their fellow soldiers. Guy took the entire unit aside and gave us this news: "Elad and Eliel are not with us anymore." (Remember, Elad was my "iron pair" and I, by God's mercy, was kept back from that mission.)

"That must have been so hard for Adam!" Ester exclaimed.
"Yeah, but thanks to God he was spared for Joy and his children."

We spent the next two days going to funerals, visiting families, and visiting the wounded. My good friend Ohad's eardrum was torn in one of the blasts. This affected his balance, and he was unable to hear out of that ear. I was able to lay hands on him in the hospital and pray over him in the name of Yeshua. Please trust with me for his complete recovery. It was very important that my focus was not on myself; I needed to be there for the others. After the final funeral two days later in Haifa, we went to the beach to clear our heads. I just sat there alone watching the sunset, internally processing all my emotions. My troop was gathered somewhere else. As I walked up to them, I found them playing volleyball and eating icecream. There was a feeling of camaraderie and relief that I have never felt before. It was very special. The Lord protected me—that's undeniable. I thank Him for this experience, for the privilege of being able to serve my country and protect our borders and my loved ones.

Thank you for your support in prayers.

Love, Staff Sergeant Adam Sovchek

FIFTY-ONE

Friday, 29 February 2008

I T WAS TEN O'CLOCK when David scanned The Coffee Bean and decided to pull up two black armchairs. Yonatan had invited him for breakfast, and David eagerly looked forward to their time together. *Just to have some time alone with this man who has become like a spiritual father to me.* He smiled. Sitting back into the deep leather seat, he picked up the newspaper. The next moment, someone pulled it down.

"*Shalom,* Davie!"

"Hey!" He got up and greeted Yonatan with a strong hug. They patted each other on the back.

"How are you?" His broad grin said that he was glad to see David.

"Good, good. And you?"

"So your bus was on time. Guess there wasn't much traffic when you came into Jerusalem?"

"No, the road was open. I was at the central bus station at 9:25 exactly."

"Great!" Yonatan took off his sweater and hung it over the chair. "Did you get coffee?"

"No. Was waiting for you. Let's order."

They walked to the counter. "We might as well get breakfast," Yoni said over his shoulder.

"*Sabbaba!*" David was starving.

When the food was on their table, the two began talking.

David took a big bite of his omelette sandwich. "No, I wasn't planning to go to the army. My mom has a friend in Scotland. He invited me to study there. We also have family in Australia. Thought I could volunteer at a veterinary hospital."

"When I saw you at Beresheet, I thought you are the kind who travels to India," said Yonatan, laughing.

David smiled. "That thought crossed my mind too: north, south, east, or west. I was heading out of Israel." He shot his forefinger toward the door.

"You speak like you have changed your mind."

"Well, the more I connect with you and your brothers, the more I feel that is what I should do."

"Do what?"

"Army."

"That's great! It'll be good for you. One's character gets shaped in the IDF."

"Yeah, a lot of discipline, right?" David said with another mouthful.

"You'll learn endurance and responsibility…actually, *many* things. One of the toughest things for me was to submit to a lousy commander."

"*Oy!*"

"Yes! Some of the officers treat their troops with respect, but others set a bad example. But the Lord gave me grace to get through it. At least there are good commanders."

"Was there any time when you felt you wanted to go AWOL?"

Yonatan thought back. "No, but I had one stinkin' experience I wish I'd never had. But it also taught me a very important lesson."

"Tell me."

"One *Erev Shabbat* there was a large group together—different companies. It was a formal occasion. The guys were very excited because girls were attending. After dinner, my company was just relaxing together. The girls had left and we were having coffee. I don't know where it came from, but before I knew what was happening, someone had popped a blue movie into the DVD player. It was raw porn. I was absolutely shocked to see what came on the screen! I immediately walked out and asked our commander to stop it. He came in and yelled at the guys to switch it off. He said he would not tolerate that kind of stuff in our unit."

"And the lesson?"

"Look, I grew up pretty sheltered. I'd never been exposed to stuff like pornography." Yonatan rubbed his hand over his eyes as if the memory was best forgotten. "I learned...I think I learned that some people like sewage water."

"Eeechs!" said David, disgusted at the picture.

"Exactly! They allow filth to mess up their minds and eventually their whole life becomes a cesspool."

David stared at his plate and pushed his olives around.

"Sorry, buddy," said Yonatan, noticing his young friend's sudden quiet.

"No, it's not what you said. It's...uhmm..."

"Spit it out."

David took a deep breath and began. "You're not going to like this."

"Nothing you say will change how I feel about you. What's up?"

"Okay." David began reluctantly. "When I was eleven, I found a magazine in my dad's workshop. It was full of..."

"Aahh, you're you talking about those 'poor' girls?" Yonatan smiled and David frowned.

"Don't have enough money to buy clothes."

"Oh!" He laughed. "Right. After looking at those...'poor' girls, I felt all charged up. I didn't even understand what was happening to my body. It was the first time I masturbated."

Yonatan looked him straight in the eye and slowly shook his head. He said with compassion, "Man, I'm sorry this thing happened when you were so young. Our eyes have a connection with our hormones.

That's why Yeshua said if a man looks with lust at a woman, he's already committed adultery in his heart."

"Only now I understand why my dad *really* divorced my mom. He said it was her faith in Yeshua that irritated him. Apparently he was already involved with other women by that time.

But as for myself—that book was not the end." David looked embarrassed. "I found some more of the same through my friends. By the time I was twelve, I discovered porn sites on the Internet. I got totally addicted to this…"

"Sewage," helped Yonatan.

"Mmm." David looked down and continued. "By fourteen I was obsessed with women. A girl would stand in front of me and I would undress her with my eyes. Especially if she wore tight pants, or her breasts were half exposed. Girls became just sex objects. I would go away and masturbate over them. This is disgusting. Why am I telling you?"

"It's okay, Davie. The Bible says we must confess our sins to one another. I'll pray. I believe God can change it completely."

"When I gave my life to Yeshua, there was a lady who prayed for me about sexual sin, and it was amazing. For three months I was free from it." He stared out the window and sighed. "But about a week ago, I stumbled. Was just paging through an innocent magazine, saw a woman in underwear, got stirred up, and I did it again. Have been battling since. I don't want to go back to that habit. It's crap!"

Yonatan's voice was a bit firmer. "You'll have to keep a few principles if you really want to be free, Davie. The first one is DON'T STARE! You couldn't help seeing that girl in the book, but when you stared at her, you burned the picture into your mind. You will not just 'by the way' forget it. Only the fire of God can scorch it out of your memory now."

David nodded with understanding.

The second is AMPUTATE! Yeshua said that if your hand makes you stumble, cut it off. Or if your eye makes you stumble, rip it out. He didn't mean literally—I mean, blind men still lust. But you have to avoid the thing that makes you stumble."

Yonatan smiled as he recalled a story. "I know of a businessman who had to travel a lot. In every hotel room, there was a television providing many channels with this kind of wickedness. After God convicted him to clean up his life, he would go to the counter and ask the hotel staff to remove the TV from his room. They would protest and say that he should not switch it on. But as a client who paid, he insisted. He would not even allow himself the option of sin, a button press away."

"Wow, that's rad!"

"I know, but being radical is the only way you'll get full victory. Avoid it like the plague. Do you still have any of those magazines at home?"

"Yep."

"Go burn 'em. As for the Internet—there's a filter you can install called 'safe eyes.'" Yoni took a pen from his pocket and wrote on the napkin "www.safeeyes.com." "If you want freedom, you need to have your mind purified of this stuff."

"And when a pretty girl walks up to me? Is there a filter for that?"

"Remember the story of Joseph running away? Potiphar's wife was constantly trying to seduce him. Every day she nagged him. Eventually, she grabbed him and said, 'Come to bed with me!' But he slipped out of his coat and ran. That's the third principle: RUN! Second Timothy 2:22 says, *Flee the passions of youth*. Don't even try to handle the temptation. Just run from it!"

David got a puzzled expession on his face. "But what I don't understand is, didn't God make sex? Isn't it supposed to be something special?"

"Of course! Sex is the most beautiful jewel given to a man and a woman who love one another, but—and a big *but*—that's why God put sex (like a valuable diamond) in a 'safe.' It's the crown jewel of marriage, and it's the only place where sex is allowed. Having sex in marriage is awesome!"

David smiled, thinking about Yonatan's five children. He should know!

YOUR SONS O ZION

"Listen, if you take that jewel out of God's 'safe,' you are a thief!
You've just broken in and stolen what God placed in the protection of
a covenant."

David thought on what Yonatan said.

"Sex is extremely powerful. When a man and a woman come together
in union, they can create something eternal."

David frowned again.

"Look. We've all been made in the image of God. People can make
things like cars, computers, cameras, etcetera. But when a child is
conceived, it's a creation that will exist for eternity. It's immortal."

David understood. Suddenly he remembered something else that
bothered him. "What happens to a baby when it dies? Does it go to
heaven or hell?"

"Heaven, for sure!"

"And when a child is aborted?"

"It goes back to God."

"How do you know this?"

"Do you know the story of David and Bathsheba? The baby they
conceived died when he was seven days old. When David mourned over
him he cried out, 'I shall go to him, but he shall not return to me.' David
knew the baby would go to heaven and that one day he would be united
with his child. Yeshua loves those little ones. He said the kingdom of
heaven belongs to children."

"That's good to know." David was relieved.

"By the way, the Scriptures also say that sexually immoral people
will definitely not go to heaven."

The idea jolted David. "No joke," he mumbled to himself.

Yonatan took a sip of his orange juice. "Okay, let's see. Can you
remember the principles?"

David counted on his fingers and said, "Run, amputate…"

"And…?"

"Uhmm, don't stare!"

"Excellent! There's one more. It's FILL THE GAP! If you only stop doing wrong things, it is not enough. The Bible says if you used to steal, you must now work so that you can earn some money and have something to give. In other words, when you uproot something, you must always plant something else in its place."

"Like what?"

"Well, instead of the bad books, read the good Book—the Bible. It is written that a young man can keep his ways pure by the Word of God."

"Yes, the other day I read in Proverbs about a prostitute leading a young man to his ruin like an ox to slaughter."

"Exactly! God is already speaking to you. It's great to hear you are reading Proverbs. That's very practical counsel. Which makes me think, when are the worst times for you? I mean in terms of temptation?"

"When I'm alone or when I'm bored."

"Then you should fill those times with something as well. Do something so you won't get into mischief."

"I know. I've started training late at night. That used to be a bad time for me. Now I go for a long run in the evenings and it serves two purposes: I'm getting fit for the army, and it makes me so tired that I don't have the strength for Internet when I come home."

"Good. I'm proud of you."

David smiled. In spite of the subject, he had a feeling of elation.

"I'm going to hold you accountable, buddy. I want you to phone me as soon as you've burned the books. Put them in a bag so you don't even see them again. And pour gas on them so they'll burn quickly."

"That's an idea," said David. He was overwhelmed to know that Yonatan was so interested in the marginal details of his life. "I'll call you," he promised.

"And when you sin again, I want you to call me and tell me about it."

"That won't be easy."

"I know, but remember what I said. God wants us to walk in the light, and when you open your sin to me, I can pray for you. That way we can walk the road together and I can pick you up when you stumble."

"I think I'd rather not stumble than have to tell you about it."

"I understand, but I still want you to promise that you will phone me."

David sighed. "I'm not ready to make that promise."

"Okay, then. If you commit yourself with all your heart, God will help you overcome this habit. Completely! Many people have crushed their habits in the power of the Spirit. You can go to the website of www.settingcaptivesfree.com and see how many testimonies there are." Yonatan wrote the web address on the napkin as well.

"One more thing." David took the last sip of his orange juice and asked with hesitation, "Is it wrong to chat with girls online?"

"Why are you asking me this question, Davie? Is your heart condemning you?"

"Well…uhmm…I don't know. Some girls are kind of inviting." David was clearly uncomfortable.

"Let me put it to you this way: Internet chatting can be a way to fellowship with other believers, or it can become a huge stumbling block. First, you can easily build an intimate relationship with more than one girl, without them knowing about one another. That's a red light. You can discuss things secretly and you can flirt without anyone knowing. That's another red light. Nowadays there are many married people who have illicit relationships in cyberspace. A woman might feel that even though her husband is never at home, there is someone out there who cares about her and who is just waiting to see her name on the screen. It excites people because it's like forbidden fruit. It satisfies their curiosity. The hiddenness of such relationships is dangerous."

"But what if it's totally innocent? And what if none of us are married?"

"Do the girls you chat with know God? That is the question you need to ask. If they don't, then they will have totally different values than you have. Be careful. *Bad company corrupts good morals.*"

David slowly nodded.

"Why don't you satisfy your desire for intimacy with Yeshua?! This is a unique time of your life, when you can dive deeply into a relationship with Him and really get to know Him. Once you're married, your attention is divided. And once children arrive—ask me! You will never have the same opportunity for undivided devotion. God is the only One who can really fill that gap in your heart."

"I've tasted His love and I know what you mean."

"There's just no Lover like Him."

"Wow, I'm glad you said that."

"Yeshua is going to help you, buddy. And I am right next to you." Yonatan put his elbow in the middle of the table and held his hand up. David did the same and grabbed Yoni's right hand in a tight grip. They pressed against one another and kept the tension until Yoni brought David's arm down in a quick, clever maneuver.

David laughed and shook his head. "Thanks again. I need to get the crap out of my life."

FIFTY-TWO

6 March 2008

Another horrible day in the Holy Land. Oh, Zion! The blood of your sons was poured out.
Eight religious young men are dead.
Two 15-year-olds.
Two of 16 years.
Two of 18.
One of 19 and one of 26.

The terrorist was an Arab driver from East Jerusalem. Came into the seminary of Mercaz Harav where the guys study and he opened fire in the library. He just shot and shot and shot. Blood everywhere. On the floor, the roof, the books. Boys shouting, "Help us! Help us!" Another man ran in and killed the gunman. God, thank You that someone stopped him!

Israel is bleeding. Her heart mourns for her sons...more than thirty wounded—some severely. Have mercy on them, Abba! Do miracles. Please do not let any more boys die. Use this horrible situation to glorify Yourself. Show Your greatness in the middle of this mess. Let Your Spirit calm those who are injured. Soften the hearts of parents who lost their sons. Comfort the brothers and sisters and protect the families from bitterness.

Father in heaven, turn the plans of hell around. Please bring Your people to Yourself, Adonai! Pour out grace and mercy, and don't stop pouring.

Psalm 28:9 SAVE YOUR PEOPLE AND BLESS YOUR INHERITANCE; BE THEIR SHEPHERD AND CARRY THEM FOREVER.

BEFORE HER SALVATION, Ester was angry with God for allowing the deeds of terror to shatter the normalcy of life and the peaceful routine in Israel. This time she realized that it was not right to blame the wickedness of man on God. Haman was an evil man, all on his own. Hitler was demon-driven. Ahmedinejad has a crazy vision to wipe Israel out with a weapon of mass destruction. All of them had the arch-murderer Satan behind them.

So many times Ester begged for someone not to die and then he did. Now she was beginning to understand that she could trust the Almighty God to do what He knows best. She would pray, yes, even beg for the preservation of life, but she was learning to accept His wisdom, whatever the outcome. The Rock of Israel is not without justice.

FIFTY-THREE

Friday, 7 March 2008

DEBRA FORWARDED A statement of the International Christian
Embassy to Ester.

Hi Es,

Wanted you to see the position of the Christians about what
happened yesterday.

Love,

Deb xxx

ICEJ STATEMENT ON JERUSALEM YESHIVA ATTACK

By ICEJ News

07 Mar 2008

The International Christian Embassy Jerusalem utterly condemns
the appalling terrorist attack on a landmark Jerusalem yeshiva on
Thursday evening. "Like the Passover seder bombing of late March
2002, this despicable assault on students at a revered institute of Jewish
learning in the name of the Palestinian cause has taken deliberate aim

at sacred Jewish traditions," said Malcolm Hedding, ICEJ executive director.

"While Israel takes great care in keeping innocent civilians out of the conflict, these Arab terrorist elements take direct aim at them, having no regard for the weak, the unarmed and that which is holy to others," continued Hedding. "We extend our deepest condolences to the families of those who lost loved ones in this horrendous shooting massacre and we pray for a speedy recovery of those wounded. We also want to reassure the people of Israel of our abiding support and concern as they struggle on against such callous terrorism amid a world that rarely understands the evil they face nor appreciates how gallantly they confront it," said Hedding.

FIFTY-FOUR

Sunday, 9 March 2008

"HEY SIS, DO you know that God wrote in His book about you?"
David hung onto the lintel of the door to Ester's room. She looked
up from what she was reading.

"What do you mean? Are you referring to the book of Esther?"

"No. I read this amazing psalm last night. It says that God has written
all the days of our lives in a book."

"Show me." Ester sat up.

He walked to his room and returned with his Bible. Paging to Psalm
139, he sat down on the double bed. Ester was keen to hear what God
was teaching her brother. She had noticed the Word open in his room,
and his conversations of late had been salted with the evidence. David
had developed a ravenous hunger for the Scriptures; and the more he
discovered, the more excited he became.

"See." He pointed to verse 16. Before he could start, Naomi came
around the corner. "David…"

"Wait, Eema!"

When he saw her face he was struck with remorse for how rudely
he used to speak to his mother in the past.

274

"Sorry! I meant, yes, my dear?"

"No, you continue. I can see I interrupted." His mother remained standing in the doorway.

David read, "All the days ordained for me are written in your Book."

There was a light in his eyes when he looked up at his sister. "This is an awesome passage. God has a plan for every one of us. He knows what He has 'ordained' for us."

"What did you think?" Ester smiled. "We're not here just for nothing. In Ephesians it says He has prepared some works in advance for us to do. We are His 'masterpiece.'"

"That is so cool!" said David. "It sounds like He kind of designed us for a specific job."

Ester joked, "Do you think I am designed to be a receptionist?"

"Perfect fit." He replied, teasing her, then he returned to the Bible. "So we're His masterpiece. Look what it says here about unborn babies: *For you created my inmost being; you knit me together in my mother's womb. I praise you because I am fearfully and wonderfully made; your works are wonderful, I know that full well.*"

Because Ester had the passage memorized, her mind trailed off while David read verses 13–15. Naomi simply stood smiling, loving her children's spiritual growth.

Ester was caught off guard when David switched gears. "Have you seen the movie *Horton Hears a Who?*"

"Ehmm...nope." She looked lost.

"Horton is this big elephant with huge ears and he can hear things other animals don't."

"So?" Ester didn't know where he was coming from or where David was going.

"Horton is the only one who can hear the voices of the little bitty inhabitants of 'Who-Ville.' Nobody else can, because these creatures are too small. So Horton begins a campaign for the "Whos" to make noise so that the other animals must take notice of them. He calls everybody to shout as loud as they can."

"It's a weird story, David. What are you trying to say?"

"Wait." He smiled, enjoying her cluelessness. "So Horton calls for a search to see if everybody is doing his part. Finally, just about the smallest Who—little Jo-Jo—contributes his noise and *voila*! The Whos are heard and rescued. Just in time!"

Ester nodded, but David continued.

"I see it as a picture of unborn babies. Somebody has to shout about them. Because 'A person's a person, no matter how small.' That's what they say in the movie."

"Exactly!" said Ester as she slapped her brother a high five. "You know what I think, Dudi? You're a perfect fit to speak up for issues of justice. Don't you think so, Eema?"

David was intrigued. "You're saying what Roi said."

"What did he say?"

"After Jake spoke at the Be'ad Chaim conference, Roi said I must fight for the unborn."

Ester wasn't sure if Roi had been joking or not. "Well, what I mean is this: either you must become a lawyer or a pastor or…I dunno. You just have a gift to make issues of righteousness clear, and people need that."

Naomi agreed.

"You really think so?" David looked questioningly at his mother.

"Yep. God can use you wonderfully in the arena of justice. But first the army, right?" Naomi reached over to touch his head.

David turned pensive. "You know, since I heard Jake, it's like I am so hurt about abortion. My heart pains me. Some nights I lie awake, thinking about it. You saw here." He tapped his finger on the Bible. "Every person is a—like a miracle! I heard that when a baby is six months in the womb, a blade appears that slices the single eyelid into two exact halves, and muscles to open and close start to develop. I mean—how wonderful is that? Where does that blade come from, anyway? I don't know how people can just cut a child out of the womb. It is a crime. An insult to God!"

"Well done, my boy. That's some sweet revelation!" said Naomi. "You've always had a mercy heart, but together with your zeal for what's right, I can see what Ester means."

David felt excited by their encouragement. "Do you really think God wants to use me?"

Thinking of how much Daniel's words of affirmation had meant to her, Ester put her hands on her brother's shoulders. "I absolutely believe that there's a place of service for you in His kingdom." She moved into a good position and started to give him a muscle rub. Purring like a lion whelp, he hung his head in a wordless request for more. Ester took the hint and massaged lower down his back.

Naomi bent down and kissed David on the head.

Being a junkie for touch, his face had a happy grin. "Whatever's in your plan, Abba. All the days of my life are in Your book!"

FIFTY-FIVE

Friday, 21 March 2008

BECAUSE OF ESTER'S BIRTHDAY in the upcoming week, Daniel had planned a special weekend for her. He didn't give her any clues about the surprise except that she had to pack for one night and one day away. When she got into the car, there was a scripture stuck on the dash in front of her seat.

> *Get up, my Love! My Beauty! Come away!*
> *For you see that the winter has passed,*
> *the rain is finished and gone,*
> *the flowers are appearing in the countryside,*
> *the time has come for the birds to sing,*
> *and the cooing of doves to be heard in the land.*

"Where we going?" she asked with contained excitement.

"You'll see," he said and winked.

As soon as they were on their way, Ester asked, "Did you hear what happened to Ami Ortiz?"

"It was in the news last night, but tell..."

"Somebody brought a Purim basket to their door, but it was actually a bomb. The cleaning lady took it inside their apartment. When she went down to take out the garbage, she heard a massive explosion. She looked up and saw smoke coming out of their place. She ran upstairs and found Ami—he was the only one in the house when it happened. His throat was slit and his body was a mess. Thank God another lady came and put a line in his esophagus; otherwise he would have drowned in his own blood."

"Where were his parents?"

"David and Leah had to be in Jerusalem."

"How did they hear about it?"

"One of their other sons phoned. You know they have six children. He said they got a message on army radio that there had been a bombing in Ariel—on their street. So they tried to call Ami, but he didn't answer. When they called the cleaning lady, the police came on the line."

"It's terrible! Where is he now?"

"The ambulance took him to Beilinson. Still in ICU."

"How's he doing?"

"My mom phoned Leah. Last night the doctor didn't know if Ami was going to make it. He has so much damage. But this morning that same doctor said that at some point in the night, Ami's condition changed and he might survive. They are going to try and put him back together."

"How bad are the injuries?"

"His lungs collapsed. Don't know exactly what happened, probably the hot air from the explosion. They operated on him for eight hours. There were chunks of muscle missing from his arms and legs. I think some nerves and veins also. Who knows? His whole body was full of shrapnel and bolts and screws. Burns and open wounds—many places he has no skin. They had to sedate him because he didn't lose consciousness. Oh, yes, and his right eye took metal—or something. He might be blind, because the eye is not responding to light."

"Wow, this is so horrible! A bomb in a Purim basket. Who could have such an evil thought?"

"I know, I'm shocked. Whoever did it probably wanted to kill the whole family. Do you know that David Ortiz led many Palestinians to salvation?"

"They think it was a Muslim fanatic?"

"Don't know yet, but David has had more than one death threat over the years. Could be a Jewish extremist too. They don't like the believers in Ariel."

"How old is Ami?"

"Fifteen. He was the basketball captain of his league."

"*Oy!*"

"I know. Leah told my mom that Ami's abba was crying to God in the night. The Lord showed him that He has a plan."

Daniel shook his head. "We have to believe that. Let's pray for them, okay?"

As soon as they were on the highway, Daniel slipped a CD with peaceful music into the player. Before long, Ester yawned drowsily.

"It's okay, sweetheart," Daniel said. "Get some rest. You've worked long hours this week."

She immediately pulled up her legs, turned sideways, and leaned her head against the seat. Daniel touched her face and she closed her eyes.

When Ester woke up, the sun was setting. "Where are we?" She looked out the window and stretched her legs.

"Still traveling on Highway 65, now close to Tabor."

"Are we going to Galilee?"

"Yes. We're sleeping at Li'or and Ruth's tonight."

"Wow, that is so fun!"

"Another twenty minutes, and we'll be there."

She brought the sun flap down to look in the mirror. Wiping the corners of her eyes, she reached to the back seat for her purse. Finding lip balm, she applied it. Then she looked in the mirror again, stuck her fingers into her hair, and turned to Daniel.

"Do I look okay?"

"Beautiful, my princess."

"You always say that."

"Because you are." He smiled, keeping his eyes on the road.

She leaned over, grabbed his upper arm, and kissed his bicep. "And you are so strong! You are head and shoulders above everybody."

"And that means?" he asked.

She thought for a while. "You're just in another category. Your integrity...I can think of a hundred things to say. But your strength to do the right thing is amazing!"

"I struggle with temptation too, sweetheart."

"I know—we all do, but it's your heart I'm talking about. You always want to please the Lord."

"This is true, but I can be really weak. My willpower melts when I'm with you. Sometimes I want to eat you up."

She nibbled his arm in a playful way.

"And the only thing that helps is when I pray hard." Daniel rubbed his upper arm. "Believe me, I've prayed a lot for this weekend."

When they turned from the highway to Porriyah, she recognized upper Tiberias. "Have you ever seen the lights of Tiveria at night?"

"You mean in town?"

"No, from the other side of the Kinneret. Once, when I was still in school, we had a tour and we slept over at a kibbutz. Dinner was at the fish restaurant, so we watched the sun setting over the lake, and then the lights came on against the mountain. It was so beautiful! Looked like a necklace with sparkling diamonds."

"Tonight, you'll also see something special."

"What?"

"Wait and see." That mysterious smile again.

When they arrived at Li'or and Ruth's, it was just getting dark. Their house was situated on the edge of the Porriyah ridge, overlooking the Sea of Galilee. The couple got out of the car and Daniel stretched himself, groaning loudly.

Ester looked at the kibbutzim at the lower end of the lake. It was still light enough to see the outflow of the Jordan River. The date palm orchards were also visible.

"The view is so beautiful!" she exclaimed.

Daniel was delighted. He put his arms around her from behind, pushed her hair aside, and kissed her on her neck. "See what I meant?"

Suddenly Li'or's voice was behind them. He opened his arms, and they both walked into his embrace. They hugged and kissed with joy.

"How was the road?"

"Great! Esti slept most of the way."

"Good. Let's go inside. Ruth is feeding the baby." They walked up three steps and into the house. The wood floor changed to tile when they stepped into a brightly lit kitchen. In the highchair sat a baby, its face smeared with orange food. Ruth got up, wiped her hands on a cloth, and hugged Ester warmly.

After the exchange of greetings, Ruth put the baby on her hip and showed Ester to her room.

There was a plush white towel and a lavender soap with a ribbon around it on the corner of a large, white double bed. The linen and curtains in shades of lilac and purple were not extravagant, but in good taste. A little vase with pretty flowers stood under the soft light of the lamp on the bedside table.

"This feels like a queen's room!"

Ruth laughed beautifully. "Be my guest, Queen Ester."

Ruth walked ahead, showing her the bathroom, and then she led out the back door. "Daniel will be sleeping in the granny flat." They walked up a few steps, and Ester noticed that the veranda looked the same as the front porch of the house. The rails were green with white iron lacework and the floor a rusty brown color. It shone as if just polished. There was a little lemon tree with fragrant white blossoms in a pot right by the door.

Once the two women were inside the flat, several surprises greeted Ester simultaneously. A round table in the centre of the dining room was set for only two people. It had a tablecloth hanging to the floor and two silver candlesticks with tall white candles in the middle. The aroma of delicious food wafted from the open kitchenette. Ester saw a hot tray with three dishes and an oval platter covered with foil.

"Wow! What's the occasion?" she asked, overwhelmed.

"Daniel told me he was bringing you away for your birthday, so I thought the two of you could celebrate a romantic dinner. All by yourselves," she added with a sparkle in her eyes.

"This is amazing, Ruth. I can hardly believe it! But what about you guys? Aren't you eating with us?"

"We have our food in the house. Don't you worry. This little one needs a bath now, so we'll be busy." Ruth gently stroked the baby's soft hair.

The next moment the men walked in with the luggage.

"Wow, Ruth! This is amazing!"

Ester burst into laughter. "I just said the same!"

After Daniel's shower and Ester's bath, they felt refreshed. Both smelled divine as they sat down for dinner.

"Where did you get this outfit?"

Ester giggled. "I improvised. The white pants and my T-shirt are tomorrow's clothes. But this," she said as she pulled on her cream satin shirt, "is the top of my pajamas."

Daniel smiled. "Looks just right for the evening."

"Yes, it's slightly chilly up here."

He passed the matches for her to light the candles. "In the summer, it's very hot in the Galilee, but now it's hardly spring."

"Baruch Ata Adonai Eloheinu, Melech Ha Olam." Ester struck a match and prayed from memory.

After a relaxed dinner of wonderful food and gazing into one another's eyes, they took their wine glasses and moved to the lounge area. A single light dispensed a gentle glow on the whole room. Ester sat down on the couch and was surprised when Daniel chose the deep chair on the left side of the lamp.

"Aren't you sitting with me?"

"Sweetheart, if I sit with you tonight, we'll get into big trouble!"

She looked a bit sad.

"I am so drawn to you, I'm almost afraid of myself."

"Why?"

"Because that couch looks too much like a bed to me."

"But we can just hold hands and sit close; we don't have do anything else."

"That's the problem, my darling. I cannot stop at just those things. You may feel okay in my embrace, but my mind works differently. You enjoy the journey—my body drives for the destination. It causes a huge frustration if a man cannot reach the goal."

Ester looked at him with tenderness.

"A man wants sex, sweetheart. And when his hormones have prepared his body for that, it's painful—until the deed is done. We become very focused when our physiology takes over, and that's when a girl can get hurt. She just wants nearness, but he can become…how shall I say it? Kind of determined. God made us that way."

"I know." She barely voiced the words.

He reached his hand across the lamp table, and she laid her fingers in his. "It means a lot that you understand."

"I also struggle with our physical-ness. When you pull me into your arms and I feel our bodies pressed together and warm, it makes me feel whole again. So many things that broke me before and used to cause me shame have become a delight and a source of healing. And it confuses me. Because when we are so close that we share breath and that breath says, 'I desire you,' I want to pull you into a lover's dance, and it feels right. But then there's a check. *Wait.* A finger wagging in my face. And I want to bite it, tear it out of my way. I want you to hold my face and whisper into my ear. I love to feel your skin on mine..."

The silence between them was saturated. She could feel his passion in the way he caressed her hand.

"Sometimes I still feel guilty about what happened with Nir," she said. "After all that you taught me, I wonder if it wasn't me who made him do what he did."

Daniel spoke comfortingly. "Sweetheart, it wasn't you who made Nir do what he did. He *chose* to do it. If you feel regret for how you used to dress or behave, then ask Yeshua to forgive you for that, and He will."

Then Daniel took a deep breath. "It's good you mention his name. Since you've told me what happened, I've had a battle. In the beginning I was very angry with Nir. But as our relationship progressed, I became more humble. Just sometimes, when I think of what he stole from you, I still want to strangle him."

"You cannot say that, Dandan. That's like murder."

"I know. I can't help myself. I feel angry enough to...to..." He drew his breath through his teeth. "My heart starts beating and my palms get sweaty. If he was close, I would do something to him!"

She stared at him, taken aback.

"That's why I'm glad you brought it up, so you can pray with me."

Ester immediately closed her eyes.

"Abba, please help Dani to forgive..." Unexpectedly her words dried up.

"Lord," Daniel's voice cracked, but he was determined. "Abba, forgive me for harboring bitterness toward Nir. I'm human just like him. I know how hard it is to control myself when I am with this beautiful girl. Please forgive the pride I had before, thinking I would never do things that other guys do. Now I know how weak I can be, Abba." He squeezed her hand. "Please help me handle this princess with care, and show me how to really love her. Never just to satisfy myself." It sounded like Daniel was going to cry.

She bent over and kissed his hand with the softest lips.

Then Ester prayed again. "And, Abba, if it was I who made it hard for Nir to resist, I am *so* sorry." She rested her head on the table.

Again Daniel was tender. "God forgave you, Esti. Now you have to believe that it is all washed away. As if it never happened. She sniffed. "I've done so many things wrong in my life, Yeshua, but You covered me with a virgin's dress, just as Jerusalem was white with snow. I believe You made me pure."

Back in the immaculate room, Ester found herself enveloped in the spotless linen of the big, white double bed. She lay on her stomach to write in her journal.

Abba, You made sex. It was Your sweet idea that a man and woman should become one in covenant. Our hearts lo-o-ong for this! But at the moment, temptation wants to shut our ears because our flesh is so hungry for each other. Teach us, Lord! Help us to know where to draw boundaries that will honor You. Sting my conscience, Holy Spirit. I do not want to be a stumbling block for Daniel. He is...I want this man to be my husband. Help us to keep our present unopened until that day. Wish Daniel would ask me to marry him...

FIFTY-SIX

Shabbat, 22 March 2008

ESTER WOKE UP very disturbed. She jumped out of bed, dressed herself in yesterday's clothes, and slipped out the back door and into the granny flat.

"Dani," she called. "Daniel!" She walked down the passage and heard a muffled moan. When she appeared in the doorway of the bedroom, he unwillingly opened one eyelid. She sat down on the floor next to his bed. His warm arm came out from under the blanket and took her hand. "Mmmm…?"

"Dan, I had a horrible dream." Her voice was thin.

He blinked hard.

"Okay, sweetheart. Go back into the house. I'll get ready and come over there."

Still shaking from the experience, Ester got up immediately and went back to her room in the house. She took her Bible and sank to her knees. Just then, Ruth's head popped around the door.

"Good morning! You rested well?" she asked with a friendly smile.

"Ehmm…yes. No. Actually, I don't know! Had a nightmare."

Ruth's face changed to concern. She walked in and sat on the bed next to Ester. "You want to tell me?"

"I dreamed it was the end of the world."

Daniel walked in and also sat down on the bed. "What's wrong, sweetheart?"

"I don't know." She began to cry when he touched her arm.

"Something shook her up," said Ruth.

"I dreamed Yeshua was coming back. I heard very loud trumpets and the whole earth shook. People panicked. They ran everywhere and shouted. The mountains were smoking and shaking like this." Ester held out her hands and shook her fists violently. "People were running and shouting, things were falling from the sky, and there was fire—like balls of fire falling on the people. People were burning and screaming. Big buildings were burning. It was much worse than 9/11. I saw my friends, Nora and Riki and Gad. And Ma'ayan. They were screaming and running. We were all afraid. I saw my abba. He was also running and calling for me to come to him, but I couldn't go there." Tears filled her eyes. "I knew I couldn't go to him because he was going to hell."

Ruth said in a serious voice, "This is a very important dream, Ester. Would you mind if I call Li'or so we can pray with you?"

Ester shook her head and wiped the tears away with her hand. Daniel sat on the floor next to her and put his arms around her. She sobbed on his shoulder. Li'or came into the room, holding the baby. He also sat down on the bed. Ruth knelt.

"I know how you feel, Esti," said Li'or. "I was born again when I was ten years old because of a dream like this. I'll never forget it!"

Ester looked up with tears in her eyes. "I am so worried about my friends and my abba! All the people who are going to hell."

Daniel grabbed the box of tissue from the bedside table and put it next to her. "Let's pray. Then you can pour out your heart." Ester immediately knelt down with her face on the floor.

"Yeshua! Yeshua!" Her voice broke and she continued to pray through the groans. "Abba, remember the blood of Yeshua. Your Son died for everyone. Have mercy, Abba! Please give salvation to my friends and my abba! Please help them to see their sin and repent before it is too late. Abba, I'm sorry that I just wanted to go to heaven and didn't care enough to tell them." There was pain in her throat when she prayed again. "I'm so sorry for not speaking to them, Abba!" She sobbed aloud. "Please help me to tell them about Yeshua."

Still in a kneeling position next to her, Daniel put his hand on her head. She immediately crawled forward until her face was on his knees. Her tears made big wet spots on his jeans. While stroking her hair, he prayed, "Abba, thank You for giving Esti this dream. We know it is because You love her family and friends. Thank You for saving David, Abba—for the way You intervened in his life. We know You can do the same for her friends and her dad. We agree with everything Esti asked. We pray that You will make her faithful to intercede for them."

Ruth began to pray. "Father in heaven, it is written that You do not want anyone to perish. Thank You for those words. We do not need to wonder if it is Your will. It is Your will that every person be saved. We pray that You will convict them of sin and bring Ester's friends and family to see the choice they have to make. Use her in this process, Father. We ask in Yeshua's name."

"*Abba shebashamaim*, Father in heaven," Li'or began, "Thank You for showing me the truth of an eternity without You, when I was only ten. Thank You for this powerful dream. I pray that Ester will never forget it, and that You will use her to give the good news of salvation through Yeshua to many, many people. We ask your peace upon her now and Your blessing for the rest of this day. In the name of Yeshua the Messiah."

Ester lifted her head and took another tissue. "Thank you so much," she said, her voice still thick with tears.

"You're welcome." The kind smile was back on Ruth's face when she left the room. "Breakfast is ready when you guys are."

"There's your surprise." Li'or pointed to a big basket covered with a kitchen towel.

"Shhh!" Daniel looked over his shoulder. "She doesn't know."

"Thank you for the *Purim* chocolates." Ruth picked up the small oval basket wrapped with cellophane and a red ribbon.

"You're welcome." Daniel smiled.

When Ester came in, they sat down at the square table and enjoyed a breakfast of scrambled eggs, toast, hummus, and Israeli salad.

"Tell us how David came to Yeshua," Ruth said.

Ester's face lit up. "My brother was using drugs and his body was wasted. He had to go to the doctor in August last year because of kidney stones. The doctor said his liver was like an old man's. He was extremely thin and pale, with dark rings under his eyes. But Daniel and I were praying for him, and I know my mom was too. Every day for three months, we just prayed and prayed." She put her hand on Daniel's arm and smiled. "And then something terrible happened. No, first something wonderful! David was traveling in a car with his best friend—they were both high on drugs. Suddenly David heard an audible voice saying to him, 'Put on your seatbelt.'"

Daniel interjected, "David said the voice had so much weight that he couldn't do anything else."

"Right," Ester said, continuing. "So he put on his seatbelt, and the next moment they had a horrible accident. Gur went into a wall and David basically saw his friend die before his eyes."

"Oh no!" said Li'or.

"Yes, it was very bad! That affected David very much. He was...how can I say? He was like a zombie for a few weeks."

"Yes, but we knew God was working on him, so we kept praying. About a month after that, he was at Beresheet and ended up at the chai tent of believers in Yeshua. Someone shared a testimony—I think a guy named Stevenson?" Ester looked at Daniel.

"Right," said Daniel. "He told how he had drowned and came back to life. God raised him from the dead."

"Exactly! As David listened to Stevenson's story he realized what he needed. So he opened his heart to the Lord."

Daniel took a bite of toast. "He was baptized on the same day."

"Wow, how wonderful!" Ruth put her palms together in front of her mouth.

"It was awesome!" Ester was her bubbly self again. "We were so glad!"

"You know," said Ruth, "when we were praying in your room this morning, I realized that this dream was making Purim extra special. It was a blessing to hear you interceding for your own people. I know that the King's scepter was extended to you and that you found favor in His eyes."

"Wow, thank you," said Ester, and her face beamed. "You have no idea how much it meant that you prayed with me."

Daniel put his hand on Ester's arm and said softly, "I want us to leave soon, sweetheart."

She took a last bite and excused herself from the table. In the room, she grabbed her things and bundled them into her backpack. After hanging a wet towel over the rail in the bathroom, she quickly brushed her teeth and sprayed on her perfume. In the meantime, Daniel put the big basket into the trunk of the car. Then he came to fetch the rest of their baggage.

It was 9h35 when they hugged Li'or and Ruth goodbye with heartfelt gratitude. As they went on the winding road down the hill, Ester asked the same question a second time in twenty-four hours.

Daniel smiled. "Today I don't know where we're going—it's an adventure. Did you read that?" He pointed to the scripture on the dash.

She read it aloud.

"Let me guess…we're going to see the spring flowers?"

"That's the plan."

With childlike excitement, Ester closed her eyes. "Great! Abba, please show us Your best in the name of Yeshua."

With open eyes Daniel filled in, "Yes, Abba, and please protect us on the road. Amen."

They traveled over the outlet of the Jordan River at the bottom of the lake, past the junction of Highway 90 to Jerusalem, and past kibbutz Ma'agan. Then they went up the narrow road to the Golan Heights. The border was so close they could see the orchards of neighboring Jordan. When they come to the top, Daniel took Ester to Peace Vista. She marveled! There are not many places where one can see the entire circumference of the Sea of Galilee.

"On a clear day you can even see Mount Hermon," Daniel said as he pointed north.

Ester shook her head and heard herself saying, "I cannot imagine our government is willing to negotiate the Golan. If the Syrian forces had to be stationed up here, look how much they can reach."

"Right," said Daniel. "Tiberias, Porriyah, all the *kibbutzim* around the lake."

"Is that Arbel?" Ester pointed toward a mountain with a sharp cliff face on the right side of Tiberias.

"Yes. And just next to it is Migdal."

"Have you ever been to the ruins of ancient Magdala, where Mary Magdalene lived?"

Daniel shook his head.

"Neither have I, but they say in the time of Yeshua, it was a fishing village with at least three thousand people. Wow! I can even see Capernaum on the opposite side of the lake. Look!"

"Yes, and there's Nof Ginnosar, where the ancient boat is. Have you seen that one?"

"Yes, when we went on the trip I told you about, we visited the educational center at the museum. They dug that two-thousand-year-old boat out of the mud, right? Do you think Yeshua really sailed on it, like some people say?"

"I think they say it just to get tourists over. Like with many other things in Israel. Have you seen the movie with the music where you fly over the whole Galilee?"

"Yes, yes! I loved it!"

"Well, that's what we're going to do today—fly over the whole Galilee. I wish I could take you in the helicopter." He grabbed her hand and pulled her into a run back to the car.

They traveled farther north, all the while enjoying the beautiful countryside. When they came to the Hula valley, Daniel turned in at the bird sanctuary. They walked on the ramparts and looked at the waterfowl and buffalos. They got some of those funny dark glasses to watch the 3-D show in the virtual theater.

When they came to the Banias they got out of the car and walked to the waterfall—it was strong and loud because of the winter rains.

At the nature reserve of Dan, they parked the car and took the circular route along the river. "The Garden of Eden," as the forest is called, had big shady trees with sunspots gracing the mosses and ferns all along the river. Ester bent down to drink from the crystal clear springs that fed the Jordan River, right at the source where it flows out from underneath the rocks. At the wading pool they took off their shoes and sat with their feet in the cold water.

Once they returned to the car, Daniel opened the trunk and took out the picnic basket.

"Oh, my!" Ester laughed. "How many more blessings?!"

He was glad to see her delight.

"I'm just going to wash my hands."

While Ester walked to the washrooms, he chose one of the wooden tables under the big trees. Lifting the dishcloth, he found a red disposable tablecloth sealed in plastic wrap. He opened it, covered the table, and began to unpack: two plastic cups, two plates, and two sets of plastic cutlery in sealed bags. There was a small container with hummus, one with Turkish salad, and one with purple cabbage. Also eggplant in mayonnaise—a favorite of Daniel's. A box with rye wafers and a few slices of seed loaf in a plastic bag came out. Next was a plastic container with chicken salad.

"Yum! One of Ruth's special recipes." He lifted the lid, pinched a nut, put it in his mouth, and reached for another. When he discovered a packet of wet wipes, he opened the seal and cleaned his hands. He took out a plastic bag with cucumber and carrot sticks and another one with cocktail tomatoes. All according to his order—Ester's kind of food. Then came a box of fruit juice. He shook his head in amazement when he took the container of "Haman's ears" cookies from the bottom of the basket. "What a spread!"

Ester was also pleasantly surprised. "Did you pack all of this beforehand?"

"No, this is your birthday gift from Ruth and Li'or." Daniel unfolded a napkin and gave it to Ester. "Sit on this."

They ate with the loud, babbling song of the Jordan in their ears. There were several other picnickers around, and as Israelis do, they filled the space. The two of them enjoyed watching the children at play. A little child dropped his sucker on the ground and put up a wail. His abba wiped it on his pants and put it back into the sticky little hand. Daniel and Ester shared their Purim cookies with the family. After the delightful time they packed up and put the basket back in the car.

Ester asked Daniel to phone Ruth so they could thank her. Once he had started the engine, Daniel dialed her number and gave his phone to Ester. "Ruthi, thanks for the amazing picnic surprise! You took all this trouble for us, and it was a feast!"

"Li'or and I had so much fun doing it, my dear. We love you, and it was a joy to spoil the two of you. Happy birthday!"

Ruth asked where they had been and what they had done, and Ester shared with enthusiasm.

Driving farther north, they enjoyed a variety of flowers on the side of the road. There were fields sprinkled with red poppies. White and yellow daisies. Purple anemones and miniature cyclamens. Small pink "brushes" and delicate lace flowers. Blue agapanthus and tall cerise hollyhocks. The glory would last only a few weeks more and then the first heat of summer would scorch it all brown in a single day. At least the verdant bed of the Jordan River would snake greenly down the Rift Valley toward the Dead Sea. This essential artery of Israel was more than just beautiful—it was life!

They turned around when they recognized the border of Lebanon. It was around 15h30 when they came to the highway turn-off to Rosh Pina. They traveled on the meandering road to the top of the hill and then took a back road on the other side of Tsfat.

"Let me show you one more spot," Daniel said and turned into an idyllic road through a pine forest. The late afternoon sun created shafts of light among the trees. The backlighting to a brown horse made it look as if the animal had a golden rim.

They came to a place called "At the Edge of the View" and parked the car. Walking down a footpath, they reached a wooden platform. The view was like a window on snow-capped Mount Hermon. As they leaned on the rail, watching the majestic northern crown of Israel, Ester shook her head. "Wow! How do you know all these awesome places?"

"My parents used to take us boys around. Dad cultivated a deep love for nature in us."

As they walked back up the pathway, Ester noticed a big black butterfly with yellow patterns flitting among the flowers. "You are so pretty!"

Daniel pointed to the opposite side of where she was looking. "That is a bohemian-type restaurant. Can you see the hammocks and cushions?"

"Oh, cool!"

"Maybe one day we'll return and have some coffee and cake. What do you think?"

"Or mint tea."

He smiled and took her hand. "Come, we have quite a way home. I don't want to travel too much of the road in the dark."

"How long will it take?"

"Ehhh…about three hours."

She looked at her watch. "Then we'd better get going."

Suddenly a small blue and orange butterfly alighted on Daniel's shoulder.

"Look!" Ester stopped in her tracks and restrained herself from shouting.

Daniel stood motionless. He slowly turned his head to look from the corner of his eye. The butterfly's wings were closed as it quietly unrolled its tongue and tasted his shirt.

"He likes you—you're sweet," she whispered softly.

Daniel stayed perfectly still. He turned his eyes back to Ester and mouthed the words, "You…are…my…butterfly."

She motioned a kiss with her lips. Then she gently put her arm around Daniel's waist and just for a moment leaned her head on his shoulder.

FIFTY-SEVEN

Tuesday, 25 March 2008

"HEY SIS, HAPPY birthday!" David caught Ester around her shoulders, with a mug of tea in her hand. He drew her into a hug.

"Thanks, man! I hardly see you these days."

"I know. Seems we're both more out than in. How was your weekend?"

"Oh, Daniel spoiled me. You know he took me to the Galilee for a surprise. It was so beautiful!"

"He told me the secret beforehand and I was jealous. I have such good memories of the Kinneret."

"Look what I got for my birthday." She lifted her hand and showed off a silver butterfly ring on her index finger.

"Wow, nice!"

"How are you doing, Dudi? What's up with the exams?" Ester pulled out a chair at the dining table, put her teacup down, and sat.

"Aargh, math's such a headache."

"When are you writing?"

"Next Wednesday."

"Can I help you? Or maybe Daniel?"

"I think I'll need it. Did Eema tell you we went to see Ami last night?"

"No, I haven't spoken to her yet. The two of you went to visit? Sit down—I want to hear. Could you see him?"

David turned the chair around and leaned his arms on the back. "No, he's still in intensive care, and he could be there for months. They are afraid he might get an infection, so only close family can go in."

"How is he doing?"

"Making progress. The doctors are quite amazed. They say, 'It's a miracle' all the time.

"Is he awake?"

"No, they haven't taken him out of the sleep yet."

"Did they induce a coma?"

"Think that's what they call it."

"He's probably doing better because so many people are praying for him."

"For sure! Ami's dad says they are receiving messages from people all over the world."

"That's great! God will turn this evil around for good in the end."

"His mom says they've had visitors from Dan to Beersheba. Even Muslims and religious Jews are coming."

"Wow!"

"You should see how the waiting room looks. There's a low table in the middle and it is stacked with food and drinks. Everybody who comes to visit can have a meal. The believers pray with the family and comfort them. It's amazing!"

"That is so good to hear."

"Yep. I met some of his school friends."

"Do you think he will ever play basketball again?"

"Don't know. Two of his toes were blown off."

"Did they amputate anything?"

"Thanks to God, no."

"Has he seen his feet?"

"No, he's sleeping."

"Oh, of course. Do they know who did it? I mean the bomb."

"His father said about a year before, the Lord told him to have security cameras installed. So there was an image captured, which the police are looking at. They think it's a Jewish religious fanatic."

"This is horrible! Hard to believe. So they saw the person who did it?"

"The investigation is still going on, but his dad says it doesn't matter who it was; they have already forgiven him."

"That's only the grace of God—to help you forgive someone." Ester's thoughts seemed to trail off a little as she was making a figure eight on the table with her teaspoon.

She changed the subject carefully. "Did you…have you processed the divorce?"

"What do you mean?"

"Well, the fact that Abba left us—left Eema—and married another woman."

"Some days it bugs me, but I'm not as miffed as I used to be."

"At first I was angry at Eema and I sided with Abba, 'cause he was blaming her," said Ester. "Now I realize it wasn't her fault. Okay, she wasn't perfect, but she tried her best. So then I became angry with Abba for all the pain Eema was having."

"I know." David sighed.

"But I had to get the bitterness out—it was poisoning my life."

"How did you get over the anger?" David leaned forward.

"I wrote him a letter and told Abba that I forgave him."

"You did?"

Ester nodded.

"What did he say?"

"He was a bit shocked. You remember last week, when he took me to buy that denim jacket for my birthday? We had coffee together and I gave him the letter and asked him to read it. Right there. He was very emotional. I thought he would be upset, but he thanked me. It is such a relief to have this thing off my chest."

"Wish I knew how to speak to Abba. We just talk about silly stuff. It's not nice." David rested his chin on his arms.

"I know, but when you forgive him for what he's done to you, to all of us, you will feel sorry for him."

David looked up. His eyes were burning. "I do feel sorry for him. He's not happy. Abba is searching everywhere for love, but only God can give him the life he's looking for."

"You're so right!"

"I'm praying for Abba to see Yeshua is the Messiah. One day I'm going to tell him what happened to me." Ester leaned forward and kissed her brother flat on the cheek. "Dudi," she said, "you are amazing. I'm sure Yeshua is proud of you."

"Funny." David squeezed her hand and his eyes lit up. "Yonatan said the same."

FIFTY-EIGHT

Sunday, 30 March 2008

MA'AYAN'S CONTRACTIONS STARTED at five in the afternoon. She gave Ester a call and then phoned Gila, the birth coach, who sent a text to Sandy. The past few months had been a mixture of joy and deep grief for Ma-ayan since her relationship with Ya'acov fell apart. As she expected, he wanted her to have another abortion, but she just couldn't. Eventually she had to choose between the life of her child and the survival of a five-year-long connection. Many days she felt like a broken tooth with the nerve of her soul dangling in exposed air. She wished she could have the security of a man in her life—like before. Especially on days when it overwhelmed her to think about raising a child alone.

Gradually the family accepted her decision not to give up the child for adoption. The other day her mother bought a little baby outfit, which told Ma'ayan that a grandmother's heart was awakening. She had not come to visit her at the apartment, but Ma'ayan still went to her mother's home. For a while she needed to get on her own two feet, but the staff of Be'ad Chaim and the other young mothers with whom she had begun to meet gave her so much hope. And Ester—of course.

Oh, Ester! Ma'ayan felt her heart warming while she rubbed hard into the pain of her lower belly. This friend had become a lifeline during the past months. Ester said she wouldn't leave her alone and she hadn't. Not even on the days when she was miserable or when she wished she had never listened to advice to keep the baby. Even when she was so emotional that she downright hung up in her ear, Ester stuck with her. She phoned Ma'ayan almost every day to hear how she was doing. No, wait a moment…there were times when she backed off for a time. But always…always Ester let her know that she loved her and was praying for her. A few times she even prayed on the phone.

Ma'ayan smiled. Weird people, these Yeshua believers! Stranger still was that after each time Ester prayed for her, a peace settled. She could always feel courage infusing her to face the next step. She smiled as she felt the movement of the boy child under her hand. *Go'el.* That was the name Ester chose. To be honest, it was the life growing inside of her that gave her the greatest motivation to go forward.

"God has a very special plan for your life, buddy!" She repeated what Ester had said a thousand times. From the time they knew the baby's gender, Ester would put her hand on her friend's belly and say those words. Ma'ayan smiled. "Wonder what he'll become?"

A sudden wrenching pain made her bend over and groan. Ma'ayan had never experienced such intense pain or emotion. She felt as if her lower abdomen and all around her lower back was being squeezed as if in a vise. For a moment between contractions, she panicked. "Tonight I'll be a mother…" Her voice trailed off in a groan.

After half an hour, Ester arrived. She had previously asked her boss if she could leave when Ma'ayan's time to give birth came, and this was it. She encouraged her greatly pregnant friend to have a quick shower, while she made them both a cup of tea. The contractions came and went.

It was a huge emotional support for Ma'ayan to have someone she loved and trusted with her. *Thank you that I'm not alone!* Ma'ayan whispered into the shower, while the warm water caressed her swollen body.

She appeared in a gown, her face wet but glowing. Ester reminded her of Sandy's warning: "When you can't smile anymore during a contraction, it's time to get to the hospital."

Ma'ayan got dressed, loosened a clip, and let her hair fall over her shoulders. Ester crawled under the bed to find shoes and helped Ma'ayan put them on. Ma-ayan giggled, resting her hands on her big stomach. "I'm so glad you painted my toenails last week. I cannot reach my feet anymore."

The clock in the hospital foyer said 18h25 when Ma'ayan and Ester walked in. They rendezvoused with Gila in the elevator on the way up to the sixth floor of Hadassah. "Perfect timing!" Gila smiled as she hugged Ma'ayan. A contraction soon followed the hug. The Hadassah midwife whisked her away for her intake and checkup.

For several hours, Gila encouraged Ma'ayan to stand up when she could and to press on the wall, rocking her pelvis from side to side during the pain. Gila gently massaged Ma'ayan's lower back and Ester cheered her on. "You are doing great girl! Just keep at it!"

Soon she was helped into the birthing position. Ester held her hand, quietly praying. Ma'ayan waited for the contraction. As Gila guided her, she pushed with all of her might. Suddenly the baby's head crowned. Someone had told Ma'ayan that giving birth is like pushing a grapefruit through a hole the size of a grape.

"This is hard work!" Ma'ayan's face contorted as she panted for air, sweat pearling on her forehead. After several more workout pushes, the most incredible miracle occurred. Her child spilled into the world. Ma'ayan looked up when the midwife lifted her baby and saw a wet head with dark auburn hair.

"You have a son!" The wrinkled, squirming little bundle let out a gorgeous high-pitched cry—music to everyone's ears. As soon as the umbilical cord was cut, the midwife placed him on his mother's chest. March 31, 2008, 3:03 A.M. Ma'ayan had never experienced such overwhelming love. It was like a giant wave of warmth, care, and compassion for the little guy washed over her. She could feel his tiny heart beating fast under her fingertips. Her whole being silently yelled "thank you" for the precious gift as tears rolled down her cheeks. After a few minutes, the baby was taken away to be washed, weighed, and checked.

It felt like an eternity, but it was only a few minutes before they brought him back. Now swaddled in a blanket, little Go'el was placed on Ma'ayan's breast to nurse. As the baby began to suck powerfully, Ma'ayan was again filled with a flood of love. Her heart wanted to burst.

"I will protect and care for you with everything in me!" she whispered as tears and smiles mixed. She admired his sculpted face, his perfect nose, the delicately crafted shell of his ear. When he wrapped tiny fingers around hers, she was filled with wonderment. Joy brimmed and tears ran down to her chin.

It had been an incredibly exciting time since coming home from the hospital. Ma'ayan phoned her family and promised to show the baby as soon as she could. The fact that her dad was bedridden and that her mom seldom left the house had been hard for them, but a relief for Ma'ayan. She didn't need other emotional things to crowd her space while she was in such a vulnerable period. For the time being, she preferred that Ya'acov did not know about the baby's birth. She was still hurt by his rejection and abandonment. She might contact him later...after Go'elli's circumcision. Too much to think about right now. If he really wanted to be a part of it, he could have figured out for himself what her due date was. He could have checked on her these months. Right now she was on her own and determined to make it.

Ester's family had been amazing! On the day after her boy was born, Ester brought her a huge bunch of yellow roses from Naomi and a card with something about sunshine and joy.

Her brother David sent a soft toy—the cutest blue elephant with big ears.

Daniel called personally to congratulate Ma'ayan and said he was praying for her. Then two days later, he came with Ester to drive her and the baby back home and to make sure she was settled. He even went to the store to buy a few basic groceries. Ma'ayan hadn't slept much the last few nights, but she could not remember a time in her life when she was happier.

It was Thursday morning, and her gorgeous little son was sleeping peacefully. Ester took the morning off work to be with Ma'ayan when the delivery of the promised gifts would arrive. She and Ester lounged on the couch, planning the baby's circumcision party a few days away. Suddenly there was a knock on the door. A team of volunteers from Be'ad Chaim, including Sandy and counselor Sharon, had brought the Operation Moses delivery. Box after box came into the apartment, including a bed, stroller, changing table, and a baby bathtub. Ester helped carry things up the stairs. Ma'ayan was overwhelmed at all the baby accessories.

"This is wonderful!" she exclaimed. Creams, baby bottles, clothes, and cloth diapers—all kinds of things appeared. "I would never have thought of buying these. Didn't even know I needed them."

She also received a supply of disposable diapers to last one month. Sandy promised that she would receive diapers every month until the baby's first birthday. Baby formula was also available. However, Sharon had encouraged Ma'ayan to continue nursing as long as she could, and that's the option she chose.

"Great!" responded Sandy. "That way your baby's immune system is strengthened while you nourish him. Breast milk is the best."

"And it creates wonderful bonding," added Sharon.

Ester made tea and they visited a bit longer. Ma'ayan drew from their wisdom and asked the most pressing questions. They tiptoed into the bedroom to "ooh" and "aah" about the sleeping darling. Again Ma'ayan's heart overflowed with gratefulness and awe.

When the visitors had left, Ester closed the door behind them. Ma'ayan opened her arms and hugged her friend a long time. Then she pulled back and looked at Ester with tear-filled eyes.

"I totally don't know what I would have done without them. Or you."

Ester smiled sweetly. "It's God who gave you this precious baby, Ma'ayan—because He loves you."

Ma'ayan shook her head. "I almost missed the biggest blessing of my life."

FIFTY-NINE

Tuesday, 4 April 2008

Hey Esush!

I was going to call you and share something Asher Intrater taught a few nights ago. He spoke on "The Connection between Worship and Spiritual Warfare." A few things really helped my understanding (in terms of the battle you and I have had with food). But I know you've been busy with Ma'ayan and the new baby, so I just wrote down what he said while it's fresh in my memory. Read it when you have time.

First the background:

Satan was involved with worship in heaven, according to Scripture. And even though he is a fallen angel, he still has the ability to trick people today and to deceive them toward worship. His main aim is to draw our worship and love away from God. In Revelation 13:4, 8, 12 it shows that he ultimately wants to cause people to worship the dragon and worship the beast. Satan said to Yeshua in the desert that he would give Him all the kingdoms of the world if Yeshua would fall down and worship him. What was Yeshua's answer? "You shall worship the Lord your God and serve only him."

Asher mentioned a few examples of how the devil causes people to worship:

A rock star that has crowds dancing and shouting about his music
A model when men lust after her body
A dictator who controls the masses by his power, and
A Muslim who says, "Alu Akbar," glorifying Allah when he commits an act of terror.

(Satan indirectly draws worship from all of these scenarios. That's why he offered Yeshua the kingdoms of this world, because he received it from people's worship.)

Then Asher used quite a blatant example. He said the metaphor for intimacy in the Bible is the relationship between God and us. Like a wife opens herself to receive her husband, we open ourselves to receive Him. Spiritual adultery is to give yourself to someone or something else.

He also said that Satan is very afraid of worship and prayer. There is power when you touch God through worship or prayer. Satan will do anything to distract or interfere, so that you will not worship—like when other people are praising the Lord and out of the blue, you feel an offence in your heart against someone in the room. Or when a woman who is not modestly dressed distracts a man's attention. He said that even our pride—like when you stand with folded arms during worship and don't want to open up—is a strategy to withhold you from connecting with God. Because when there's intimacy, there's power!

Do you remember when I was visiting with you in January and we talked about the Temple Mount? The final question is "Who will you worship?" That is the place where the Antichrist will sit and extract worship from the deceived masses. It seems this is the biggest scheme of Satan in all the earth—to divert worship away from the one true God. But his scheme is also to battle my daily choices. Small things: Whether eating, or doing whatever…to do all to the glory of God. Can you relate?

The idea of an unfaithful wife is disgusting! And yet I know that I have been unfaithful to Yeshua many times. This picture was like a mirror to me. Well, seeing that I'm confessing my sins now (compromise and unfaithfulness), will you pray for me that I will be changed? Glad I can be transparent with you.

Sh'ma Isra'el, Adonai Eloheinu Adonai echad!

> Love u lots!
> Yours,
> Deb xxx

SIXTY

Motze Shabbat, 5 April 2008

WHEN THEY FINISHED dinner, Ester sighed with delight. She shifted into her high-backed chair and looked at the posh silverware and beautiful white crockery. Not being able to contain her curiosity any longer, she took hold of the tall candle stand, leaned across the dark wooden table, and whispered, "Prince, why did you bring me to the Cordelia tonight?"

"Because I love you." There was a hint in his smile. "Did you forget that it's a year since we first met in Debra's kitchen?"

"Really?"

"Yep, exactly a year ago I first laid my eyes on you."

The live music of a violin and clarinet danced an intimate melody in the background. He came close enough to rub her nose against his own. "Don't you think it is a date to celebrate?"

"Mmm…" She closed her eyes and yearned, but he didn't kiss her.

"That reminds me…" He sat back and removed his slim digital camera from his shirt pocket. "Let's make a memory." He waved their waiter over. They leaned toward one another. Ester's lacy blouse and elegant pearl earrings were the epitome of femininity. Her hair was held up with a single pin—a few loose strands caressed her graceful neck. The candlelight caused a soft glow as they smiled cheek to cheek. Their confident waiter suggested a few more poses, captured them, and handed back the camera.

They thanked him and Daniel slipped it into his pocket, fastening the button. They shared a delectable treat of tahini ice cream with date-honey syrup and spun halva. Daniel's insides trembled as he watched Ester licking the sweetness from her lips. His voice was soft, yet he asked with calculated restraint,

"Anything else, sweetheart? To drink maybe?"

"Thanks ahuvi, I'm done."

After settling the bill, Daniel got up from his seat, took his daypack, and swung it over his shoulder. He pulled Ester's chair out. "Shall we go for a walk, my lovely?"

The spring air was fresh and laden with fragrance when they went outside. They strolled leisurely through ancient Yafo, leaning on the walls, looking at the lights of Tel Aviv. Ester was relaxed and beautifully alluring. Daniel could feel his heart pounding. He tried his best not to let her detect the shiver in his hands when he offered her some gum.

"It's a new moon tonight."

"Yes.

"First of Nissan. "

"Mmm…" He nodded. Biblical new year—an appointed time!

They walked a little downhill until they came to the street leading to one of the oldest ports in the world. All the while Ester hung on his arm, trying to keep her balance with her high heels on the cobblestoned surface. The small harbor had a variety of boats. There were big spotlights providing enough light to see that most of the boats had the name *Yafo*—"Beauty." Some vessels were old and rusted. Others looked fairly new. There were motorboats and fishing boats with brown, green, and blue nets draped over the sides. One even looked like a small cruiser. Also, there were yachts and vessels with masts and sails.

"Wow, I forgot Yafo is so nostalgic"

"Great! I was hoping you would find my choice romantic."

Her intuition told her there was a reason why he said that, but she gently smiled and leaned into his shoulder. She was wearing a knee-length skirt and the terrain was uneven. As they stepped down to walk onto the pier, his strong arm supported her securely. Although it was late, they noticed an old skipper fiddling with a torch on his boat.

"Good evening," they said in greeting.

"*Shalom!*" He looked up, and his face seemed glad at their arrival. They began to talk, and, knowing Daniel's warmth with people, she was hardly surprised when Yossi invited them for a boat ride. What was unexpected was that Daniel agreed for them to do it—right then. Before she knew what was happening, he picked her up and lifted her over the side of the boat.

"You're an endless adventure!" she exclaimed when the noise of the motorboat's engine started. They headed out of the harbor and into the open sea. She enjoyed the fine spray on her face as they sped into the darker deep. When the lights of the city were far behind them, Yossi turned off the engine. She looked around and saw him stepping out of the cabin and going to the back. The stars were bright against the moonless sky.

"You cold?"

"A little."

Daniel pulled a navy-blue sweater from his backpack and helped Ester get it over her head.

She undid the pin from her hair, and soft brown waves cascaded over her shoulders. She sighed and smiled into his face. Putting one leg over the bench, he drew her into his arms.

"I love you." Daniel kissed her forehead and hugged her tightly, his heart pumping wildly.

She heard the sound of the water splashing, but Ester didn't realize that Yossi had slowly turned the boat around. Feeling a little self-conscious, she looked to see where the old man was.

Then her eyes caught something unusual. "Look!" Her arm shot out, pointing toward a rainbow light blinking in the water nearby.

"Uh-huh." Daniel smiled. Everything was going according to plan.

She got up quickly and held onto his arm to balance herself. "Can we get a bit closer?" she asked, loud enough for Yossi to hear.

The skipper took an oar and rowed the boat gently in the direction of the colored light, which blinked on and off, on and off. She stared at the novel object. When they were right next to it, Ester took a firm grip on Daniel's hand, leaned over the edge of the boat, and grabbed the bobbing container.

She shook off the water. It was a kids' rubber ring stretched over the neck of a plastic bottle.

"There's something inside!" Ester was beside herself. "Wow! It looks like...what? A real message in a bottle!"

There was a broad grin on Daniel's face.

She used the bottom part of her skirt to dry it and, taking his arm to stabilize herself, she sat down again.

"What on earth? A treasure hunt!" she exclaimed, removing the rubber ring and giving it to Daniel—the light had stopped flashing.

She gripped the top and unscrewed it. Shaking the bottle upside down, Ester pulled the scroll out by one corner. She unrolled the letter and squinted her eyes in the dim light from the cabin behind them.

My one and only Princess!

Her mouth dropped open. "It's *your* handwriting!"

"Right!" Daniel smiled broadly and dug in his daypack for the little flashlight.

"How? What? How did it get in the water?"

He enjoyed her surprise to the marrow of his bones. She stared into his eyes, awestruck.

"I paid Yossi."

"You mean you arranged all this?"

Daniel nodded, his smile not waning a bit. Either Ester was truly surprised, or she was playing along wonderfully. He swung his leg over the bench, sat down in the same position as before, and switched on the flashlight. She began to read aloud:

My one and only Princess!

For the past nine months, at least one day out of seven, we've had amazing times together. We went to the beach, we walked in the parks. We just chilled.

As we dreamed, we found our hearts beating like one.

You and I decompressed about the week behind us and prayed about the one to follow. After Yeshua, you have brought the deepest joy I've ever known. Shabbats have been the best days of my life, and the peace I felt has left me an addict. To it and to you.

Week by week we rested and we were brimmed with new strength. My closeness to you has helped me go much deeper with God.

She looked up and smiled. "Me too."

He kissed her cheek as she continued to read:

For a while I've been thinking…

God's sign of covenant with Israel was Shabbat—one day out of seven to strengthen relationship. To refresh LOVE.

That really worked for us, right?!

How would you feel about continuing the pattern for life?

We've spoken about marriage…

A ring on a finger is not enough for me. I want a TIME guarantee. I want to know that with my challenging responsibilities and your schedule, we'll survive the pressures. I want the reassurance that we can STOP once a week, have time together to look at Yeshua to get our compasses true north again.

What the future will bring, I don't know. You neither. Days ahead may be difficult. But if we can debrief one out of seven, I have faith that we will not only survive, but also have a quality connection.

Do you think you can agree to such a commitment?
I want to be joined to you all the days of my life.
But one out of seven, I want you to myself. Exclusively.
I want a time to romance and enjoy you.
Can you say "I do" to that?
If so, then...

Will you marry me?

"Oh...oh, Dani!" Ester's eyes filled with tears. She threw her arms around his neck and hugged him so hard he almost choked. When her grip loosened, he pulled back a little. With his face very close to hers, he whispered the question again.

"Ester Tal Davidor—will you marry me?"

"With all my heart!" She looked into his eyes and said softly, "I've been dreaming about this moment forever!" He pressed the rubber ring so the rainbow light activated again and slid it onto her forefinger. It was way too big. Her laughter filled the night like a burst of birdsong.

Daniel held her beautiful face and brought his lips tenderly to hers.

"So have I," he whispered and kissed her for the longest, longest time.

"Wait!" she said suddenly. "I have a question."

She bent down and picked up the scroll from the ground. Unrolling it, she pointed to the bottom.

Double oval circles with a *shin* in the middle.

"What's this?" There was a sparkle in her eyes.

Daniel smiled, drew his breath, and looked up to heaven. He embraced her again and breathed the longing of a lifetime.

"That means—it's official!"

GLOSSARY

A

Abba/Abba shebashamayim—Dear Father in heaven
Adonai—Lord
Adonai Tsva'ot—God of Armies
aliyah—immigration to Israel

B

balagan—mess
bar/bat mitzvah—when Jewish children come of age, boys at thirteen
and girls at twelve
Beit Lechem—Bethlehem
Beresheet—New Age Festival held at Succoth (meaning "Genesis")
Boker tov—Good morning

C

chai—tea
chutzpah—guts, cheekiness

D

Daiyenu—It is enough/sufficient
dreidel—a spinning top for the Hanukkah game

E

eeechs—yuck!
eema—mom
Erev Shabbat—Friday night

G

gibush—rigorous testing for the selection of elite troops in the army
Go'el—Redeemer

H

hallah—braided Sabbath bread
Hanukkah—Feast of Dedication
hanukkia—the nine-armed menorah, used during the Feast of Hanukkah
hashish—marijuana
hateech—hunk
HaQirya—headquarters of the Israeli Defense Force in Tel Aviv
hummus—chickpea paste (most common Israeli food)

I

Intifada—uprising

K

Katyushas—Russian made rockets
kibbutz/kibbutzim—communal farm
Kinneret—Sea of Galilee
kipa—skullcap

Kita Gimmel—grade three

kosher— "pure" according to religious food laws

L

Laila tov—Good night

Le'chaim!—To life! (a toast offered when glasses are raised)

M

matza—unleavened bread

Mazel tov—Congratulations

mezzuzah—a small container of a scripture scroll on the side of a Jewish door (see Deut. 6:9)

moshav—a communal farm (a later model than the kibbutz)

Motze Shabbat—Saturday evening ("after Shabbat")

Mashiach/HaMashiach—Messiah/the Messiah

N

nana tea—peppermint tea

nargila—a water pipe, instrument for smoking (also called hubbly bubbly)

nesher—eagle

Nissan—first month of the biblical New Year

O

Oy/oy va'avoy—Oh, dear!

P

Pesach—Passover

pita—round flat bread like a pocket

R

Rosh Hashanah—Jewish New Year according to tradition

S

sabbaba—cool!
seder—order at Pesach (that is, Passover meal)
Shabbat—Sabbath
Shaddai—Sufficient One
shalom—peace (greeting for "hello" or "goodbye")
Shaldag—an elite unit in the Israeli army, similar to US Navy Seals
Shavu'ot—Feast of Weeks (Pentecost)
Sheket—Be quiet!
Shekinah—manifest presence of God, sometimes used for "glory"
shin—a letter of the Hebrew alphabet, שׁ usually found on the small oblong case to the side of a Jewish door (mezzuzah). The letter shin represents "Shaddai" (the All-sufficient One), but it is also a symbol of God's presence (the Hebrew word is Shekinah).
shofar—ram's horn
Simchat Adon—Joy of the Lord (name of congregation)
succah—shelter/hut
Succoth—Feast of Shelters (or tabernacles or booths)
sufganiot—Hanukkah doughnuts

T

tahini—crushed sesame seed paste
Tanach—Old Testament
Torah—Pentateuch (first five books of Moses)

Y

Yeshua/Yeshua HaMashiach—Jesus/Jesus the Messiah

Yeshu—a curse word in Hebrew (acronym meaning "May his name [Jesus] be blotted out")
yeshiva—seminary of Judaism
yoffi—great!
Yom Kippur—Day of Atonement (literally "Day of Covering")
Yom Tru'ah—Feast of Trumpets (literally "Day of the Blast")

Expressions, Prayers, and Songs

Ani ohev otach—I love you (man to woman)
Ani ohevet otcha—I love you (woman to man)

Baruch Ata Adonai, Eloheinu Melech HaOlam—Blessed are You, O Lord our God, King of the universe

Be'shem Yeshua HaMashiach—In the name of Jesus the Messiah (said at the conclusion of prayer)

Kol Israel ivasha—All Israel will be saved (Rom 11:26)

Lo etbayesh—Not ashamed (of the gospel of Jesus Christ; Rom 1:16)

Sh'ma Israel Adonai Eloheinu, Adonai Echad—Hear, O Israel, the Lord our God, the Lord is One

ACKNOWLEDGMENTS

TO ALL THOSE who helped:

    soldiers & students
    interns & intercessors
    proofreaders & professionals
    leaders & little ones
    artists & advisors
    family members & friends
    Pillars of support—
    THANK YOU!

This is your book. I picked the grapes but like in an ancient winepress, we trampled it together, we strained and bottled the wine. You watched over its quality and you paid for its value.

Sons and daughters of Zion—le'chaim!

Theodorah Villion

September 2011

In learning how a Cobra helicopter is operated, we researched much. Amongst the simulated DVDs, internet sources, and conversations with a heli pilot—*Chicken Hawk*, written by Vietnam war veteran Robert Mason, deserves special mention.